S0-COP-564

and crying out for more of his touch. A warm need stirred deep down in her belly, intensifying, along with the kiss, into a burning ache. Finally breaking apart, Tony led her up the staircase. At the top of the stairs, he let go of her to move away in the dark. He switched on the lamp in his room. Standing by the wide bed, he held out his arms.

Susan walked into his arms and they closed tight around her. Cupping her head between his hands, he leaned it back gently for another impassioned kiss. She welcomed the languid probing of his tongue even as her knees weakened.

With his eyes never leaving hers, his hands smoothed the red wool of her suit top. "I do love this on you," Tony said, undoing the first shiny black button. "But I'm gonna love taking it off even more."

ABOUT THE AUTHOR

Judith Yoder decided at age thirty that she wasn't going to deny herself anymore her lifelong secret desire to write professionally. With that decision made, and with the help of an encouraging husband, Judy had her first romance novel published in 1984. And she hasn't stopped writing since.

Books by Judith Yoder

HARLEQUIN AMERICAN ROMANCE

228–SEPTEMBER GLOW

Don't miss any of our special offers. Write to us at the following address for information on our newest releases.

Harlequin Reader Service
P.O. Box 1397, Buffalo, NY 14240
Canadian address: P.O. Box 603,
Fort Erie, Ont. L2A 5X3

JUDITH YODER

A MATTER OF COMPROMISE

Harlequin Books

TORONTO • NEW YORK • LONDON
AMSTERDAM • PARIS • SYDNEY • HAMBURG
STOCKHOLM • ATHENS • TOKYO • MILAN
MADRID • WARSAW • BUDAPEST • AUCKLAND

Published March 1992

ISBN 0-373-16432-7

A MATTER OF COMPROMISE

Chapter One

Susan O'Toole knew there was trouble as soon as the train came to a screeching halt.

"Ladies and gentlemen, there is a disabled train on the tracks at the next station. We expect a delay of ten to fifteen minutes. We apologize for this inconvenience."

A collective groan rumbled through the crowded subway car. The Metro train was stuck, stalled in a dark underground tunnel somewhere between the Foggy Bottom and Farragut West stations. And no one was going to get to work on time this morning, Susan realized with a frustrated sigh. At least this was the third day on her new job instead of the first. She'd be *very* nervous by now if this had happened Monday morning.

The conductor's announcement over the public address system did little to appease the rush-hour passengers. Annoyed grumblings and muttered complaints ran up and down the length of the car.

One would have thought the small D.C. subway system would have improved during her four-year absence from town. After all, it was no longer new. And this was Washington, not New York, she mused, wishing she was sitting down. By the time she'd boarded the train all the seats had been taken. Shifting her weight from one foot to the other, she accidentally brushed against the man standing beside her.

"I'm sorry," she said immediately. "The car is too crowded. A person can scarcely breathe."

The stocky man glanced at her with mild curiosity and mumbled something incomprehensible before turning back to his newspaper.

Without anything on hand to read she made a quick study of the other passengers—at least of the few she could actually see. No surprises there. It might have been four years since she'd been a regular commuter on the Metro, but her fellow travelers were still the same mix of government workers, lawyers, secretaries and businessmen. It was as if she'd never left town.

A sudden spurt of movement through the crowd caught her attention. What was going on? The train hadn't budged an inch.

But then one particular voice rose above the disarrayed hum of the others. "Excuse me, please. Sorry. Could I just get by here?"

Susan lifted her eyes to the ceiling in amusement. Some cockeyed optimist was actually trying to get from one end of the subway car to the other, not a very easy nor reasonable thing to do considering it was jam-packed.

The voice drifted closer. "Pardon me. May I get by? Excuse me..."

This man's voice sounded familiar. Did she know it? Or was it just her imagination? Unfriendly comments followed the person through the crowd. Tempers were short enough, she thought. This guy had better watch it or someone might take a swing at him.

The next thing she knew the guy was wedging himself between her and the man next to her. "What the hell?" her stocky neighbor began sputtering. "You've got some nerve, buddy."

But the intruder ignored the man as he turned toward her. Her eyes widened with recognition. It hadn't been her imagination, after all. She did know that voice.

"Susan? It *is* you."

"Tony." It was all she could think to say. She realized his antics had attracted a lot of attention, yet she was too stunned to feel embarrassed. He was the last person she expected to see during her first week in town. Although Washington was a small town in many ways, she simply didn't travel in the same lofty circles as Anthony Brandon II.

"I thought I caught a glimpse of you from the other end of the car. Then I thought, no, it couldn't be. But once the train stalled I had to find out for sure."

"Well, now you and the entire car know for sure it's me." Susan cast a quick glance over her shoulder before leaning closer to him to whisper, "Let's just not mention any last names, okay?"

Tony's responding laugh sounded low and rich. She felt drawn to it. But a stark quiet seemed to settle over the crowded car, forcing her back to a total awareness of where she was and who she was with. She couldn't understand it. Despite a train full of disgruntled passengers, all she could hear was the hum of the air conditioner. And all she could see was Tony's expectant face. It was as if all the other passengers had taken it upon themselves to discreetly disappear.

She tried to hide the awkwardness she was feeling by saying something. Anything.

"You're lucky you didn't get your head knocked off."

He didn't smile. He just peered at her through gold wire-rimmed eyeglasses. They were something new. At least she didn't remember Tony needing glasses when they worked together at the legal aid office.

"What are you doing here?" he finally asked.

"Trying to get to work." Glancing up at his wavy sandy brown hair, she regretted her self-conscious stab at humor. What an inane thing to say to a man she hadn't seen in over four years.

"I thought you were back in Baltimore working for the consumer affairs office. At least that's what I heard through the grapevine." His tone sounded a tad curt.

"Hey, I was director of the division," she corrected with a teasing grin that she hoped would mask her nervousness.

He nodded, a wry smile twitching his lips. "Of course. I'm not surprised. You were destined for great things, Susan."

She studied his expression for a moment, deciding that, except for the glasses, Tony hadn't changed much. Oh, his face might have filled out a little, but handsomely so. The slight cleft in his chin, barely perceptible to less observant eyes, was as intriguing as ever. The cut of his gray suit might be a bit more conservative, but he wore it well. After four years his compact, athletic build remained slim and vital. Susan hadn't known Tony very well back then, but she had thought him good-looking and charming. He also was sought after—and rich. And out of her league.

"You still haven't told me what you're doing in Washington," Tony said, interrupting her study of him.

"I've moved back." Her manner softened. "I'm with the consumer affairs office of the National Senior Citizens' Association."

Tony smiled. "As the boss, no doubt."

"Yes, they hired me to be the director. I started on Monday."

"Congratulations. I'm glad your career's moving right along." He sounded as if he meant it.

"Thanks. And you? Still with your father's law firm?"

"Yes. I'm a full partner now."

"That's great," Susan acknowledged with a neutral nod of her head. She wasn't surprised to hear it. Anthony Brandon II might be the boss's son, but he was a brilliant attorney in his own right. "Still living in Foggy Bottom?" she asked quickly to get off the subject of his current job.

"Still there. And where are you now?"

"Renting a place over in Rosslyn, not far from my old apartment."

Without warning the train lurched back to life, jolting Susan off balance. She felt herself swaying against Tony's chest as the car slowly moved. He curved an arm around her shoulders to help steady her. Although she regained her balance immediately, his firm grasp had felt oddly reassuring.

"Thanks," she murmured, moving away from him.

"What about on the home front, Susan? Are you married now?"

"Me? No, haven't had much time for things like that." What did it matter to him, anyway? Still, in spite of herself, she asked, "And you?"

"No, I haven't gotten around to it myself."

Somehow this surprised her. During the four or five months they had worked together, Tony had seemed to date a lot—especially the more socially prominent young ladies around town. Besides, a successful, personable and *eligible* man like Tony was a sought-after entity in Washington. His family was of the city's old guard. He surely could have his choice of women. Then again maybe he had made a choice. Just because he wasn't married didn't mean he wasn't involved with someone.

"Susan?"

She looked up at Tony. A pained expression had crossed his face, yet he looked her right in the eye. "You know, I *was* upset that the university closed down the legal aid office."

Susan stiffened. "We all were."

Grimacing, he looked away. "I know it's long after the fact, but I was sorry."

After the fact, her mind echoed as she tried hard to swallow back the resentment she thought she'd buried long ago. She couldn't believe he was saying this now, not after the way he had left the office high and dry. She forced herself to stay calm. It was all water under the bridge. And there was no point in starting an argument with a man she would rarely, if ever, see. "You're right. It is long after the fact."

Mercifully the train pulled into the next station. "This is my stop," Tony announced. The train's door slid open and a crowd of disembarking passengers moved forward. "Well, good luck with you new job," he said as the momentum of the crowd edged him toward the door. "Welcome back to D.C."

"Thanks," she barely had a chance to murmur before the car door snapped shut and the train began to move.

As the train glided out of the station, she could see him walking on the platform, headed for the escalators to the street. His forthright gait reminded her of their last encounter, the last time she stood gazing at his back as he walked away. Now he was quickly disappearing from view as the train sped into the darkened tunnel, and Susan found herself remembering.

Even as the rumbling rhythm of the subway car reassured her of the present, Susan winced when she recalled the afternoon Tony had told her he was quitting legal aid. Since she'd been managing the office for only a few months, his resignation had come as a real blow. He was their best lawyer, and she had hit the roof.

How strident, how cynical she had sounded! How inflexible she had been. She shook her head at the memory. Things hadn't been easy back then: her mid-twenties had been a confusing time for her. She was no longer a student, secure in her accepted position within the known boundaries of university life. When, finally, she was on her own, she had found herself unprepared for the complexities and the frustrations of the working world. Back then her ideals and standards had been fairly lofty—perhaps too idealistic for anyone to live up to. Certainly Tony Brandon hadn't.

Well, the intervening years had knocked some of the wind from her sails. She'd learned a few lessons along the way. She still threw herself into causes, and she still worked hard for what she believed in. But now she could bend a little. She had more confidence in herself. She was pleased about that.

The Metro train pulled into the next stop at Mac-Pherson Square. Stepping onto the station platform, Susan threaded her way through the crowd of commuters. She was glad to be back in Washington, glad to be facing it on new terms. She'd grown up enough to realize she couldn't change the world with good intentions and noble gestures. She'd learned how to work within the system, how to make compromises. Although the process could be slow, her steady work could produce realistic solutions for a lonely widow with a limited income trying to pay the ever-increasing taxes on her home, or for a retired couple being bilked by unscrupulous workmen.

Minor though her contributions might be, she was able to make a difference in some people's lives, and that gave her a tremendous amount of satisfaction. The small victories did count and they did add up. Riding the escalator up into the sunny Indian summer morning, she couldn't help wondering if Tony Brandon had found as much satisfaction in his work at Conners, Brandon and Moffet.

Despite the delay on the subway, Susan arrived at her office in time to telephone her mother in Baltimore before she left for work.

"For heaven's sake, Susan, I was just leaving for the bus," Fay O'Toole sputtered into the phone. "Is something wrong?"

"Nothing, except you weren't home when I called last night."

"Oh, that—I worked late. Mrs. Harrison's sister-in-law from Pittsburgh is visiting for a few days—you know, the one she doesn't get along with? Well, Mrs. H. practically begged me to stay to serve dinner, and I felt so bad for the poor thing..."

"I know all about it. I called the Harrisons, but you had already left by then."

"Oh. So why call now? Morning rates are very high, you know, and—"

"Mama listen! I want you to come down to D.C. for the weekend. I thought you might ask Mrs. Harrison for Friday or Monday off so you could stay longer," she explained. "It'd be fun to go shopping together for some of the things I need for the apartment. Besides, I miss you."

"And I miss you too, Suz." Yet her mother's ensuing sigh made her suspect a "but" was in the offing.

"You can't come?"

"I wish I could darlin'. Except Mrs. H. is giving a party Saturday night for her sister-in-law, and I said I'd help out."

First she worked late last night, and now she'd be working on her usual day off. Susan didn't know who she was madder at—Mrs. Harrison or her mother. "Mama, didn't we have a long talk about cutting back on your hours? Now that I have this new job you don't have to—"

"I know, I know. And I did mention it to Mrs. H."

"You did?"

"It sorta took her by surprise. She said the timing couldn't be worse, what with the fall parties and the holidays coming." Her mother hesitated for a moment. "She asked me to hold off until after the first of the year."

"Oh, great. By then she'll have come up with another excuse," Susan fumed. "Mama, you've got to be firm with her. You don't realize what a demand there is for good housekeepers like you. Why, you could go just about anywhere, name your salary and hours and be snapped up on the spot."

"Just a minute here," Fay bristled. "I do owe a certain loyalty to the woman. She's been good to me for over eighteen years. And you may recall that I worked for some pretty bad apples before Mrs. H. came along."

"I know."

"And I shouldn't have to remind you that she pulled the strings that got you into Carlisle Academy."

Susan never could think of a good response to that line.

"So, in light of everything, I don't think Mrs. H. is being unreasonable in asking me to wait. She's taken awfully good care of me over the years."

She sighed deeply. "Mama, *I* want to take care of you now. Don't you know that? I'm finally making pretty decent money, and with raises and promotions it'll be even better. Why, in a year or so you probably can flat out retire."

"I appreciate the sentiment, darlin', really. But I'm too young to retire," she insisted. "Besides, what if you lost your job?"

"Oh, Mama."

"It could happen, Suz."

She was getting nowhere, and she knew it. "You could take things a little easier, though."

"I'll cut back in a few months. I promise."

Frustrating as the situation was, she knew it was pointless to argue further. She just wished she could make her mother understand how strongly she felt. All Susan wanted was for Fay to enjoy her daughter's success—a success that was in no small part due to Fay's Irish determination and years of hard toil.

Susan was also certain of what she didn't want. She didn't want her mother cooking meals and cleaning houses for rich women much longer.

SUSAN O'TOOLE. Of all the people to run into. Tony couldn't believe it. And damn! Those incredible navy blue eyes of hers still could make him feel as guilty as hell. He jabbed the up button at the bank of elevators in his office building. "Eyes of an angel, heart of stone," he muttered to himself as he impatiently hit the elevator button again.

"Talking to yourself again, Counselor?"

The familiar voice with its lilting accent caught him by surprise. He turned around. "Guilty as charged, Maria Lopez."

"No way around that plea, sir. You've been talking to yourself for as long as I've known you." An elevator arrived, and he followed Maria into it. "I see we're both late this morning," she noted. "Luis and I got caught in Beltway traffic. What's your excuse?"

"Breakdown on the Metro. Serves me right. I should be walking to work, anyway." Again he thought of Susan. "By the way, I ran into an old friend of yours on the train this morning."

"Who?"

"Susan O'Toole. Did you know she was back in town?"

"I had no idea," Maria claimed. "Of course, she and I lost touch a couple of years ago. But I never thought Susan would come back. She was so disillusioned when the bureau was shut down."

"She's with the Senior Citizens' Association now."

The elevator arrived on the tenth floor, the doors opening up directly to the main reception area of Conners, Brandon and Moffet. He and Maria both worked on the tenth, although the firm occupied four full floors of the building.

"Susan O'Toole. What memories she brings back," Maria said with some fondness as they walked together down the center corridor. "The all-night work sessions before an important court date. The cases she used to literally find on the street. Like that drugstore clerk who was being fired because the manager wanted to hire someone younger for less pay and Susan just happened to be there buying panty hose...."

"And overheard the manager doing the firing," Tony continued. "Susan convinced that poor guy that he was a victim of job discrimination and dragged him back to the office. I ended up representing him. Got him his job back, too."

He couldn't help smiling; the memory made him feel good. At legal aid he could often see how his work actually helped people. The end results weren't delayed by years of intentional court postponements, nor buried under thousands of documents and briefs filled by an army of faceless lawyers.

Maria stopped at the work area she shared with three other legal assistants and plunked her briefcase down on the first desk. "I'll never forget those gorgeous birthday cakes she used to make for people in the office."

He had forgotten about that. "You know, Susan couldn't have been managing the office for more than a week when she sprung one on me for my birthday." He failed to add that today—after he mentioned the bureau's closing—Susan had looked as if she'd wanted to *throw* a cake at him. Tony guessed he'd be forever a deserter in Susan's eyes. And that irked him.

His secretary greeted him with a cheerful "Good Morning" and handed him his messages. "Paul Church from the FAA called already."

"Already?" Tony gave a heavy sigh. "I've got to talk to him."

"He said he'd try you again this afternoon. He sounded very irate, though. Says USA-WAY Airlines is headed for more trouble if they don't shape up fast."

Tony rolled his eyes in disgust. "Just what we need," he muttered as he entered his office. Although he loved his job, there were aspects of it he could do without.

He found it hard to get worked up over Paul Church's warning. USA-WAY had been down this road before, and the firm had pulled it out smelling like a rose. They'd do it again, Tony concluded with some ambivalence, not sure if he approved of the way his client was working around safety regulations.

Suddenly Susan came to mind again. She wouldn't share his ambivalence; she'd know exactly which side to be on. After working with her for a while, he had realized that everything was black and white for Susan. He had admired her strength of conviction at first. But within a few months of her arrival at legal aid he had come to view this characteristic as sheer inflexibility. And this flaw had made his resigning from legal aid more acrimonious than he'd expected.

That resignation stirred uncomfortable memories. He slammed his briefcase down on his desk, snapping the locks open with a swift, angry jerk. He was almost sorry he'd run into Susan O'Toole at all. After removing some file folders from the case, he decided he needed a cup of strong black coffee. He paused at his secretary's desk. "I'm off to the coffee room, Kathy. Can I get you a cup?"

"I've already had my quota this morning, thanks. Did you see that message from Mr. Brandon? I think he wants you to go home for dinner tonight."

"Tonight?" He had been planning to work late—*needed* to—if he was going to make any dent in his backed-up work load.

"Shall I call his secretary for you?"

"I'll take care of it. You've got enough to do."

A few minutes later, with a cup of fresh, hot coffee in hand, Tony stopped by his father's office. The secretary waved him into the stately corner office where he found John Brandon poring over a legal brief. The older man was oblivious to everything but the work before him. To attract his father's attention Tony rapped lightly on the open door. "Morning, Dad."

Slowly the senior Brandon dragged his eyes away from his reading. "Ah, there you are. Keeping bankers' hours these days?" he chided in the refined baritone that was well-known for its power to challenge witnesses and mesmerize juries. As a youth, Tony had found his father's distinctive voice intimidating and distancing. Now, as an attorney himself, Tony could appreciate its booming richness as a finely honed tool of the trade.

"Got stuck in the Metro, Dad, that's all." Tony shrugged, no longer a fearful child. He sat down in a black leather club chair, one of the few nonantique pieces of furniture in the room.

A slight smile curved the older man's lips, bringing much needed warmth to a man with icy silver hair and cool gray eyes. "Is that the best excuse you can come up with for being late to work?"

"Best and only."

His father laughed and leaned back in his high-backed desk chair. "Be at the house tonight for dinner. William Leland is joining us."

"The William Leland of Laser Media? You know him?" His father knew many rich, powerful people, but the controversial founder of the world's largest communications conglomerate was someone out of his strata.

"No, we don't know him. But his new wife, apparently, was at Vassar the same time as your mother. Ever since she heard Leland would be in town for the Smithsonian gala, she's been networking like mad to make a contact. His

New York office accepted the invitation for him just last night.''

"This is Mother's doing? What's got into her?''

His father shrugged. "Looking out for our interests, I suppose. Whatever the reason, she deserves a partnership for it. Just think what this can mean for the firm.''

The implications of Leland's visit weren't lost on Tony. Power was what made D.C. spin. That was a lesson his parents had been drumming into him for most of his life. Yet it had been only in the past few years that he had come to accept the fact. One couldn't work in one of the most influential law firms in Washington and not realize the truth of it.

"Of course you're coming," his father added.

He thought about all the work he had planned to catch up on that night. He was always trying to get caught up. But then again, the William Lelands of the world didn't cross his path every day. "Guess I can't afford to miss it.''

"Good. Wear your tux." John began shuffling the few papers on his incredibly uncluttered desk. Tony knew this was his father's way of dismissing him. It used to bother him, being sent away as if he were just another young partner instead of the man's only child. Even now it seemed rather cold, as if his father was dead set on maintaining a distance between them.

Tony stopped at the coffee room to refill his cup before returning to his office. Maria was there, trying to choose a Danish from a large bakery box. "I wish they'd stop bringing these in," she declared as she pulled out a cheese Danish. "By the way, did you say Susan O'Toole was at the Senior Citizens' Association?''

"So she told me.''

"I think I'm gonna call her. I'm dying to hear how she is.''

"Whatever," Tony mumbled, walking off without further comment. He felt oddly out of sorts this morning and he didn't want to discuss Susan O'Toole anymore.

Kathy handed him three more phone messages as he passed her desk. Damn! It wasn't even 10:00 a.m. and he was hopelessly behind already. He stared at the dozen or so pink message slips, the neatly typed letters waiting for his review and signature, his crowded appointment calendar. For the first time in a long time he felt overwhelmed.

Even hours later, when he dashed home from the office, he was still running behind. It had been a long day, and the last thing he felt like doing was getting all dressed up for dinner at his parents' home. At least his tuxedo was back from the dry cleaner. He could just imagine his mother's horrified silence if he showed up wearing a perfectly good blue suit instead of a tux.

He'd been practically born into black tie. When he was little more than a toddler, his nanny would let him peek through the stair railing as guests arrived at his parents' innumerable parties. When he reached the appropriate age, his mother had marched him downtown to be fitted for his own tux.

Yet tonight, driving up to his parents' large old house, aglow with its dramatic lighting, Tony was filled with dread. Expensive cars lined the driveway, and the purple truck of the city's most respected caterer was parked off to the side. This was to be another of Letitia Brandon's small but perfect dinner parties.

Estelle Case, the family housekeeper, took his coat at the door. "Thank goodness you're finally here, Mr. Tony. The missus has been asking for you every five minutes."

"That late, am I?"

"Not really. The Lelands arrived about five minutes ago. But you know your mother. She's got something on her mind, and it obviously has something to do with you."

"Oh, great."

"Better get yourself into the living room. That butler from the caterer is serving cocktails. I'm just the hatcheck girl tonight."

"Consider yourself lucky."

"I do, honey, I do," she trilled, walking away with his topcoat.

Now Tony could hear the lively chatter emanating from the living room. He hesitated for a moment. Although he'd been introduced to formal dinner parties at an early age, his tolerance for them was diminishing. Lately his tuxedo had been feeling like a stiff, superficial uniform.

The big Brandon living room was more like an elegant great hall. Still, his mother spotted him as soon as he set foot in the room. "There you are, darling," she called, her arms stretched out to him.

Tony planted a kiss on her well-made-up cheek. She was perfumed, powdered and dressed in one of her favorite designer dresses. Her faded blond hair was perfectly coiffed. And she was "on"—playing hostess to the hilt. Only Tony wouldn't call his mother's behavior *acting*, because she had always seemed to relish the role.

She curled her arm through his. "Why didn't you bring a young lady with you, dear? It would have rounded out the party nicely."

"Not enough notice, Mother." Actually, bringing a date for this evening had never even entered his mind.

"I must tell the butler to remove a place setting from the table," she muttered to herself. She led him farther into the room. "You know everyone here, I believe. Except the Lelands, of course."

Tony scanned the room. The faces were familiar. Former Ambassador Charles Ring and his wife, Muriel, from next door were chatting with the Blair Mitchums from Middleburg. Then he spotted Carter Bolton, a senior partner at the firm, and his wife, Elaine, talking with a rather plain but expensively dressed middle-aged woman.

Mrs. Leland probably. Finally he saw his father standing near the unlit fireplace. He was deep in conversation with a man Tony recognized from photos in newspapers and business journals—William Leland.

"Looks just like his pictures, doesn't he?" Letitia remarked. "Can't say he's the most charming man I've ever met. Very reserved."

"Dad seems to be getting on with him."

Letitia lowered her voice. "Of course he is. The man's a potential client. Father very much wants you to talk with him—he may need some help over at Justice."

"Tony, dear, we haven't seen you in so long."

He turned to find Muriel Ring standing next to him. Always pleased to see her, he walked into her motherly embrace. He had known her all his life, and she was the warmest and sweetest of all his mother's friends. Her son, McKay, was one month younger than Tony, and the two of them had been best buddies growing up. They'd probably be close even today if his parents hadn't always been comparing him—unfavorably—to McKay Ring. Somehow McKay had always managed to follow the "right" path, while Tony had always fallen short of expectations—at least in his parents' eyes.

"I hear McKay's been assigned to the embassy in London," Tony politely noted. "Sounds like quite a promotion."

Muriel beamed. "Isn't it wonderful? Charles is just so proud. He's unbearable."

"Charles should be proud," Letitia interjected. "That son of yours is going to win an ambassadorship by the time he's forty." Leaning closer to Tony, she added, "McKay and Sally have just had their second baby—another boy."

Tony offered Muriel his congratulations.

His mother, however, was bound to have the last word on the matter. "Here you already have two grandchildren, Muriel, and I can't even get this son of mine to marry and settle down." After a deep sigh, she gave her friend a knowing look. "At least he's with the firm now—you know we suffered a few anxious years over that."

"Oh, for goodness' sake, Letitia. You've nothing to complain about." Muriel placed a hand on his arm. "You've plenty of time to start a family, Tony. I think you're wise to devote yourself to your career now."

Muriel turned to his mother again. "And speaking of careers, Letitia, why are you worried about grandchildren when your writing career has just taken off? Did you say your book will be in the stores in time for Christmas?"

God bless Muriel Ring, Tony thought with a smile. She sure knew how to change a subject. The upcoming publication of his mother's first novel was certain to hold her attention long enough for him to move on. Letitia loved to talk about her book. And why not? She had every reason to be proud of her accomplishment. It took her over three years to write and then sell the murder mystery to a paperback publisher. Tony was proud of her. Also, he was glad that she now had something of her own to focus on besides the law firm and the state of his career.

Except tonight Letitia seemed quite concerned that he make a good impression on her guest of honor. She interrupted the conversation about her book just long enough to catch him before he slipped away. "Your father's waiting."

He looked across the room to where his father was standing with William Leland. John caught his eye right away. At this point Carter Bolton had joined the two men and he was talking quite intently to Leland. John gestured for Tony to come over.

He wished he could step out to the terrace for some fresh air. He wished he had time to fix himself a drink. Mostly he wished he could take this imminent introduction in stride. But his father's frown of impatience beckoned.

So he took a deep breath and resolutely squared his shoulders. With a businesslike smile on his face he marched over to the three older men, knowing the pressure was on him to perform.

Chapter Two

"Kathy, I've got to get the hell out of here," Tony said, whisking by his secretary's desk. He'd been on the phone all morning, and now he was running late. "Leland's expecting us at twelve-thirty, exactly."

He rushed out to the firm's main reception area to meet his father. The previous evening with William Leland had produced the desired result: a business luncheon to discuss what Conners, Brandon and Moffet could do for the billionaire. John Brandon had high hopes for this meeting, and there were still details to be talked over during the cab ride to Leland's hotel.

When he reached the reception area, however, his father hadn't yet arrived. He relaxed a bit, glad for a moment to catch his breath. He glanced at his watch, checking it against the clock on the wall. Then he remembered he'd set his watch five minutes ahead in order to keep on top of things today.

He decided to use the few extra minutes to review his notes. Heading for a seat near the receptionist's desk, he spotted a dark-haired young woman sitting in the far corner of the room. She was reading a magazine, her long, slim legs crossed in a rather fetching pose. Only when the woman's lithe figure shifted slightly in the chair, did he realize she looked familiar. He grabbed the glasses out of his breast pocket and quickly pushed them into place. The shiny dark brown hair and the fine-featured face came into focus.

Susan O'Toole. What in the world was she doing at the firm?

Intrigued, he approached her slowly. Since she was reading the latest issue of *Time* with such concentration, she took no notice of him. Something was different about her hair, he decided. She used to wear it pinned back in an efficient ponytail, and now she wore it loose and smooth to just above her shoulders. It was so shiny dark that it made him think of black silk.

Suddenly Susan glanced up from the magazine. She was so startled to find him standing there that the magazine slipped out of her fingers and onto the floor.

She reached down just as he stooped to get it for her. Her flowing hair grazed his fingers when he picked up the magazine, and it did, indeed, feel as soft as it looked.

"Thank you," she murmured, easing back into the chair.

He peered up at her face as he handed her the magazine. She was rather pretty, he thought, more so than he'd ever realized. Why hadn't he noticed before?

Slowly he straightened. "So we run into each other again," he remarked, his voice so matter-of-fact she'd never guess how he'd just been admiring her. "What are you doing here?"

"I'm having lunch with Maria." She closed the magazine on her lap and looked around the room. Then, as if remembering exactly where she was, she quickly explained, "She asked me to meet her here because her schedule's so hectic today. Otherwise I—"

"Otherwise you'd rather not be here."

She didn't answer. Her mouth straightened into a tight line, and she looked away.

He wished he hadn't made the crack. "Susan, forget it. You don't have to feel uncomfortable here." Ironically enough *he* was now feeling uncomfortable. What was it about this woman that put him on edge? "Look, I'll go tell her you're here."

"She already knows." Susan nodded toward the receptionist.

"Of course." He felt weary. He wished his father would hurry up. "I'm glad you and Maria got in touch. She was pleased to hear you were back in town."

At last Susan smiled. "Thanks for telling her. I felt sort of guilty about letting our friendship slide while I was away."

Tony drew odd comfort from the fact that Susan O'Toole felt guilty about something. Maybe she actually had feet of clay, just like everybody else. He turned the thought over in his mind for a second and then decided to ask, "Maybe we could—"

"Tony, let's go!" his father bellowed as he emerged through the double doors leading to the office suites. Like a whirlwind, he whipped through the reception area without a backward glance. "We can't keep William Leland waiting."

"*The* William Leland?" Her deep blue eyes were wide with surprise.

"A potential client," he admitted, his adrenaline rising as he prepared to leave. His father was already out the door.

"Well, one *can't* keep a billionaire waiting."

Oh, brother. Yet he knew there was no time to respond to Susan's dry remark. And no point, either.

"I'M GLAD YOU CALLED me yesterday, Maria. I was planning to get in touch with you once I got settled in," Susan told her former co-worker. They had just given their order to the waiter at the small sandwich shop and were sitting comfortably, sipping iced tea. "And I am sorry for not answering your letters."

"Forget it. That was a long time ago."

"Yes, but it wasn't very nice of me. It's not good to let friendships slide—good ones are hard to come by."

Maria gave her a sympathetic smile. "These things happen."

But she still felt the need to explain. "I was pretty traumatized by the closing of the legal aid office. For the longest time it was painful to even think about it. I guess I developed a mental block against anything or anyone connected with it." She gazed across the table at Maria. "Which unfortunately included you."

"I thought it might be something like that."

"I managed the occasional note or call to a friend or two from my old apartment building. But when it came to you, I'd keep telling myself—I must get in touch with Maria before she wonders if I've dropped off the face of the earth. Still, I kept putting it off until it seemed pointless to answer."

Maria reached across the table to pat Susan's hand. "Well, we've gotten together now. That's what matters."

Maria's understanding was gratifying. As they continued talking, Susan felt as if the two of them were picking up where they'd left off four years before. Conversation flowed freely, laughter came easily and memories revived quickly.

"I really wish Luis could've joined us," Maria said, her gentle smile gleaming white against her golden-honey complexion. "But since he teaches three classes at the university on Thursdays, it was impossible for him to get away."

"Well, I hope to meet this husband of yours soon. He sounds wonderful."

Maria's smile widened considerably. "Oh, he is, Susan. He's everything my first husband wasn't—and more. Luis is all for my getting my law degree. He helps with the housework. And, more importantly, he's a good influence on my son—at least he is when Roberto lets him get close enough."

She couldn't help feeling envious. "You're lucky to have found someone like that."

"I know. Everything would be perfect if—" Maria shook her head and continued in a low voice "—I knew Roberto was really all right. We worry about him so much."

"Surely things are better now that he's at boarding school."

"Yes, we've managed to separate him from the neighborhood toughs." Maria looked across the table at Susan, her deep brown eyes clouded with concern. "Only now he's having problems fitting in at Oakridge. He's not happy. I can tell from his phone calls. He's a smart boy, Susan, but already he's doing poorly in some classes. I don't think he's made any friends."

"Fifteen is a difficult age." Especially if you're a scholarship student at an exclusive private school, Susan added silently.

She knew something of what Roberto was going through. She'd attended an exclusive boarding school herself. Being the only poor, fatherless girl living with the offspring of steel magnates, Wall Street tycoons and Mayflower descendants had proved to be brutal on the adolescent psyche. A scholarship might pay one's tuition to the finest school, but it didn't pay for fancy clothes, expensive vacations and the sundry other accoutrements of the wealthy. It didn't buy one a background—and prevent unspoken prejudice.

But Susan had endured four years of Carlisle Academy by studying very hard and by covering her sense of inadequacy with dry, insightful remarks. And she'd never allowed any kid to get close enough to matter to her. She'd gotten smart about that fast. Why put herself in a position to be hurt? Besides, the type of girls she'd gone to school with would have suffered some kind of culture shock if they'd ever stepped foot inside the O'Tooles' third-floor walk-up.

She'd stuck it out because her mother had desperately wanted it for her. How could she drop out when Fay practically moved heaven and earth *and* Mrs. Harrison to get her into Carlisle in the first place? So she had stayed, worked hard and gotten one of the best prep school educations available.

And she'd hated every single day of it.

But Susan knew Maria didn't need to hear that. "You've got to give Roberto all the support you can," she said instead. "Try to understand what it's like for him there. It's hard to feel like an outsider, like you don't belong—especially at such a vulnerable age."

The waiter arrived with their food, the interruption allowing the two women to move on to other subjects. They munched on turkey club sandwiches and talked enthusiastically of their new lives. Over the years much had changed for them both. And it was clear the changes were, predominantly, for the better.

Because her lunch with Maria lasted longer than expected, Susan worked late that evening. It was dusk by the time she exited from the Rosslyn Metro station. The end of September had brought early darkness and a sharp nip to the evening air. Susan shivered as she headed up Wilson Boulevard. Her blue suit jacket, plenty adequate for the sunny and often balmy fall days, was much too light for these cooler evenings.

Unfortunately tonight she had to stop at the supermarket on her way home. There wasn't one decent thing in the refrigerator for dinner, and she was starving. When she reached the supermarket, she wheeled a cart directly to the frozen foods aisle and selected several low-calorie gourmet frozen dinners. Thank goodness her kitchen came furnished with a microwave, she mused as the first enervating strains of fatigue licked at her limbs. Unfortunately she had five good-size blocks to walk before she reached home.

As the automatic exit door swung open for her, a young man, wearing jeans and a threadbare denim jacket, stood outside. He held out a handbill to her. "Help save the Somerset."

"The Somerset?" Susan stopped, shifting the grocery bag and briefcase around in her arms. She wanted to get a good look at the sheet of paper the young man had thrust into her hand. "I used to live there."

"Yeah? Well, only people with plenty of bucks will be living there if these developers get their hands on it. The rumor is a purchase agreement has already been signed," the youth revealed. "Then the Somerset will become either a luxury apartment building or condos, just like everything else in Rosslyn."

Susan knew what he meant, because *she* was renting a condominium apartment from an investor-owner. Scanning the handbill, she noted a landlord-tenant meeting was scheduled for the following week. "Do you know Alice McGraw?" she asked.

"Yeah, I know Alice. Seventy years old and about as spry as they come."

"She was my next-door neighbor."

"No kidding? Well, Alice and her cronies are really in deep trouble with this thing, you know. Me, I'm just a student. I'll roll with it if I have to. But what about these old guys who've been living in the building for decades? Where can they go?"

Susan knew the options were limited and that something had to be done. "Is this meeting next week open to the public?"

The young man nodded.

"Has the local press been notified?"

"Absolutely," he said, excited by her show of serious interest. "Can we count on your support? Will you come to the meeting?"

"You bet your boots I'll be there."

By the time she reached her apartment, Susan was all fired up. Fatigue had disappeared along with the growling in her stomach. Even before she unpacked the groceries she was on the phone to Alice McGraw, arranging to visit her the next morning. She wanted to see and hear for herself what was happening at the Somerset.

After calling Alice, Susan found it difficult to relax. Ideas and plans and fears for the not-so-faceless residents of the Somerset rushed through her mind. The familiar sensations of apprehension, excitement and outrage were coursing through her body. She knew she was preparing emotionally to do battle for her former neighbors.

Although her hunger had dissipated, she also knew she had to eat. She popped a frozen dinner into the microwave, then retrieved a TV tray table from the coat closet. Unfolding the table, Susan groaned as she glanced around her living room. It looked positively Spartan. Before she had left for work she had planned to spend this evening unpacking the several moving crates sitting in the middle of the room. Of course, that had been before she'd learned about the Somerset, and before she'd had the long lunch with Maria, and before she had run into Tony at his office.

Tony. For the first time that day she allowed herself to think about their chance meeting in the reception room. It was certainly different from their encounter on the Metro. Friendlier? Maybe not. But there was also something about the way he'd looked at her. His bespectacled green eyes had focused on her with a curiosity that had confused her, while an unexpected awkwardness and giddiness had swirled from her head to the pit of her stomach.

She'd felt more relieved than startled when he dashed off to meet William Leland.

What a day, she thought as she plopped herself down on the bottle-green sofa bed. It was the only solid piece of furniture in the apartment. One of these days she'd have to get herself motivated to make the apartment into a home. She thought of her mother. Susan really was disappointed she couldn't come down for the weekend. Going out to eat, shopping, even working on the apartment together would have been fun. For, if nothing else, Fay O'Toole was one great motivator.

Just then an aching twinge in her back reminded her of the torturous nature of sofa beds. "At least buy yourself a real bed," she ordered herself out loud.

SUSAN SAW right away that the Somerset had fallen victim to neglect. Peeling wallpaper in the lobby, cracked plaster on the ceilings and stained carpeting in the corridors were clear signs of cosmetic deterioration. She could only imagine what shape the plumbing and heating systems were in. The Somerset had never been anything more than moderate-income apartments, but when she was living there it had been well managed and maintained. Now she could see by its condition that the owners had let maintenance slide, a sure sign they were just waiting for a buyer to take the building off their hands.

At first Susan thought she had knocked on the wrong door. "Alice?" she asked the elderly woman who opened the door as far as the latched chain lock permitted. This woman looked somewhat different from the way Susan remembered.

The voice, however, deep and brassy, was instantly recognizable. "Susan O'Toole, come in, come in. Let me get a good look at you." Unlocking the door, Alice pulled her inside the apartment.

As Alice looked her over, Susan realized the intervening years had altered the seventy-year-old woman's appearance considerably. Most noticeable was her hair. It was pure white now where before Alice had kept it dyed dark brown. She also remembered her as being big-boned, husky. But Alice had lost weight. Her cotton house dress fit loosely, and her frame seemed almost frail.

"Susan, I can tell by the way you're looking at me that you're wondering if I'm feeling poorly."

"Well . . ."

"Well, I'm not. I've lost some excess baggage," Alice claimed with a light slap on her hip, "but I'm as fit as a fiddle. My mind is clear, and although I'm wearing my hair au naturel these days, in my heart I'm still a stunning brunette."

Susan chuckled. She could see that Alice's cheeks were a healthy pink and her hazel eyes were clear and bright. "Okay, I'm convinced. It is good to see you again, Alice."

"Same here, honey. And something in that bag sure smells good."

She held up a large white paper bag. "I brought us breakfast."

They sat in Alice's immaculate kitchen. The building might be crumbling around her, but Alice kept her apartment as clean and neat as possible. Alice explained that two burners on the electric range were broken and plaster was cracking and peeling off her bedroom ceiling. And Susan could see for herself that the entire place was badly in need of a fresh coat of paint. Still, it was cozy. She knew Alice would never find another halfway decent apartment in the Washington metropolitan area for the same low rent she was paying here.

Over ham and cheese croissants, juice and coffee, she filled Alice in on the past couple of years.

"I can tell you're disappointed your mother decided against moving here with you," Alice commented. "But I can understand her wanting to stay in Baltimore. Everything she's ever known is there.''

''Not to mention that my mother guards her independence like a hawk. I think she was afraid I'd cramp her style.''

Laughing heartily, Alice leaned back in her chair. ''And more power to her, God bless her. She'll be visiting often enough, I imagine.''

''I certainly hope so.''

As Alice drank the last of her orange juice, Susan dug into her purse for the handbill the college student had given her. ''Looks like we're going to have some trouble around the Somerset,'' she said, smoothing out the paper with the flat of her hand.

Alice's face fell at the sight of the handbill. The brass and the humor were gone. A fretful expression made her look every bit as old as her seventy years. She started shaking her head. ''I don't know what's going to happen to all of us.''

''Well, somewhere, somehow we're going to have to find an answer to that,'' Susan replied calmly. ''Tell me what's going on.''

Alice revealed what she knew about the pending sale of the building. All the current tenants could rerent their apartments, once renovated, at greatly increased rates. If they didn't rent, then the new owner would pay them a sum of money for relocation expenses as required by the law.

''The problem is, I can't afford this place no matter how much of a break they give us. The starting rent will be just too high,'' Alice said. ''And where can I relocate? Everything around here's the same—condominiums or fancy apartments. I can't afford those kinds of places on Social Security. None of us can.''

''Are Gerald, Eva and Sally still living here?''

''Yes. And several more retirees have moved in since you left. There's this new fellow who lives on the fifth floor. I don't know him too well, but Eva said he's been forced to move out of four buildings that were slated for conversion." Alice raised her eyes to the ceiling in exasperation. "One couple, Nan and Lonny, have been turned out of their homes twice in five years because of condos. This will be the third time for them. Except now there's no place else to go. The Somerset was the last."

Her voice broke, and she took a deep breath before continuing. "This has been my home for thirty years, Susan. Where does someone like me go? I'll be homeless, just like those poor souls who sleep on the grates near the subways." Tears filled her frightened eyes.

Susan felt like crying herself. People like Alice had worked hard all their lives and had given so much to the community. They deserved better than to be fearing for the roof over their head.

Swallowing hard, she willed her voice to be steady. "You've got to hold on and be strong." She placed her hand on Alice's trembling shoulder. "Believe me, there are solutions. I'll help you find them. I promise."

Chapter Three

"The poor woman is scared to death she'll end up homeless."

"And with good reason, I'd say." Neil Stecker shook his head, obviously disturbed by the truth of his remark.

Although Susan had met Neil only briefly on her first day of work at the association, she sensed he was the type of man who would want to help the Somerset tenants. As the association's director of housing affairs, Neil was an expert in the field. As soon as she called him, his concern was apparent as he generously offered to come downstairs to her office to discuss the situation.

Tall, with thick blond hair and beard and dark, interesting eyes, Neil didn't mince his words about the situation. "This kind of thing is happening all across the country. The expanding redevelopment of cities and the inner suburbs—like Rosslyn—has its fallout. Unfortunately it's the elderly and other disadvantaged groups who get left out in the cold."

He sank comfortably into a chair, his lanky legs stretching out to their full length. "Tell me, has your friend been in touch with the county's human services department?"

She nodded. "Most of the senior citizen residences have long waiting lists. All the county can find for her right now is a bed in a nursing home. That would practically be living death for a healthy, independent woman like Alice.''

"Short-term solutions are often the only solutions, even if they're not very palatable.''

"Well, she can't go to a nursing home. I'd have her move in with me first.''

"That's all well and good—if Alice would even consider it. But what about the others?''

She felt frustrated. "I know, I know. So how can we help?''

He mentioned strategies, ranging from alerting the media about the situation to lobbying state and federal officials. "But as far as I'm concerned,'' he added, "the most direct way to solve this particular problem is to take legal action against the owners. If nothing else, this would buy Alice and her friends some time.''

"Buy them some time,'' she repeated thoughtfully, "until alternative housing can be found.''

"That's the idea.''

"Of course, I'm sure they'd rather remain just where they are.''

Glancing at his watch, Neil stood up. "Susan, I've got to run. Perhaps we could discuss this further over dinner—say on Saturday? That is, if you don't already have plans.''

"You wouldn't mind? Giving up your Saturday night, I mean.''

He smiled. "I'm not being completely selfless. I'd like to get to know you better.''

So he was asking her out on a date. She found the idea appealing. After all, he was friendly, knowledgeable, sincere, attractive. And it wouldn't be a boring evening by any means because they had their work in common. "I'd be delighted.''

After Neil left, Susan considered his suggestions for helping Alice. Taking legal action probably was the wisest course. But going to court would cost a small fortune, and that was something she was sure Alice and her friends didn't have.

It made her sad when she considered that Alice wasn't much older than Fay. Only Alice had no close relatives, no one to turn to for financial assistance. But if it weren't for Susan, Fay would be alone, too, and could, quite conceivably, find herself in the same dilemma. Although her mother was a scrappy, independent woman, she was only one child away from being as vulnerable to such a crisis as Alice. This thought made Susan shudder.

It also made her want to see her mother.

DRIVING UP to Baltimore first thing Saturday morning, Susan knew her mother would already be at the Harrisons' house. Indeed, she found Fay in the big shiny kitchen, polishing silver for the night's dinner party.

"For heaven's sake, Susan, what's gotten into you? First the phone call the other morning, and now you show up here unannounced."

She joined her mother at the kitchen table. "I just wanted to visit with you. And I figured if you couldn't come to me, I'd come to you."

"Is that so?" Fay looked skeptical. "Well, I'm not sure how much visiting I'll be able to do, dear. Mrs. H. is already on edge about tonight."

Poor Mrs. H., Susan thought wryly. Then she grabbed one of the soft white cloths by her mother's elbow. "I'll help," she offered, reaching for the silver polish. "We can talk while we work."

Her mother sighed and shook her head. "Suit yourself, dear."

Fay reheated the breakfast coffee and they talked for a while about her new apartment and job. As always her mother was anxious to hear about the people with whom she worked.

"Sounds as if the new job's working out well," Fay said. "Now aren't you glad you decided to take it, after all?"

"Yes, Mama." She wondered if hers was the only mother who was always right. "Still, I wish you had moved down with me."

"You're not to feel guilty about moving an hour away. It's like I've said all along—my life's here in Baltimore. Always has been, always will be."

"I know, I know." Yet, as she sat in the Harrisons' kitchen, a room in which she'd spent countless hours as a child, her present life in Washington seemed light-years away.

"Besides, you'd be miserable in Washington without Cousin Iris and your cronies from St. Mike's," Susan conceded. Then she thought of Alice and *her* cronies from the Somerset, and an earlier fear revived itself. "Mama, you'll let me know if you ever need anything or run into any problems, won't you?"

"Of course I will, Suz."

"Promise me."

"Promise?" Fay looked puzzled.

"No keeping secrets, no hiding bad news."

She heard her mother's exasperated sigh loud and clear. "All right, I promise. Okay? Now, would you mind telling me what this is all about?"

Susan explained about the crisis facing the elderly Somerset tenants. As always she was completely truthful with her mother, knowing it was useless to try to spare the grittier details. Fay wanted facts, clean and simple. She'd learned to deal with life head-on shortly after her husband died, leaving her the sole support of their baby girl. From then on, as she always told Susan, she believed that she'd suffer more from what she didn't know than from what she did.

Fay finished rubbing the last ornate fork. "I hope those poor souls get this straightened out."

"Me, too, Mama. It looks as if they'll have to retain a lawyer."

"A good one." Her mother nodded knowingly. "They say having a good lawyer can make all the difference."

"They also can be very expensive. I'm not sure what these people can afford, but we'll try to find someone."

"You used to work with a bunch of lawyers at that legal aid office, didn't you? Maybe you could call one of them."

This idea had occurred to Susan. But she had lost touch with the people she used to work with, and it would take time to find them. Of course, Maria Lopez might be able to help her track down a former co-worker or two, might even know who was still active in tenants' rights. Susan made a mental note to call her when she got back to Washington that afternoon.

"How many guests are we expecting for dinner tonight?" Susan asked, deciding it was time to change to a less depressing subject.

"Only ten. But Mrs. H. is really putting on the dog for her sister-in-law from Pittsburgh." Her mother raised her eyes heavenward. "You'd think she was the Queen of Sheba or something."

"The two ladies still don't get along, eh?"

Fay chuckled. "Don't ask."

As if on cue, Mrs. Harrison bustled into the kitchen. "Fay, I'm about to leave for the hairdresser. Do I need to pick up anything for—why, Susan, what a surprise!"

Susan wasn't sure what kind of a surprise Mrs. Harrison meant.

"Suzy drove up to say hello," Fay interjected. "Now wasn't that nice of her?"

Mrs. Harrison cleared her throat. "Very nice, indeed. I'm just sorry I can't stay to chat, dear, but with this dinner tonight we're all frantic." Glancing from Susan to Fay and back to Susan, she hastily added, "Your mother's just a doll to help me out tonight. I don't know what I'd do without her." Then her eyes landed on the newly polished silverware. "Oh, good, the silver's done. What about the table linen, Fay? It's back from the laundry, isn't it?"

"Yes, I just haven't gotten it from the linen closet yet." Fay stood and started edging her boss out the door. "Now you don't want to be late for your hair appointment."

Mrs. Harrison glanced at her watch. "Thank you, dear. And on my way out I'll fetch the linen and leave it in the dining room." She tossed Susan a careless goodbye wave.

Fay let out a long, slow breath and peered down at Susan. "See what I mean?"

"I don't think she was too thrilled to see me, Mama. She's afraid I'll keep you from your work."

"You're always thinking the worst of her," her mother said, shaking her head.

"What?"

"It's true," she insisted. "Ever since she got mad at you for turning down the job offer at Mr. H.'s firm after you graduated from law school."

"She just couldn't accept that I'd decided practicing law wasn't for me."

"Sometimes I still find it hard to understand."

"Fay!" Mrs. Harrison's shrill cry sounded from the next room.

"Oh, heavens, now what?" Fay muttered as she pushed through the swinging door leading to the dining room.

Susan thought it best to stay put in the kitchen. Pouring herself a second cup of coffee, she could only half hear what Mrs. Harrison was complaining about. Something about the table linens. Her mother was quick with her replies, though, she thought with satisfaction. Fay never took these things lying down.

"I asked you before not to use Nickerson's Laundry, Fay," Mrs. Harrison barked. "See that you don't again."

Susan heard this loud and clear, and her blood boiled.

Fay returned to the kitchen, the tablecloth in question draped over her arms. She shot Susan a sharp glance. "Don't say a word, Suz. The woman's on edge, that's all."

Susan let her anger simmer away. Her mother had gotten enough flak from Mrs. H. already. Instead, she took the tablecloth from her mother's arms. "What's the problem?"

"Needs a good pressing. The cleaner botched it."

"I'll do it."

Susan retrieved the iron and ironing board from the rear laundry room and set them up in the kitchen in order to keep Fay company while she cooked. They both worked quietly for a while. Susan derived a therapeutic pleasure from steaming out the creases in the heavy white linen as she watched her mother move around the kitchen through the iron's mist.

Yet, as Fay's plump body stooped in front of the open refrigerator, childhood memories clouded Susan's thoughts. She could see herself sitting in this very room, eating supper while Fay ran in and out to serve the Harrisons in the dining room. She also recalled doing her homework at the kitchen table while Fay washed and ironed the family's clothes. And she'd never forget those Saturday mornings when Mrs. H. dashed off to the beauty parlor while Fay cleaned her bathrooms and changed her bed sheets.

Now, from Susan's standpoint, it seemed little had changed. True, Fay was older and rounder and her salt-and-pepper hair had turned white. As for herself, she was now well educated and had a great job, but her mother was still keeping another woman's house. And this filled her with an ambivalence she didn't know how to deal with. So she buried it inside her, along with this latest rash of unwelcomed memories.

Knowing her mother would insist on making lunch despite how busy she was, Susan decided to leave shortly before noon. As she prepared to go, Fay, as always, reminded her to eat right and lock up at night. "And, honey," Fay continued in her best "now listen to Mother" voice, "I'm real proud you're helping those elderly tenants. But don't be too busy saving the world to pay attention to your social life. Sometimes you do forget."

She should have known this was coming. "Mama, you'll be pleased to hear that I have a date tonight."

"Well, hallelujah," Fay declared, making no attempt to contain her delight. "Maybe there's hope for you yet."

Shortly after she arrived back at her apartment, Susan telephoned Maria Lopez. During the drive home, she'd mulled over her mother's suggestion for finding an attorney to help the Somerset tenants and now was anxious to get moving on it. Unfortunately Maria didn't answer her phone.

Frustrated, Susan dialed Maria's number every twenty minutes or so, busying herself with household chores between calls. She hated delay of any kind, especially when it came to something important like this. God, she hoped Maria and her husband hadn't gone away for the weekend.

Three hours later Maria picked up the phone on the fifth ring.

"Finally!" Susan gasped, rushing into a detailed rundown of how long she'd been calling. Only when Maria defensively explained she'd been out doing her Saturday shopping did Susan realize how intense—and foolish—she must have sounded.

She apologized by explaining the situation at the Somerset.

"Gosh, I suppose I could locate a couple of the guys from the old office. But, Susan, have you forgotten Tony Brandon?"

She was startled. Tony hadn't entered her mind. But had she actually forgotten about him? Or had she just blocked him out?

"You said these people are in a critical situation," Maria continued. "I think Tony could help them."

Susan shifted the receiver to her other ear. "But—he's probably not licensed to practice in Virginia."

"I believe he is. Besides, when it came to tenants' rights, Tony was one of the best."

"I think *was* is the operative word here. Can you tell me when he last worked on this kind of case?"

"Honestly, I don't keep track of the man's caseload. I know he's extremely busy."

"He handles quite a few big cases for the firm, doesn't he?" Susan suggested thoughtfully.

"Of course. He's very important to the firm."

"I'm sure he is," she said, not sure she meant it the way it sounded. Tony was an excellent, dedicated lawyer, and she had never believed otherwise. That, however, was beside the point now. "Working all those billable hours must make it difficult to fit pro bono work into his schedule."

"He tried. But it was a lack of time, not a lack of desire to help that held him back," Maria said immediately. "Let's face it, Conners, Brandon and Moffet is a business with demanding clients and cases that are often so complex they take years to resolve. It's easy to get caught up in that."

"I know it happens. It's just a shame that it happened to Tony." She remembered how Tony had tried to temper his resignation from the legal aid bureau by insisting that pro bono work would be a priority for him at his new firm. She'd been skeptical then. It gave her small satisfaction to know now that her doubts had been well-founded.

"He could make such a difference in people's lives," Susan added in wistful afterthought. But then she caught herself. "Will you listen to me? Getting on my high horse again, aren't I?"

Her bright, self-mocking tone did the trick in easing any tension between Maria and herself. Maria chuckled. "Okay, Susan, I'll look around for you. I'll even mention it at work. A few people at the firm do take on cases for little or no fee, and some do have experience in tenants' rights cases," she advised. "I wish you wouldn't rule out Tony, though."

"Even if he wanted to do it, what makes you think he'd have the time?"

"I think he'd make the time—if it was important enough."

Ah, yes, but who knew what Tony Brandon considered important these days?

"Look, Maria, if I thought Tony was the best man for the tenants, I'd swallow my pride," she conceded. "I'd put up with the awkwardness between us. All I know is that he hasn't done this kind of law in quite some time. And he's probably too busy, anyway."

Maria didn't argue further, much to her relief. As far as Susan was concerned, she and Tony Brandon were like oil and water. It would be best if the two of them simply kept their distance.

Still, a twinge of guilt nagged at her. But what would be best for the Somerset tenants?

ALTHOUGH TONY had enjoyed her company in the past, the lovely Taylor Peters was having a definite numbing effect on him tonight. She had begun the evening by giving him a blow-by-blow account of how she had managed to wangle them a coveted Friday night dinner reservation at the newest eatery in the District. Over appetizer and entrée he heard every excruciating detail concerning her hot pursuit of a partnership at the law firm where she worked. By dessert and coffee Taylor was going on and on about the expensive Eastern Shore cottage her father was helping her to buy.

Something was wrong here. Tony suspected it was him. Taylor may be getting carried away with herself right now, but she was usually a friendly and interesting lady. If Taylor was half as shallow as she sounded tonight, they wouldn't even be dating as casually as they were.

No, the fault was his. He wasn't keeping up his side of the conversation; Taylor probably felt obliged to rattle on. But he was tired. It had been a particularly grueling day at work, yet he felt he'd accomplished little. William Leland's interest in the law firm was still up in the air—much to his father's chagrin. And for some inexplicable reason he couldn't forget the look of disapproval on Susan O'Toole's face the other day when she heard the firm was courting Leland. Would that self-righteous woman haunt him for the rest of his life?

He felt better when they joined Maria and Luis Lopez at the Kennedy Center after dinner. The pre-Broadway musical they were seeing at the Opera House was diverting enough to keep thoughts of Susan O'Toole at bay.

Then came the intermission.

As soon as they stepped down to the center's great red-carpeted lobby, Taylor excused herself and headed for the powder room. Maria sent Luis off to buy her a soda. "I've got something to discuss with you," she announced, leading him through the crowd toward one of the massive floor-to-ceiling windows overlooking the Potomac River.

"Susan O'Toole" were the first words out of her mouth.

The irony of it would have amused him, except he was quickly caught up in Maria's tale about Susan and the Somerset tenants. "She's probably going to kill me for telling you about it," Maria admitted, "but the way she described the situation to me this afternoon—I thought you might be able to help."

"Sounds like those people have big problems."

"Apparently morale is very low."

"And Susan doubts my ability to handle this even though I have more tenants' rights cases under my belt than any other guy in the firm." The irony in that did amuse him.

"Not recently you haven't," Maria reminded him. "You've been so wrapped up in all the corporate and government stuff, you haven't had time for much else. Face it, you are a bit rusty."

He was painfully aware of how little pro bono work he had done these past few years, and he didn't like being reminded of it. "You really believe that's her only reason for nixing me?"

He didn't have to elaborate; Maria knew exactly what he meant. "You can't really blame her. Leaving the legal aid office when you did caused a lot of problems for her."

Despite Maria's defense, he couldn't help feeling indignant. "That was years ago. Besides, why should Miss High-and-Mighty put her personal feelings ahead of someone else's best interests?"

"Forget about Susan for a minute, would you?" she insisted with a harsh whisper. "Look, I'm saying this to you because we've been friends for a long time. I've noticed a restlessness in you these past few months. At the office I can see how these cases you're handling are leaving you empty. You do a good job, but it's not satisfying anymore, is it?"

"What are you getting at?"

"You, my friend, are a man who is not happy in his work."

"For Christ's sake, what has this got to do with Susan?"

"Very little as far as I'm concerned. It does have everything to do with you."

"Explain that, please?"

"Maybe this kind of challenge will shake you up a bit, get you out of the doldrums." She gave a sigh of exasperation. "And, personally, I think you're the best man for the job."

"Thanks for the vote of confidence." He cracked a wry smile.

"Think about it, please? I did promise Susan I'd mention it to some of the other guys in the office."

"No one else in the firm has the kind of expertise this case requires." He didn't say this to boast; he said it because it was the truth.

Maria grinned. "Now that's what I like to hear."

The last act of the musical passed before his eyes in a blur. He couldn't concentrate. Maria's assertions had been right on the money. Lately he *had* been just going through the motions at work. He knew it, and yet he had avoided reflecting on the cause of his discontent. Perhaps he feared the questions any soul-searching might ask. Perhaps he'd be embarrassed by the answers.

Then, with Susan's return to Washington, all the brash declarations he'd made four years ago about his career, his life, came back to haunt him. Things hadn't quite turned out the way he'd expected. Susan's return, Maria's lecture, the Somerset's legal woes all suddenly seemed to bring into focus his underlying sense of failure. It wasn't failure in a professional sense, but a failure of his hopes and dreams.

Although he was mildly annoyed by Maria's chastisement, she was a dear friend. Tony knew she had meant well. But he was outright irritated with Susan, although he'd be hard-pressed to explain why. It wasn't her fault that he perceived her mere presence as a voice of conscience, taunting him for not living up to his promise.

He was relieved when the play ended. Trying to make up for his lackluster behavior, he was extra attentive to Taylor while he drove to her home in Georgetown. Once he had said good-night, however, he began contemplating strategies for the Somerset situation. He could help Alice McGraw and the others; he was certain of it. What was more, he *needed* to help them.

SUSAN SNEAKED a peek at her watch as she tried to suppress a tired yawn. She couldn't help it. Her day had been hectic, and now it was almost midnight. But because he had a long drive to the Maryland suburbs ahead of him, she had offered Neil a cup of coffee for the road. That cup of coffee had stretched into three.

She liked Neil, and they'd had a nice enough time together. Nothing fancy—a light dinner at a popular café near Dupont Circle followed by a movie. Frankly this kind of uncomplicated evening suited her. She didn't need the extra flourishes like flowers or expensive wine. Nor did she want to be taken to a "romantic" restaurant with dim lights and soft music designed to spawn an intimacy she wasn't ready to feel.

Neil wasn't trying to impress her with anything, and that was just fine. And she'd probably go out with him again if he asked. But right now she wanted him to go home so she could go to bed.

Finally Neil finished his last cup. "I better hit the road," he announced, getting up from the sofa. He searched around the meagerly furnished living room for somewhere to put his empty coffee cup.

"How long did you say you've been living here?" he asked as she took the cup from him.

"A few weeks."

"Waiting for your stuff to be delivered from Baltimore?"

"Actually, I'm starting from scratch. I haven't had time to shop for furniture yet," she said, feeling somewhat defensive.

"I'd be happy to help. This place has a lot of possibilities. I know a great furniture store out in Rockville."

"Thanks, Neil. I'll give it some thought."

"I'm free on Sunday if you'd like to go shopping then."

She cast him a playful look. "Hey, do you get a commission for bringing in customers or something? You sound awfully eager to get me there."

He laughed. "No, no, nothing like that. I guess when I move into a new place my first impulse is to settle in," he explained. "I feel if my home is in order, then order in other parts of my life will naturally follow."

Susan gradually guided Neil toward the door. "You're probably right. I'll get my act together sooner or later." Although she liked Neil, he was sounding rather pushy about the unfurnished state of her apartment. She disliked feeling pressured, especially about something that—in the overall scheme of things—seemed fairly inconsequential. She didn't need external things like furniture to give her a sense of order.

As she opened her front door, the telephone rang, saving her from any more of this discussion, and from a dragged-out goodbye. It was probably a wrong number, she thought when she quickly closed the door behind Neil. A wrong number with good timing.

"Susan? This is Tony Brandon."

Surprise made it hard to catch her breath. Finally she managed to say, "Pretty late to be calling, isn't it?"

"You sound wide awake to me."

Even with the distracting background noise of passing cars and chattering pedestrians on his end of the line, Susan detected belligerence in his tone. "Tony, what's this about?"

"I've been talking with Maria."

She didn't have to guess about what. "So she told you about the Somerset." Maria certainly didn't waste any time, she thought dryly.

"I think we should talk about it. Now."

"Right now?"

"Over the phone or in person, if you prefer. I'm at a phone on M Street in Georgetown. I can be in Rosslyn in a matter of minutes. Either way is fine with me, as long as we talk."

He sounded angry. She was getting annoyed. "You've got a lot of nerve. In case you haven't noticed, it's well after midnight. I'm too tired to do anything but go to bed."

"Won't work, Susan. As I recall, you used to work around the clock with energy to spare, if something was important enough."

"I'm a little older now. I don't have that kind of stamina anymore," she cracked testily. "Besides, I dislike talking about something as important as the Somerset over the telephone."

"Fine. I'll be right over."

"Now wait a minute. I—"

"Susan, it's the Somerset tenants who can't wait. If you sincerely want to help them, you'll hear me out."

She held her tongue. Tony was hitting her where she was most vulnerable, and he knew it. Yet, when he put it like that, how could she refuse to see him? "All right, come. I'll give you fifteen minutes."

"That'll be more than enough time for what I have to say to you, Susan O'Toole."

Chapter Four

"Glad to see I didn't drag you out of bed."

Tony breezed through Susan's front door. He wasn't expecting a friendly reception from her, and he certainly wasn't expecting her to be all dressed up—and looking gorgeous.

Susan ignored his remark. "I see you had no trouble with my directions." She nodded toward the sofa. "Won't you sit down?"

"After you."

As she led the way, his eyes settled on her back, taking in the graceful sway of her walk and how the dark purple sash wrapped around her waist made her slim figure seem curvier. He appreciated the way her dress clung softly to her waist and hips. It wasn't a revealing garment by any means, but on Susan it was very much a sexy little black dress.

She sat down first, crossing her long legs in one fluid movement. It was such a womanly gesture and rather unexpected from someone like her. Every muscle in his body tightened, making him, again, all too aware of a Susan he hadn't known before. When he sat beside her, he realized how good she smelled. Her fragrance was sophisticated, maybe exotic, definitely feminine. Like Susan herself? he wondered.

"Tony, you've come to have your say, so say it."

She broke her own spell. He leaned back into the sofa, physically distancing himself from her and her provocative perfume. He struggled to get his mind focused on the matter at hand. His head clear of her fragrance, he was then distracted by another pleasant aroma hovering over the room. He grabbed at it as a chance to pull himself together. "Is that fresh coffee I smell?"

"Not too fresh. I made it for a friend before he drove home." She sighed before adding, "There's a little left if you want it."

Coffee for a male friend? All dressed up late on a Friday night? Of course, she had been out on a date. The woman actually had a personal life! And he'd been worried about waking her up.

"No thanks," he replied curtly, her revelation having snapped him back to reality. "My allotted fifteen minutes don't allow for a cup of coffee."

Her reply was a cool stare.

"Okay, no more beating around the bush," he began. "Maria told me about the Somerset problem. And the first thing I want to know is why you would sabotage their case just to suit some petty need of yours to shut me out?"

"Sabotage? Petty? Where do you get off—?"

"Isn't it true? Because I left legal aid for reasons *you* disdained, you've determined that I can't or won't help these people. Even when you know—probably better than anyone else—that I may be their best chance."

"You're pretty sure of yourself." Her voice was testy. "Especially for someone who, as I understand it, has been handling nothing but huge corporate and government cases."

His eyes narrowed. "Is that supposed to be some sort of indictment against me?" He rose from the sofa and started pacing in front of it. "I don't want to see old people out on the street any more than you do."

Susan stared down at her hands. "I know."

"Then why are you intent on denying me not only the chance to help them, but also the chance to prove to you that I still take my moral responsibilities seriously?"

"Maybe it's not me you need to prove that to."

Now he wished he hadn't said that. "Maybe yes, maybe no," he said with a shrug. "It's not the issue here, anyway."

She avoided looking at him. "This is really awkward."

"Only if we keep allowing it to be." He joined her on the couch again. "Surely after four years we can put our differences aside in order to help people who need us both?"

"In theory we should, but I have my doubts. Guess I'm just skeptical by nature."

He couldn't help but grin. "Tell me about it."

Susan didn't smile. "Look, how do I know you won't bail out again if something more prestigious or lucrative comes along?"

Her words stung. He always knew that was how she perceived his resignation from legal aid. But hearing it so bluntly stated stung nevertheless.

She didn't wait for him to defend himself. "Tony, do you really have enough time to devote to the Somerset tenants? Your caseload at Conners must be quite heavy."

The insinuation rankled. "I wouldn't shortchange them just because they're pro bono, if that's what you're getting at."

"It's a natural concern."

"Come on Susan. No matter what you think of the choices I've made, you ought to know I'd do nothing less than my best for a client."

"Your intentions may be good, but your skills may be rusty."

"Not on something like this. I can do it."

"There you go again, sounding so sure of yourself."

"I have to be if I want to win." He turned to her with imploring eyes. "And another thing of which I'm darn sure is that when you and I put our heads together, we make a heck of a team. I remember at least two cases at legal aid that we managed to pull out of the hole. We can do it again."

His assertions seemed to catch her off guard. Confusion shadowed her face. "I don't know. That was quite a while ago."

"Sure. And presumably both of us are not only older, but wiser." He eyed Susan's expression thoughtfully. He could tell her doubts about him were slipping. "Remember the Marley Apartments? We managed to keep the university from buying it and turning it into a dorm. And what about the Beacon House?"

Her eyes lit up at the reminder. "We persuaded the mayor's office to get involved."

"And they had a rather stern talk with the developer who wanted to tear it down. Remember how thrilled the tenants were when the owners 'decided' to renovate instead?"

She threw up her hands. "Okay, okay. You make a persuasive case for yourself, Counselor."

"I don't expect us to be bosom buddies, Susan. But working together again could be fun."

"Well, I guess it might."

"Good. Because I think my fifteen minutes just ran out." Smiling, he leaned back against the sofa.

"Oh, I'm sorry about that." Half groaning, half laughing, she covered her face with her hands in embarrassment. "I know I can be a jerk sometimes."

He gently pulled her hands away from her face. "That seems to be part of your charm, Susan," he teased, keeping her hands between his. They felt soft. Warm.

She laughed. "Thanks a lot."

When she slipped her hands from his grasp, he realized he was reluctant to let them go. And this startled him.

He quickly moved away from her. "So what do you say, Ms. O'Toole? Should we arrange a meeting with the Somerset seniors to see if they want to retain me?"

"Sounds good." Her expression then turned solemn. "But I'm warning you, Tony, if they decide to hire you, you'd better not let them down. Understand?"

"Completely."

Her smile returned, warm and relaxed, flooding him with a sense of relief. He'd come here prepared for a ranting, raging argument and, instead, ended up making friends with Susan. If a week ago someone had told him he'd be sitting in her apartment actually laughing with her, he would have said impossible.

"How about a cup of coffee for the road?" she offered.

He nodded and watched her go into the tiny kitchen. His mouth curved into a thoughtful smile. Who said life wasn't full of surprises?

SUSAN COULD TELL by the rapt expressions of the dozen or so people crammed into Alice McGraw's living room that Tony had won himself some clients. As well he should have. From the moment the meeting started he had taken control, exuding confidence and providing encouragement without misleading the elderly Somerset tenants about their prospects.

"As you know, the building has been sold to the Hammond Group," Tony was saying. "Their plans for the building haven't been made public yet. From their past transactions, however, we might assume that they plan to renovate the Somerset into luxury apartments."

"Yeah," a man piped up from the rear of the room, "the Hammond Group were the ones who booted me out of my last apartment. They don't give a tinker's damn about anything but making money.''

"That may well be the case, sir," Tony acknowledged, his tone respectful. "Still, I should contact them regarding what, if any provisions, they intend to make for current residents.''

"Forget it," the man remarked with a disdainful wave of his hand. "They'll never come across.''

Susan spotted Alice craning her neck toward the back of the room. When she located the man speaking, she narrowed her eyes. "Why don't you hold your doom-and-gloom tongue, Mr. O'Brien, and give this young man a chance to explain.''

"Thanks, Alice, but Mr. O'Brien may be correct," Tony said, giving the short elderly man a knowing look. "The Hammond Group probably will not, of its own volition, 'come across' for you. Well, not with anything substantial, anyway. That's when it's up to me to really get down to work." Tony continued. "Let me reassure you all— you're not powerless by any means.''

Susan nodded in silent agreement. That was just what these elderly tenants needed to hear. The group's sense of relief was almost palpable. Their determination to fight for their homes was growing with Tony's every word.

How could she have doubted him so? she wondered. Watching him now as he patiently responded to questions, she felt as if time had slipped a gear. This was the man she had known and admired back at the legal aid office.

"As I mentioned earlier, Susan O'Toole once lived here at the Somerset, so some of you already know her," he announced, pulling her attention back to the present. "She'll be helping me collect the background data on you that I'll need to build our case.''

She acknowledged Tony's comments with a smile and a nod at the people in the room.

Slipping off his tweed sport jacket and loosening his necktie, he asked the tenants to split up into two groups so that he and Susan could start interviewing them. Alice helped Susan get situated at the kitchen table while Tony ensconced himself in the middle of the living room sofa. As each person sat with her at the table, Susan repeated the same questions concerning income, assets and possible housing opportunities. She took copious notes on a thick yellow legal pad. Every now and then she peeked through the kitchen doorway to see Tony scribbling his own notes as he listened to each tenant.

By the time the last tenant had left Alice's apartment, long afternoon shadows crisscrossed the old woman's kitchen. Alice switched on the ceiling light. "You two certainly accomplished a lot this afternoon."

Susan stood at the table, organizing her papers. "Well, we got the ball rolling, anyway. I think some of them are skeptical, though. Like that Mr. O'Brien. He left without talking to us."

"We've still got a long way to go." Tony entered the kitchen, leather briefcase tucked under one arm and his jacket slung haphazardly over the other.

"Well, I can tell you most people left here feeling a heck of a lot better than when they arrived," Alice said. "You two kids are giving us hope. As for Tom O'Brien, he's a crab apple, that one. Lived here for over a year and hardly talks to anyone. A widower, I think."

"I hope he comes around. No one should be forced out of his home," Tony said, dropping his briefcase onto a kitchen chair. He curved his free arm around Alice's narrow shoulders. "But now I'd like to discuss a more pressing concern—I'm starving. What would you two ladies say to an early supper? My treat."

Alice shook her head. "Thank you, Tony. I'd love to, really. But Saturday night is bingo night at the senior citizens' center. Gerald, Eva and I never miss it. Afraid I'm hooked.''

"A gambling woman, are you?" he said with a playful glint in his eye. "Then I guess I'm honored you're taking a gamble on my representing you."

"True, I like a game of chance, but not when it comes to my home. You're what I call a sure thing."

Tony's gaze turned somber as he gently squeezed Alice's shoulder. "I'll try my damnedest."

His thoughtful tone struck a chord of compassion in Susan. Having the fate of elderly people resting on his shoulders had to be daunting, no matter how confident or talented a lawyer he was. For the first time that afternoon she could see how much he took this responsibility to heart. The long, complex meeting seemed to have taken its toll on him. Lines of fatigue masked the usually healthy color of his face. And after talking to many different people for several hours, even his voice sounded tired, raspy.

Alice turned to give Tony's cheek a maternal pat. "I have faith," she said. "And you know what? I think I'll go knock on Mr. Grumpy O'Brien's door and see if I can drag him out to play bingo. That'll give me a chance to work on him for you."

The three of them laughed together. Tony hugged her. "Alice, with you on our side, we can't lose."

"Yeah, like a secret weapon, right?" she joked, obviously relishing the camaraderie. "Now don't let me keep you two from going out to eat," she added, pointedly looking at Susan.

Tony turned to her. "Care to grab a bite with me?"

"Sure." She wasn't going to back away from him this time. His responsibility to these old people was indeed formidable; maybe she could keep it from seeming like a lonely one. At least for today.

She suggested a small Chinese restaurant located around the corner from the Somerset. As they sat down in one of the wide red vinyl-covered booths, she glanced around the dining room. "I used to come here often when I lived at the Somerset, but the name's different now. Must be under new management. Hope it'll be all right."

"We'll take a chance."

"Well, the food used to be good. And back then—for some mysterious reason—I liked their zombies."

Tony looked surprised. "Zombies? You?" A teasing grin spread across his face. "Susan, I never would have guessed."

"What can I say?" She shrugged. "I was young. My tastes were unrefined. But, to reassure you, I don't drink zombies anymore."

"I imagine that's not the only thing about you that's changed since then."

"Four years is a long time," she said quietly, feeling a slight shyness coming over her. "Of course I've changed—as I'm sure you have."

"Yes. Probably." Then he shook his head, a slight trace of a smile remaining on his lips.

"Something funny?"

"I was thinking about last night. When I came over to your place, I was very annoyed with you."

"I could tell."

"I was prepared to do a few rounds of battle. I wasn't expecting things to work out so amenably."

"What you mean is you didn't expect me to break down and give in so easily. Right?"

He laughed heartily and nodded.

The resonance of his laughter, and the ease with which it came to him, chased away her earlier sense of shyness. She was beginning to feel comfortable with him. "Maybe it's not so hard for me to admit when I'm wrong anymore," she confessed, lazily leaning back against the firm vinyl bench. "Most of the time, anyway."

His green eyes settled on her with a look she found difficult to decipher. There was almost a lawyerly skepticism about his gaze, as if he'd found her admission hard to believe. She wanted to ask him if this was true and, if so, why. Yet she wavered, and then lost her chance when the waiter came to take their order. She had held back too long, and the moment had passed.

During their meal, talk strayed back to the Somerset tenants and the information they'd gathered at the meeting. She and Tony batted possible strategies back and forth. Later, when the busboy came back to clear the few remaining plates from their table, she checked her watch. "We've been talking for over two hours."

"Yeah, it's getting busy in here. Looks like they're going to need this table soon."

He was right. The dinner crowd was quickly filling up the restaurant. Tony had paid their tab at least fifteen minutes ago, and the waiter had come back once since then to ask if he could get them anything else. Clearly it was time to move on.

"We haven't even gone over the notes I took on some of the tenants," she pointed out. "Do you think you can understand them on your own?"

"Not unless your handwriting's improved considerably over the years. The entire legal aid staff had declared your handwriting illegible. Remember?"

"I do now," she admitted with some embarrassment.

"Look, why don't I stop by your place on my way home? We can do a quick once-over on your information there. If it's all right with you, of course."

The expression on his face was straightforward, sincere. So why was she hesitating? What was she afraid of? After all, they had spent an entire afternoon together without a hitch. They both had gotten over their initial awkwardness. Being alone with him in her apartment shouldn't be a problem.

Yet it was a problem. For if she was to be honest with herself—and she always tried to be—she'd have to admit she wouldn't mind spending another hour or two with Tony. And her reasons had nothing to do with the Somerset Apartments.

"Well?" He peered at her from across the table.

"Sure, why not?"

He shot her a dazzling smile that made her feel warm all over. She wished she could say it was an artful, well-practiced smile—because that would be easier to deal with. She wasn't attracted to insincerity. But the smile was genuine and very appealing.

He stood and extended his hand to her as she slid out from her side of the booth. His touch was warm, his grasp careful but firm. Suddenly she was aware that her heart was beating a little faster.

"Maybe you could make me some coffee," he suggested as he released her hand.

She had the fleeting impression that he had grabbed the first subject that came to his mind. Had he guessed what she was thinking? She struggled to speak clearly, but her reply still sounded lame to her. "I gather you still drink a lot of coffee."

As they passed through the restaurant door, he shrugged with forced airiness, "I guess that's something about me that won't ever change."

When Tony showed up at her apartment the previous evening, she had been too annoyed to feel nervous. Now, as she unlocked the front door, with him standing right behind her, she was jittery. It was silly, she knew. They were getting along too well today to start arguing again. So what could possibly happen? she asked herself as she switched on the lights.

She took his jacket and hung it in the closet. As she placed it on a hanger, she stroked the fabric. The tweed felt cool from the crisp autumn air, and it held the fresh, light scent of his cologne. Realizing what she was doing, she snatched her hand away.

When she returned to the living room, she found Tony sitting on the carpet with his paperwork and her notes spread out before him. Where else could he put them? She had no table to work on—all she had was the bottle-green sofa.

She noticed he had put on his eyeglasses again. Before the meeting at Alice's he had told her he needed them mostly for reading. Though she found his wearing glasses hard to get used to, she liked the rather professorial air the round gold frames gave him.

Realizing she was standing over him, he glanced up. "Into minimal decorating these days, Susan?"

Lord, not him, too, she thought. Apparently he'd been too preoccupied last time to notice or at least to comment on her apartment's lack of furnishings. "Don't ask," she muttered, turning toward the kitchen to make him his coffee.

As she turned, she noticed that he had rolled up his shirtsleeves. His lean forearms caught her eye. Their muscular smoothness held her attention for a moment as she let her gaze travel along his tanned skin to his hands and long, elegant fingers. She found herself recalling how, back at the restaurant, their touch had made her skin tingle.

Hurrying into the kitchen to start brewing the coffee, she knew she had to get a grip on herself. If she was going to come unglued at the mere sight of this man's bare forearms, she was in big trouble. And this work arrangement could turn into a farce. She took a peek at Tony through the opened kitchen door. He was sitting there on the floor, reading, his golden brown head bowed over her pad of notes, pencil in hand. He seemed oblivious to his surroundings—and to her.

He looked wonderful.

With butterflies dancing defiantly in her stomach, Susan was scared and annoyed with herself at the same time. She was reacting as a teenager would to a cute new boy in homeroom. Yet, in reality, she wasn't even sure she approved of what Tony represented to her: old family money, a last name that opened doors in D.C. and the access to power, which went hand in hand with that privilege.

By the time she brought Tony a mug of coffee, she had her emotions under control. Still, she was uneasy. "I'm sorry we have to use the floor," she offered quietly, sitting down beside him. "I don't know why I haven't gotten around to fixing this place up."

Taking his first sip, Tony gazed at her over the rim of his cup. "Why be sorry? You've probably been busy with more important things—like helping Alice. As long as you've got a bed, a bathroom and a coffeepot, you're all set."

She didn't bother explaining that her only bed was the sofa behind them. She felt better, though, not so much about the apartment, but about Tony. She did rather like him. Maybe they could be friends despite their differences.

"Good coffee," he said after a second sip. "You know, I think I'm going to like working with you again."

"'Cause I make good coffee?"

"No, although it's a definite plus." His grin seemed to deepen his handsomeness in her eyes. "I mean, it's been a long time since I've been involved in a dispute over something as basic and as crucial as the roof over a person's head."

"Too long."

"Maybe so." He looked down at his cup, his grin gone. "Susan, when I joined the firm, I had every intention of doing as much pro bono work as possible. As time went by, though, my work load grew and I never really accomplished that." He returned his gaze to her. "Your return has made me realize that's no excuse. You've galvanized me out of this . . . this paralysis."

She doubted she was the actual catalyst. Something else in his life must have driven him back to this path. But she was curious about the whys and wherefores.

"We only worked together a few months at the legal aid office," she began tentatively, "yet I could see how effective you were. Then, to just up and leave the way you did and why you did—it was hard to understand."

"I imagine it was, but if you knew—" He looked her straight in the eye and then stopped himself.

"If I knew what?" she coaxed, eager to hear his explanation.

But he shook his head. "Look, I'm not going to lie to you. I was attracted to the kind of power my father's firm wields. And I guess I decided it was finally time to take my place in the family business, so to speak. Isn't that understandable?"

"I suppose it is."

Yet she wondered if that was really all there was to it.

Shifting the set of papers in his hands, Tony didn't appear inclined to discuss the matter further. "I've taken up enough of your time tonight," he said, his tone unrevealingly even. "We should get back to these notes."

It didn't take long to review her notes from the Somerset meeting. They discussed what needed to be done on the case that week. He planned to call on officials from the Hammond Group; she would start looking into possible rent subsidies and housing alternatives.

Then, with a promise to call her on Monday and a simple good-night, Tony left. Susan closed the door behind him, feeling unsettled, even a bit let down, which was ridiculous.

She busied herself by straightening up, hoping this sudden flash of restlessness would fade. She picked up Tony's empty coffee mug off the floor. As she gazed wistfully at the cup, her finger encircled its smooth, cool rim. Then she took another look around her practically empty living room. It looked as lonely as she felt.

Chapter Five

Her mother would be disappointed in her, she knew. But over the next two weeks Susan could only manage time for one evening out with Neil. Instead, she spent every spare hour helping the elderly Somerset tenants. The urgency of the situation and the energy needed to meet it added to her sense of purpose.

Going out on more dates would take time away from work she found edifying. The string quartet concert at the National Gallery that Neil took her to on their second date was the kind of understated outing Susan preferred. Yet she begged off his further requests to get together. Her after-work hours were all she had to devote to the Somerset case.

Tony worked hard on this case, as well, impressing Susan with the amount of time he spent on it. Working with him again reminded her of the better days at the legal aid office, and the awkwardness between them ebbed as she felt increasingly at ease with him. His wry humor during dull meetings and his optimistic outlook even on the most trying days never failed to lift her spirits. She found herself looking forward to their work sessions more and more.

Only when she caught herself jumping at the chance to hand-deliver some documents to Tony's office late one afternoon did she realize something new was motivating her: another chance to see him. The notion gave her pause, but it didn't stop her.

"I'm going to run a quick errand," she advised the department's secretary on her way out. "It's such a nice day out and I can do with some fresh air."

This was true, she told herself as she headed down L Street with the packet of financial statements tucked under her arm. Winter was just weeks away. Soon the crisp, sunny days would be history. She should take advantage of the good weather, even if only for a six-block walk.

As she rode the elevator up to Tony's office, a stab of apprehension caused her to reconsider her actions. If she was interested in the man on a more personal level, she should be frank—both with him and herself. Playing this sort of "drop-in" game really wasn't her speed.

Yet she wasn't sure she *wanted* to be personally interested in him. And if she did want to, she didn't know how to go about making it known to him. Talk about arrested development, she taunted herself ruefully.

Perhaps it would be best to simply drop the documents off with the receptionist. She didn't actually have to *hand* the envelope to Tony. Yes, that was the sensible thing to do, she decided.

The receptionist recognized her immediately. "Oh, Miss O'Toole, Mr. Brandon said you'd be delivering this. But I think he wants to see you," the young woman said before Susan could rush off. "You can go in now," the receptionist added as she reached for the telephone. "I'll tell him you're on the way."

Although her plan had gone awry, she was secretly pleased Tony wanted to see her. Having been to his office several times during the past two weeks, she had no trouble finding her way through the maze of corridors and offices. When she reached his secretary's desk, he was already walking out of his office to meet her.

His shirtsleeves were rolled up to his elbows; a conservative striped necktie encircled his collar loosely. And he looked positively exuberant. "Susan, your timing is perfect." Taking her by the hand, he practically waltzed her into his large corner office. "I've got great news."

"So I gathered." She couldn't help giggling.

He reached for her other hand and looked her square in the eye. "Guess who just called me?"

She couldn't seem to catch her breath, but it didn't matter because Tony answered his own question. "Bart Tompkins from the Hammond Group."

"The CEO?"

He nodded.

"You're kidding."

"Not about this. Seems old Bart and some other key executives think we should sit down and talk about this Somerset 'thing.'"

She couldn't believe it. "But you've been after them for weeks to meet with you."

"Bart insists it's been a matter of miscommunication."

"Miscommunication, my foot," she scoffed. "They've just finally realized you're not going to let them get away with ignoring the tenants." She glanced down to see he was still holding her hands. She didn't pull away this time, but looked up to find him watching her. Warmth glimmered in his eyes as his thumbs gently stroked the back of her hands. Her knees felt weak.

"All that matters is that I'm meeting with them later in the week." A satisfied grin lit Tony's face as he finally released her hands and spread his arms out wide. "This could be a real breakthrough."

"I know. It's wonderful." His excitement was contagious, and she smiled broadly. "I can't wait until you tell the tenants at tomorrow morning's meeting."

"Yeah, it'll be nice to have something tangible to report for a change." Gesturing to her to have a seat, he sat down and leaned back into his chair's rich black leather. "But by then I'd better temper my enthusiasm with some caution. As we both know, one meeting does not a settlement make. Anything can happen."

"True. But it is a start." She chose a chair directly in front of his big mahogany desk. As she sat, she carefully placed the packet of documents on her lap where they caught his eye at once.

"The tenants' financial statements?"

"Three copies of each." She lifted the heavy envelope to hand to him.

Even after he reached across the desk to take the packet from her, his gaze lingered on hers. "You didn't have to bring these over yourself," he finally said, his voice low. "I could have sent a messenger."

"I know," she said quietly, about to add something about fresh air and the beautiful day. But they were only excuses, and she didn't want to be coy.

His green eyes flickered for a second. With realization? Acceptance? Acknowledgment? She wasn't sure. She only knew that this fleeting look made her heart skip a beat.

A sharp, intrusive buzz from his telephone broke apart their gaze. Obviously startled, he hesitated a moment before he answered it. "Oh, right. Thanks, Kathy."

He hung up the receiver. "My four-thirty appointment should be arriving soon."

"Oh." She glanced at her watch. "I need to be getting back to the office. They'll be wondering what happened to me."

She rose quickly and was halfway to the door when he caught up with her. "I'll walk you to the elevator," he said, his hand on her elbow.

She nodded, glad that their time together would be extended a few extra minutes. As they made their way out of the suite of offices, walking side by side, she liked that he didn't tower over her. His height seemed to suit hers nicely as her shoulder brushed against his arm from time to time and he slowed his stride to match hers. Still, neither of them spoke a word until they reached the elevators in the outer hall.

Feeling self-conscious, she pressed hard on the down button. "Guess I'll see you tomorrow at the Somerset."

"Right," he said, nodding. "Thanks for delivering the statements."

She told him it was nothing, and then they stood together in a silence she found unbearable. She racked her brain for a way to indicate what she wanted, what she was feeling right now—before the elevator arrived. But the words didn't come, and her mind spun in frustration. She prayed the elevator would get stuck on another floor or, at the very least, arrive so packed with passengers that she'd have to wait for another.

"Damn! I can't stand this."

His outburst zinged her like a jolt of electricity. "What?" she gasped.

"This. You and me." He looked as surprised by his outburst as she felt. "Look, I want to go out with you."

"You do?"

He nodded, lifting his palms in a gesture of uncertainty she found touching. "Have dinner with me tomorrow?"

"I'd like that."

She detected relief in his smile. "Great," he said. "Tomorrow, then, after the meeting?"

"Fine."

She was rewarded with another of his smiles. This one, however, had a new aspect to it—a mischievous glint in his eyes that made his whole face seem younger. He placed a hand on her shoulder, carefully looking to his right and then to his left. Before she knew what was happening he had lifted his hands to her face and held it gently between them. He peered into her eyes, moving nearer and nearer to her until she instinctively closed them as his lips touched hers with smooth, lingering pressure. Soon she was caught up in a floaty feeling of surprise and pleasure. Tony's kiss was as sure and as graceful a first kiss as she thought there could be.

The suddenness of it made her light-headed. She was grateful when Tony continued to hold her face gently after he ended the kiss. She needed to get her bearings. Yet when the chime of the elevator announced its arrival, she was still in a daze.

His hands dropped from her face. "See you tomorrow, Susan," he said, nudging her into the empty elevator car. She was still trying to find her voice as he reached inside to press the lobby button for her. He grinned at her speechlessness. "Just say goodbye, Susan."

This made her smile. "Goodbye, Susan!" she said, feeling her smile widening until she was sure she was beaming. Then the doors snapped shut and the elevator carried her away.

Susan's smile dazzled him. He remained by the closed elevator doors for a moment, extremely pleased by what had just happened. Kissing Susan right then and there had seemed natural and felt right. *Felt great.*

Besides, it was bound to happen sooner or later, he realized. There was a compelling quality about Susan that he'd become increasingly aware of over the past couple of weeks. This quality wasn't easily defined, since it was a combination of things.

Whatever it was about Susan, he liked it. More and more each day.

He strolled back to his office, feeling mellow. This was turning out to be one hell of a good day. His mood must have shown on his face, because his secretary gave him a curious look when he reached her desk.

"Your four-thirty just canceled. And don't you look like the cat that just swallowed the canary," Kathy added.

"Just having a good day," he mused as he leafed through the message slips she had handed him.

"Hmm." With a disbelieving smirk she turned back to her computer terminal.

He had just settled in again at his desk when Kathy quickly opened the door and poked her head in. "Forgive me for telling you this in person, but I think your good day is about to get better." Grinning, she pointed to his phone. "William Leland's secretary is on line two. Mrs. Everly."

"Leland?" Immediately he reached for the phone. As he greeted Mrs. Everly, he motioned to Kathy to come inside. The conversation with Leland's secretary was brief and to the point. He scarcely had time to think. "I'll catch the 6:00 p.m. shuttle," he promised before hanging up.

The call was over so fast that he almost thought he'd imagined it. He looked up at Kathy's expectant face. "Leland wants me to fly up to New York tonight," he revealed, his voice a combination of amazement and disbelief. "I'm having dinner with him and then meeting with his staff lawyers tomorrow." He paused as the implications of the phone call set in. Shaking his head because he still didn't quite believe it, he added, "Wait until my father hears about this."

Kathy was suitably excited, and she started preparations for his trip right away. "I'll cancel tomorrow's appointments," she said on her way out the door. "Good thing your four-thirty canceled out."

Only then did he remember: the meeting with the Somerset tenants tomorrow morning. And his dinner date with Susan. Damn! Still, he wasn't about to turn down a meeting with William Leland.

"Wait. Let me deal with the Somerset meeting. You cancel the rest."

With a groan he leaned so far back in his chair that it practically tilted. He stared straight ahead, focusing on nothing in particular as his perfect day dissolved before his eyes. Breaking a date less than a half hour after making it was bad enough. But telling Susan he'd be missing tomorrow's meeting—and why—was going to be touchy. Very touchy indeed.

"GEE, TONY, this must be some kind of record for breaking a date. I just got back to my office," she said breezily, trying to mask her disappointment. "But if you have urgent business in New York, I understand."

"There's more, Susan."

The edginess in his voice caused a twisting sensation in her stomach. She waited.

"I'm having dinner with William Leland later tonight and then I have to stay over for meetings tomorrow," he explained. "So you see..."

Suddenly she saw things all too clearly. "You'll miss the meeting with the tenants." Now her stomach was in knots. "Oh, Tony," she said with a breathy sigh.

"I'm sorry, Susan, but it can't be helped. This is important to the firm. I have to go."

"I see." When William Leland calls, you come running, she thought. "What do I tell the tenants?"

"I know it's too late to reschedule the meeting, so I've asked an associate from the firm—Rob Berns—to step in for me. He's got a solid background in tenants' rights, and he's driving with me to the airport so I can fill him in on the details."

"You really think he's capable?"

"I'm sure you and Rob can handle the meeting just fine."

She wished she could be as certain as he sounded. At the beginning she had feared something like this would divert his attention from the Somerset tenants. Then the past weeks had lulled her into a false sense of security. Now that this fear was realized disappointment overrode her initial anger. Somehow she had led herself to believe that he wouldn't allow this kind of thing to happen. Had she been unrealistic?

"I guess we have no choice but to handle things."

"I *am* sorry."

"I hope the tenants will understand."

"Frankly, Susan, I bet they'll be more understanding than you seem to be."

She frowned. Maybe he had a point. "Look, Tony, I realize you have to tend to your other work. I really do. I guess I'll just have to get used to the occasional disruption." She knew this was the understanding, common-sense thing to say. And she meant it, mostly. Still, doubts remained.

Although the palpable tension of his phone call with Susan disturbed him, Tony had little time to dwell on it. Rob Berns had a taxi waiting downstairs for the drive to National. Considering it was evening rush hour, they'd still be cutting the timing pretty close. He couldn't afford to miss that flight. Thank goodness experience had taught him to keep an overnight bag and a change of clothes at the office.

He didn't relax until he arrived at Leland's Midtown Manhattan office. Even then he wasn't completely at ease. A lot was at stake here, as his father had made a point to remind Tony before he'd left for the airport. As if he could forget. From the moment William Leland greeted him with a handshake, Tony knew he had to be careful of every word and gesture.

Even though the renowned entrepreneur was short, wiry and balding, he was still an intimidating figure. He was impeccably groomed. Tony noticed that Leland's suit looked freshly pressed, even though it was eight o'clock at night. The garment itself had to be the work of an exclusive London tailor.

An accepted genius, Leland wasn't the most gracious of men. His choice of words was precise, his manner distant.

As they ate in the private dining room adjacent to his penthouse office, Leland kept the conversation impersonal. He made a passing reference to Tony's parents and said nothing at all about himself. They talked mostly about the politics of power in Washington, a topic Leland seemed to find fascinating.

The limited conversation caused them to finish the meal quickly. Tony scarcely knew what he was eating, anyway. His focus was on William Leland. As soon as the waiter poured the coffee, Leland turned his attention to business.

"I'm going ahead with the purchase of Central Satellite Systems. I want your counsel on executing the deal starting tomorrow morning."

"I see." Tony sipped his coffee.

"I've given serious thought to your earlier comments about a Justice Department review of the sale. It is inevitable, isn't it?"

Tony returned the fine china cup to its saucer. "When the owner of one of the largest TV cable systems in the country plans to buy a company that controls seventy-five percent of the country's communications satellites, one has to assume Justice will want a review for possible violation of antitrust laws," he explained. "As I suggested before, they'll be concerned that you'll be able to control other networks' access to satellite service stations."

"I agree. And your representation of private industry in Washington is impressive." Leland's clear-eyed gaze fixed on Tony's eyes. "I only hire the best, which is why I want to retain you to handle this matter."

Leland bestowed this praise in an offhand manner without any hint of emotion. Still, Tony was flattered. A quiet, inner excitement buoyed his spirit. For the first time in his career he felt he'd finally come into his own and made it on his own hard-won reputation.

He thought of his father. Landing William Leland as a client would mean a lot to him, too—in terms of prestige for the firm and, he hoped, in terms of a father's pride.

William Leland concluded their dinner promptly at ten o'clock. "Mr. Collings has called the company limousine to take you back to your hotel," he said, nodding at the butler standing guard by the door. "I will drop in on your meeting with my attorneys at some point tomorrow."

"Of course," Tony said as Leland rose from the table.

"Until tomorrow then." He held his hand out. "Thank you for coming."

He shook Leland's hand and then, right away, the butler began to usher him out of the dining room. Before Tony could turn back to say good-night his strange host had already slipped out a different door. Without further pleasantries or even a simple goodbye, Leland was gone. The man's odd departure left Tony with the disturbing sensation that the past two hours had been a figment of his imagination.

But when he settled into the long black limo waiting for him on the street, he knew his meeting with William Leland had been very real indeed. For the first time that entire evening he relaxed. And he smiled all the way back to the hotel.

His euphoria carried him through the day-long meeting with Leland's staff. Putting his antitrust expertise in high gear, he felt very effective and in control as he conferred with his fellow attorneys. It was a heady feeling. Only when he was flying back to Washington did he finally come down to earth. Alone with his thoughts on the short flight home, Tony, at last, had time to reckon with logistics.

Representing Leland Industries in this kind of case was every Washington lawyer's dream. Tony knew his schedule was already heavy. But he also knew the firm would move mountains to free up his time to work on this. Being linked with Leland's massive empire in an antitrust review meant both high visibility and high fees not only for him, but for Conners, Moffet and Brandon, as well. Not to mention the enormous potential for future business.

Of course, there was the Somerset case to consider. He had made a commitment to the tenants, one he took very much to heart.

Tony felt the aircraft's plunge into descent. He stared out the small window while the plane circled above the city as it prepared to land at National Airport. From his vantage point the well-lit monuments glowed like majestic jewels in the darkness. He gazed down at the shimmering lights of the White House and the Capitol dome beyond, and he felt the familiar twinges of awe and excitement. More landmarks came into view. He even thought he detected the shadowy outline of the Somerset Apartments when the plane curved along the Virginia side of the Potomac.

Washington had always been his home. And this home was a city of power and grandeur. And this city was home to the people who made it run, present and past: people like himself and the retired residents of the Somerset. If he was going to help make the system work for the William Lelands of the world, wasn't he honor-bound to make it work for the elderly tenants? Yet did this mean handling it himself or finding the tenants another competent, less-distracted lawyer who wasn't about to embark on the case of his career?

He stopped at the first public phone he found after disembarking from the plane. He wanted to talk to Susan. Her phone rang several times before being answered with fumbling confusion.

"Hello?" Her greeting was a drowsy rasp.

"I woke you. I'm sorry." Feeling clumsy, he checked his watch. It wasn't even nine o'clock.

"Tony," she half whispered. Then she cleared her throat with a cough. "You didn't really. I was reading and I must have dozed off."

Still, her voice was soft, warm with gentle sleep. The sound of it aroused a tender memory of yesterday's kiss. Had it only been yesterday? he wondered in disbelief. He apologized again for disturbing her. "I should have waited until morning."

"No, I'm glad you called. Are you back in town now?"

"Just got off the plane, actually."

If Susan was surprised by this fact, she didn't sound it. "Then you've had a long day. You must be tired."

"A bit." He waited. Her concern was soothing, and he wanted to hear more of it.

"Was your trip a success?"

At this point the question would have cut him to the quick if any tension or sarcasm had marred the receptive timbre of her voice. But her question was sincere and without double meaning. He wanted to tell her everything.

"Can we talk about it tomorrow?" he said instead. He didn't want to risk her disapproval tonight, not with the way her sublime sweetness was enveloping him with warmth. It would seem she'd gotten over her annoyance about his missing the tenants' meeting. "I owe you a dinner. Can we meet after work?"

"Sure."

His relief was immediate as they arranged to meet at her office at seven. The thought of seeing Susan again made him smile as he hung up the receiver. Speaking with her tonight had resharpened their connection, a link blunted by the circumstances of the past twenty-four hours. Now tomorrow night couldn't come soon enough as far as he was concerned.

Yet, when they did get together, the main topic of conversation could turn into a mine field of fatal blows. Tony winced at the thought.

God, he hoped he could make her understand.

Chapter Six

Susan was tense.

Tony sensed this the moment he walked into her office. She greeted him with a smile but remained seated behind her desk, her posture stiff, both hands tightly gripping a black felt tip pen. Her small talk was impersonal and distancing. Long gone was the soft warmth of last night's telephone conversation.

This didn't bode well for what he'd hoped to accomplish this evening.

Wary, he sank into an armchair by her desk. He disliked this aloofness of hers, especially after the kiss they'd shared the day before yesterday.

"I thought you wanted to see me tonight," he said, deciding that being direct was the best way to go.

"I did...I do..." His bluntness caught her off guard. "What do you mean?"

"You're acting like a person who's *pretending* she's not annoyed."

"For heaven's sake, what are you talking about?"

"Susan, I feel a distinct chill in the air."

With a sigh she dropped the pen onto her desk and leaned back in the chair. "All right, I admit I've had second thoughts since we talked." She glanced across the desk to check his reaction. "Your call sort of caught me off guard."

He'd been afraid of something like this. At least she had the grace to admit it. "So you're still put out with me."

"Not put out," she objected. "Disturbed maybe. And concerned. Definitely concerned."

She *was* mad. In the interest of mending fences, however, he decided to keep calm. "Fair enough. Let's clear the air right here and now."

"Right now?"

Her startled response surprised him. "Don't you think we should?"

"Yes, but here? And what about dinner? Aren't you hungry?"

"Famished, but—" Suddenly it dawned on him—the tension when he arrived, the hedging, the reluctance to talk now—she wasn't ready. No doubt she had plenty to say, but he was beginning to realize that Susan wasn't a woman who could be pushed.

Well, if she needed an hour to unwind or to feel more comfortable with him, he was all for it. "Maybe we should have dinner first. But promise me something?"

"Yes?" She looked wary.

"Ease up on me a bit? It's not going to be a heck of a lot of fun eating across from someone who's as 'definitely concerned' as you."

"I think I can manage that." He could tell she was fighting back a smile. He wished she wouldn't; her smiles were smashing.

Unfortunately her effort was successful and she continued on. "As a matter of fact, why don't I cook dinner for us? It'll be easier to talk at my place. We'll have to stop at the supermarket, though."

After weeks of working with her, Tony knew better than to read anything into her suggestion. Susan was just being her eminently practical self. Still, he protested about her going to the trouble of making dinner.

"I really like to cook," she insisted. "I don't get much chance to these days. And now that I have a new dining room table it'd be a shame not to use it. Besides, it'll help me relax."

"Then by all means," he agreed.

Grocery shopping with Susan was an enlightening experience. He marveled at how choosy she was about each item: checking each vegetable and fruit for ripeness; sending a choicer cut of beef back to the butcher to fillet instead of selecting a precut package in the meat case. She even sent him back to the dairy aisle for a different brand of sour cream, claiming she preferred it to the one he had chosen. He couldn't get over it. For him, buying groceries meant a dash to the corner market for staples like coffee, juice and bread. But he and Susan had spent almost half an hour shopping for just one meal. He couldn't help chuckling.

"What's so funny?" she asked as they carried the two light bags out to his car.

"I've never spent so much time in a supermarket before."

"What do you mean? We couldn't have been in there more than fifteen, twenty minutes."

He unlocked the trunk of his car. "Thirty minutes. I clocked it." He placed the paper sacks inside the trunk.

She looked puzzled. "So? How long does it usually take you to shop?"

"I don't. I usually bring home take-out meals or eat out. Otherwise it's a quick stop at the corner store." He unlocked the passenger door and held it open for her.

"Oh." She still seemed confused. "Well, didn't you ever go grocery shopping with your mother when you were a kid?"

He slid behind the steering wheel, forcing himself not to laugh at the idea of his mother doing the family food shopping. "Uh, the housekeeper did that."

Her eyes widened suddenly, and then she looked away. "I see."

"Is something wrong?"

"No. I just forgot that you're from a wealthy family."

"Well, don't hold it against me," he quipped with a smile.

She didn't respond, and the drive back to her apartment was silent. That bothered him, but he decided not to push it. People often didn't know how to react to his family's wealth. So Susan's apparent uneasiness wasn't too surprising. He hoped she'd get over it soon, though. He didn't want to have to prove to her—in addition to everything else—that he really was a regular sort of guy despite his Brandon name. Yet she *had* momentarily forgotten his wealthy background, and he took that to be a good sign.

While Susan unpacked the groceries, he doffed his suit jacket and tie. Rolling up his light blue shirtsleeves, he joined her in the kitchen. "What can I do to help?"

She looked at him with a speculative eye before smiling for the first time since they'd left the supermarket. "Can you put together a salad?"

"I think I can manage that."

Her smile broadened. "Great. You can start that while I change out of this suit," she suggested as she pulled a clean white chef's apron from a low drawer. She handed it to him and told him where to find the necessary utensils.

His eyes followed her out of the kitchen, admiring the way her long legs moved beneath her outfit's slim dark red skirt. His muscles contracted pleasurably as he realized the scent of her perfume had lingered behind. There was much about Susan to discover, and he suspected the process of discovery would be tantalizing.

When she returned, he was busy chopping celery. "How's it going?" she asked, peeking into the almost full salad bowl. "Mmm, looks good."

Taking a step back, he pushed his slipping eyeglasses higher on the bridge of his nose and took a long head-to-toe look at her. She had changed into black slacks and a rosy pink turtleneck jersey. Her dark hair was freshly brushed, and it fell, soft and full, against her high collar. "You look good, too," he murmured.

"Thanks," she said with a shy nod. Then she quickly added, "Need your glasses for cooking, too?"

"Only if I don't want to chop off my fingers," he said lightly, hoping to put her at ease.

Susan lifted her gaze again, a slight grin curving her fine, thin lips. "Well, we can't have that." She placed her hand over his for a gratifying instant. He was amazed at the effect this had on him.

When he finished with the salad, she gave him place mats, napkins and directions on where to find the silverware, glasses and dishes needed to set the table. As she busied herself preparing the main dish, he wondered if this was the time to bring up the Somerset and his trip to New York. But Susan had finally loosened up, and the two of them were getting on rather well. He didn't want to do anything to disrupt that—not yet. Instead, he let himself be distracted by the appetizing aromas wafting through the apartment.

At her request he uncorked the bottle of red wine and set it down to breathe for a while on the dining room table. Then, leaning against the kitchen doorjamb, he studied her as she moved expertly from pan to pan. She was confident, in control, and she was obviously enjoying herself. He enjoyed watching her.

"I guess cooking is the closest thing I have to a hobby," she revealed when they sat down to eat. "I find it relaxing and fun."

"I noticed." He watched her fill his plate with steaming noodles. "You know, Maria reminded me about the birthday cakes you used to make for the people at legal aid."

"Really?" She seemed pleased.

He nodded as he took his first taste of the beef Stroganoff. It was delicious, a wonderful melt-in-your mouth blend of textures and tastes. He complimented her profusely. "Where did you learn to cook like this?" he added, digging in for another bite.

"From my mother. Some of my earliest memories are of helping her in the kitchen."

"It shows."

"I'm glad you like it." Susan lifted her wineglass to her lips, her gaze remaining on him. The red wine seemed to make her dark pupils gleam with warmth, intriguing him as an ache stirred low in his body. He tasted his own wine, all the while wishing for a taste of her lips.

They ate in companionable silence for a time until Susan offered him a second helping. As she refilled his plate, she asked, "What do you do to relax, Tony?"

"With my caseload who has time?"

"Come on, you don't work *all* the time."

"Sometimes it seems that way," he said with a shrug. "But let's see—I play racquetball for the exercise. I go to the theater, and in the summer I take in an occasional ball game up in Baltimore. I wish I had more time to read than I do. And I like to drive."

"Drive?"

"Yes, long drives out in the countryside—when I can."

"Sounds nice," she said with a nod. "The only real driving I do these days is home to Baltimore. I'm afraid to take my old Honda any farther than that."

"Go up there often?"

"Not as often as I'd like. I'll be going this Sunday, though—if the Honda cooperates," she added, knocking on the oak table for luck. "My mother's giving a birthday party for our cousin Iris."

Thinking it would be a great opportunity to get to know Susan better, he offered to take her.

"You're much too busy for that."

Her response surprised him—not so much what she said but how she said it. Cool. Abrupt. End of subject.

A polite "No, thank you" was one thing. But her answer? He was unable to leave it at that. "I wouldn't have offered if I didn't have the time."

"I didn't mean . . ." She flushed with embarrassment. "All it is, is a small get-together with friends and a cake. Nothing grand."

"Sounds nice to me."

"You might find it dull, what with Iris's old cronies sitting around the parlor chattering on about the good old days. And their good old days happened long before you or I were born."

Her argument lacked conviction; he didn't believe a word of it. "I don't think I'd be bored. In fact—"

"Tony, you must have something you'd rather do on a Sunday afternoon." Her voice was edged with frustration. "You just said you don't get much free time."

It was clear that she didn't want him along. But why not? The day before yesterday she seemed plenty interested in spending time together. What could be better than a leisurely drive to Baltimore and an hour or two at a cousin's birthday party?

But the day before yesterday was *before* he went to New York to meet William Leland. Of course, that must be it. Yet he was so caught up in being alone with Susan and enjoying their dinner together that he'd blocked out the reason they were here in the first place.

"Susan, you're still mad that I canceled out of the Somerset meeting."

"The meeting?" Her eyes flickered with ambivalence. "Well, I . . ."

He sighed. "We've put off talking about it long enough, haven't we?"

She looked at him with an uncertainty he found perplexing. After a moment, she lowered her eyes to her hands. "Yes, you're right."

"It's only getting in the way."

Her head jerked up, eyes wide. "In the way?"

"Between you and me," he added, reaching across the table for her hand.

Before he even touched her Susan edged away. Pushing her chair out, she lifted their emptied dinner plates off the table. "Let me make coffee first," she murmured quickly. "Then we'll talk."

Tony watched her disappear into the kitchen. He shook his head in disbelief. This was going to be harder than he'd thought.

For the longest time Susan just stared at the gurgling coffee maker. Now what? she asked herself as the nutty aroma of fresh-brewed coffee filled the kitchen. In her hands she twisted, then untwisted a blue-and-white-checked dishtowel several times before she realized what she was doing. She was anxious, uneasy. And torn. Now she was doing to the towel what she'd been doing in her head all night long: twisting her concerns into neat arguments and then untwisting each angle of the argument as new doubts crept into her head.

Yet she had agreed they should talk, and talk they would. Only she wished she felt more sure of herself.

Knowing she'd be seeing Tony, she'd taken extra care with her makeup and hair this morning and had selected a particularly flattering outfit to wear tonight. She wanted to look attractive for him, plain and simple. Even she couldn't fool herself on that account. As much as she'd like to submerge her personal feelings about Tony into her subconscious—at least until the Somerset situation was resolved—she couldn't. Her attraction to the man was the monkey wrench in the entire works as far as she was concerned. It was making her lose her objectivity.

Susan had been less than thrilled at the way he'd taken off for New York. She had stewed over it from the moment he'd told her about it, and she'd been prepared to read him the riot act when he returned. But then he'd called her from the airport. Just hearing his voice had overridden her displeasure with his actions. Suddenly outside concerns had faded; all that mattered was the quiet talk, the give and take between man and woman.

Except that wasn't how she should have reacted at all. She shouldn't have forgotten about the Somerset. She shouldn't have forgotten just who and what Anthony Brandon II was. And she shouldn't have forgotten the lessons she'd learned at boarding school years ago.

By the time the coffee was ready, Susan had resolved to keep her head on straight. Mind over matter. Substance over attraction.

Returning to the dinner table, she couldn't bring herself to look him in the eye—partly due to anger, partly due to fear. Yet his physical presence filled her awareness—broad shoulders beneath a beautiful gray vest, the slight wave of golden brown hair combed back off his forehead, the clean scent of soap and shampoo. The last time they were together he had kissed her.... Enough! she scolded herself.

Silently she poured the coffee—all the while reminding herself to stick to priorities.

Tony didn't move, but she could feel him watching her. She sipped her coffee, forcing herself to look at him over the rim of the earthenware mug. He continued to stare at her with his dark green eyes. She stiffened. "Have I forgotten something? You take yours black, don't you?"

"I think I've underestimated how put out with me you are," he said at last. "After last night I thought—never mind." He straightened his shoulders. "It just doesn't make what I have to tell you any easier."

"I knew it." Susan put the mug back down on the oak table, and it resounded with a heavy thud.

The green eyes narrowed. "Knew what?"

"You're going to back out on the tenants."

He muttered a curse, throwing the navy blue napkin onto the matching quilted place mat. He stood up and yanked his chair over to hers. "Sorry, but this time you're wrong."

"Am I?"

Although he was sitting right beside her, he leaned closer, elbows resting carelessly on his thighs. "Listen, Susan, I'm very committed to representing the Somerset tenants. And you know that. But I'm not about to give up my entire career to do it."

"No one expects that," she snapped, trying to mask her alarm. He was so close that she could almost feel the tension rippling through his body. It was disconcerting in more ways than one. She needed to keep him at arm's length. She needed to keep her perspective.

"No? Sometimes I wonder."

"And *I* have to wonder if the tenants will get enough of your attention. You can't blame me for that, Tony. Not with the way you just flew off to New York."

With a sigh that seemed a mixture of frustration and weariness, Tony pulled back. She felt a slight reprieve from the intensity of his closeness.

"Let me tell you what I want to do," he said, looking down at his hands. His voice was low, the anger dissipated. "Let me explain."

She felt herself softening a bit. "Please. I want to understand."

He told her about his meeting with William Leland. He sounded so excited about the prospects and so proud that she felt her resentment subsiding. She couldn't help feeling pleased for him.

"But it in no way lessens my commitment to the tenants," he continued. "If anything, it reinforces it. I'm determined to see it through."

"But how?" Right away she felt guilty about getting caught up in his excitement. It seemed disloyal to the Somerset tenants. After all, *someone* had to give them priority.

Tony met her gaze. "With your help, of course. And with Rob Berns's."

"I see."

"Rob says the meeting with the tenants went well." He tilted his head slightly, his eyes questioning.

"It did," she conceded. "Rob held his own."

"And the tenants?"

"They seemed to like him." Then she hastened to add, "That doesn't mean he can take your place."

The beginnings of a smile touched his lips. "I guess I should take that as a compliment."

She frowned. "What I meant was he doesn't have your expertise. And, anyway, the tenants agreed to your representation, not Rob's."

"Yes. And that's what they'll get. I'll give them my best," he assured. "But under these new circumstances I can only do my best if I have Rob's help."

"Circumstances seem to change quickly for you."

"It seems that way. Especially lately." He let his hand rest on hers and smiled. "Like meeting you again."

"Don't change the subject." She slipped her hand off the table and away from his touch. "My concern is for the tenants."

He got to his feet, pushing his chair out of the way. "So is mine. I want to help them, and I've been working damn hard toward that end, and you know it. That's not going to stop."

She didn't know how to respond. She felt he was being sincere, yet something held her back.

He peered down at her. "You don't believe me."

Oh, she wanted to. She wanted to give him the benefit of the doubt. Yet it seemed as if he was changing the rules in the middle of the game—changing them to suit his own gain. Mistrust from the past taunted her. Still, her common sense argued that this time the situation was different. Wasn't it?

"And you don't trust me." His voice was matter-of-fact, but his eyes were troubled. He looked wounded.

Susan got up from the table and turned away. She stood at the large window in the living room and looked out at the purple evening sky. She needed to be careful. So many thoughts were running through her mind; she felt confused. Did she trust him?

"Susan?"

Still gazing blankly out the window, she took a deep, cleansing breath. "I've had misgivings from the start," she said at last. "I told you as much."

"Yes, you certainly did."

"But things have been going so well these past weeks that I thought I'd been wrong about you and that you were really committed this time."

Tony stood by her side. Turning her by the shoulders to face him, he reached down and took her hand between his. His grasp was reassuring. It felt good to be touching him. He looked into her eyes for a few moments and then spoke in a low, encouraging voice. "We have to get beyond that now. You've got to trust me—not just for the tenants' sake, but for our own, as well."

The promise in his words thrilled her. But almost immediately she pushed this feeling aside. It would complicate everything.

"Maybe we should keep the two separate—until the case is settled at least." She lowered her eyes to their clasped hands. His long fingers were strong and graceful and they fitted around her hand nicely.

"I can't do that. We're in this thing together."

"Oh, Tony, I want to trust you. But I'm afraid—"

"Don't be afraid," he urged with a tender whisper.

"No, listen. I'm afraid you're the one being unrealistic now about your ability to do justice to the Somerset case while you're representing William Leland."

He squeezed her hand. "You're just going to have to trust me on this. I'm a good lawyer, Susan, and I know my limitations. That's why I'll need your help. And I'm afraid if I don't try now, I might never again."

She wasn't sure if it was the urgent tone of his voice or the imploring glint in his eye, but in that instant she believed he was sincere. Yet her renewed faith in his intentions couldn't completely erase her concern that somehow power and prestige might win out again.

She couldn't bring herself to express this concern—not now when he was being so honest, so hopeful. And by keeping this fear to herself, she realized she had already taken a leap of faith. And, heaven help her, she couldn't turn away from him now.

She reached for his hand. "I'm with you."

Chapter Seven

Tony held Susan's hand tightly, relieved and grateful for her support. Yet words failed him. He simply looked into her lovely eyes, as dark as midnight, and felt she understood his silence.

This sense of connection with her stirred feelings within him that had long been unmoved. Susan O'Toole. A woman who wasn't so single-minded, after all. She had her vulnerabilities, her doubts, her questions. She also had warmth, empathy and sparkling eyes. And at this moment he felt very close to her.

Wanting only to be closer, he instinctively leaned toward her until their faces were mere inches apart. His lips ached to possess hers. Her eyes held his captive even as her delicate black lashes fluttered hesitantly.

He felt her warm breath against his cheek. "Susan," he murmured, his hands cupping her shoulders to close the last dividing gap between them.

But her body stiffened in his arms and she turned her face away.

"Susan?"

"Not now," she gasped, stepping back. "Not yet."

"Why not?" He reached out to her again, but she took another step back.

"Please."

Dropping his hands to his sides, he stayed where he was as she moved farther away. "I thought—" He stopped. He hadn't thought anything—he'd only felt close to her. So close.

Torn between cursing himself for pushing her and shaking her for pulling away, he forced himself to continue. "I'm sorry. I didn't mean to press you."

"I know. And I meant what I said—I'm with you on the Somerset case," she added, sounding nervous. "But let's take one thing at a time. Okay?"

"Of course." He looked around him, awkwardness setting in. Damn, he wished he could extricate himself from the situation by saying something reassuring, something smooth. But this woman... this woman. "I should go."

She fetched his suit jacket for him, and he shrugged it on as he headed for the door. Reaching for the doorknob, he turned back to her. "Look, don't worry about this."

She nodded, her face expressionless.

"Thanks for the great dinner." He pulled the door open. "See you at the meeting."

After Tony left, Susan immediately began loading the dishwasher. She had to keep her hands busy or drive herself crazy thinking about the mess she'd just made of everything. Why did she hold back like that? Why not just kiss the man? Heaven knows she'd wanted to.

The busywork wasn't helping. She wondered what it would be like seeing Tony at the tenants' meeting the day after tomorrow. Would he still be uncomfortable about what had happened—or rather hadn't happened? Would she? If nothing else, it would be awkward.

Lord, she must have been out of her mind to get involved with him—he was an associate, and he was Anthony Brandon II. She should have kept her distance. Now part of her wanted nothing more to do with seeing Tony socially; the other part feared he might feel the same way about her.

SHE WAS VERY NERVOUS.

Even Alice's welcoming hug when she arrived at the woman's apartment couldn't calm her. The meeting had already begun and Tony was speaking to the group. "We waited a while for you, honey," Alice whispered, "but Tony was anxious to get started. He has to go back to his office tonight."

Susan quietly edged her way to the back of Alice's living room. It was impossible to be inconspicuous in such small quarters, and Tony saw her right away. His eyes held hers in an endless moment of awareness. Her spine tingled with undeniable attraction, and she couldn't help wonder what he was thinking. Was he glad to see her? Acknowledging her presence with a smileless nod of his head, he then returned his attention to the tenants. She hadn't a clue as to what he was thinking *or* feeling. Apprehension overrode nervousness.

She forced herself to concentrate on Tony's talk. He was explaining how he wanted to increase Rob Berns's role in handling the tenants' grievances against the landlord. He was quite frank in telling them why.

When he asked if anyone objected to Rob's joining the team, Eva Knowlton was on her feet at once. "Mr. Brandon, you've been very generous to us so far. And honest, too," the petite woman said, her blue-gray curls fairly bouncing as she nodded emphatically. "If having Mr. Berns's assistance will make it easier to do your job *and* help us, then so be it."

"We trust your judgment, Tony," a man called out. A few people clapped their hands in agreement.

Then Alice stood and faced the crowd with a cheerful grin. "Everybody knows two heads are better than one, so having two lawyers on our side may be just the ticket we need."

An outburst of laughter followed, and Tony smiled broadly. "Some might argue otherwise, Alice," he teased. "We, however, thank you for your support."

To Susan it looked like quite a mutual admiration society between Tony and the elderly tenants. He dealt well with them; clearly he had their trust. As Tony described his strategy for his upcoming meeting with the CEO of the Hammond Group, she could see that he meant to give one hundred percent, just as he'd said he would.

At the completion of the meeting a few tenants approached Tony with questions while others chatted among themselves before leaving. Susan sighed wearily, uncertain if she was disappointed or relieved by the momentary delay. She remained seated in the back of the living room, waiting to catch him alone.

"There you are, Susan." Alice's deep voice startled her. "I thought you had snuck out on us."

Alice was gently clutching Tom O'Brien's elbow with her large hand. She seemed excited, and Tom actually had a slight curve of a smile on his usual poker face.

Alice nudged him forward. "Our lone dissenter has decided to join the fold. I finally convinced him he should fight for his home this time."

"I'm really glad to hear it," Susan said, regarding the older couple with interest.

"This lady here is some talker." Tom leaned closer to Alice. "She made me see the light."

Although Alice was a good head taller than her less outspoken friend, Susan detected an air of togetherness about them. It would be nice to see Alice and Tom form a friendship—something good had to come out of all this trouble.

"Now, Tom, you'd better go get ready for the dinner," Alice said before turning to Susan. "The Golden Age Club is having a potluck supper at the recreation center tonight."

"Sounds fun."

Alice nodded. "It is in a way. Mostly it's just nice to get out—away from these four walls. Believe me, honey, it pays to stay active."

After Alice and Tom excused themselves, Susan looked across the living room. The last of the tenants had cleared out, and Tony was nowhere in sight. His overcoat and briefcase were gone. He had left without even speaking to her. Shaking her head in disbelief, she turned to get her coat.

"Looking for me?" Tony asked, standing behind her.

She composed herself quickly, determined to sound calm. "As a matter of fact, I was."

Tony held out her trench coat. "Walk me to my car?"

Slipping her arms into the coat, Susan felt his closeness keenly. His clean, subtle scent filled her head as he drew her coat around her. The fleeting touch of his hands on her shoulders sent a quiver of longing through her. Except for Alice, who had gone to her bedroom, she and Tony were alone in the apartment and so physically close that all she had to do was reach out.

"Ready?" he said, starting for the door without waiting for a reply.

Although he moved away rather abruptly, she was relieved to have some distance between them. Gathering her wits, she followed him. Now was the time for calm, rational thought. Sentiment and attraction had to be kept at bay, or how else could she endure being with him? Working with him?

Once they stood outside on the sidewalk, the cool air washed over her. Her clenched hands uncurled as her tensions eased. She could see that Tony was feeling just as awkward as she. He had said only a word or two since they'd left Alice's, and that wasn't like him. Empathy and tenderness rose from her heart. This was difficult for him, too.

Midway down the block she stopped and turned to him. "Why don't we just talk about what happened the other night? We'll both feel better."

He looked down into her eyes, relief softening his expression. "Amen," he murmured as his fingers tenderly touched her hair. Then he pulled his hand away. "The last thing I want is for you to be uncomfortable with me. I like you, Susan. And I'm very attracted to you. That's not going to change." He looked away, his eyes staring aimlessly at the night sky. "I don't want it to change."

"You don't?"

Tony returned his gaze to hers. "Do you?"

She froze. She didn't know. "Things are happening quickly," she tried to explain. "Is it smart to get involved right now? We could be making a mis—"

She stopped as two men walked by. "This isn't the best place to discuss this," she added in a low voice after the men passed.

"I'm parked around the corner." Tony took her by the arm.

They walked to his car in silence. As soon as he sat behind the wheel, he resumed the conversation without hesitation. "It's no longer a question of getting involved. I am involved." He turned to her, his green gaze as adamant as his voice. "So are you, Susan. It's no mistake."

Excitement rushed through her. His eyes, his voice, his words—she was totally drawn to him. And she knew he was right. She had no argument. Anything she said now would be just an excuse. "No, it's not a mistake," she whispered.

Tony looked as if he wanted to pull her close. Instead, he took her hand.

"What now?" she asked.

"Whatever you want, Susan. It's up to you."

She lowered her eyes, uncertain if she wanted it left up to her. Part of her wanted to fall into his arms, allowing attraction and feelings to lead her where they may. The possibilities made her insides flutter with excitement.

"Perhaps we should take it slowly," she said, wondering if she sounded at all convinced.

"If that's what you really want." Tony's words whispered with disappointment.

"I think it is." She steeled herself against the teasing urge to say, "Oh, what the hell." Closing her eyes, she sighed. "I wish I could be different."

"Don't." He squeezed her hand. "You're fine this way."

"Sometimes I wonder."

"Besides," he shrugged without releasing her hand, "if the truth be known, my work schedule is pretty tight. It'll be tough to find time to spend together during the next few weeks."

"The pressure's already on."

He nodded. "Which is why I have to go back to the office tonight instead of taking you out for a nice quiet dinner."

"Maybe it's just as well," she suggested halfheartedly. "To give us breathing room, I mean."

He shot her a skeptical look. "Maybe. But why do I feel as if I should ask you to wait for me?"

She laughed. "Don't worry. I'm not going anywhere."

"I'm not worried about *where*. I just don't want anyone snatching you away while I'm buried in legal briefs."

That was unlikely to happen, but Susan didn't feel she needed to state the fact. Besides, she was flattered by Tony's concern, even if he might have said it half in jest. A satisfied smile twitched her lips. "You just take care of the tenants and—"

"And Leland?"

She rolled her eyes. "And Leland. The rest will take care of itself."

"I hope so." He leaned across the seat to kiss her.

It was a light kiss, and a brief one. She knew this was deliberate on his part. Still, it filled her with a giddy happiness.

Half an hour later Tony was back in his office trying hard to concentrate on work instead of thinking about Susan. It was tough going. He even thought he still smelled her perfume.

The sharp knock on his open office door was a welcome distraction. His mother stood there, grinning. "It must do your father's heart good to see you working this late."

"What are you doing here tonight?"

She strolled in, wearing a black silk suit that made her look slender and younger than her sixty years. "I was supposed to be going out to dinner with your father, but it seems another eleventh-hour crisis has claimed him. We have reservations at Marseille. Have you tried it yet?"

"No. Though I've heard it's excellent."

"Since your father's standing me up, why don't you and I go? It'll be lovely."

"I wish I could. But I just came back from a meeting, and now I've got a long night ahead of me. Sorry."

Letitia dismissed his explanation with a wave of her hand. "I understand, darling, believe me. After all, I've been a lawyer's wife for over thirty-six years."

"Maybe we can do it another time," he offered, spurred by a stab of guilt.

"Of course we will." Letitia came up behind his chair. Glancing at the papers on his desk, she rested a bejeweled hand on his shoulder. "Hard at work on Leland business?"

"Actually, no. I'm prepping for a morning meeting with the new owners of a Rosslyn apartment building." He thought for a second before adding, "I'm representing the tenants." She'd have asked, anyway.

Her hand dropped from his shoulder. "Is that the pro bono case you were discussing with John a few weeks back? The one that girl from the Senior Citizens' Association got you involved in?"

He nodded. "The Somerset."

"Surely someone else in the firm can take it over now that you're representing William Leland." With shoulders straight and back stiff, Letitia walked around to the front of his desk. Tony could tell she wasn't pleased.

"I made a commitment to these people, Mother."

"What about your commitment to Leland?" she asked. "He deserves your utmost attention."

He stirred uneasily in his chair. What was his mother getting so hot about? "I know that, and he's getting it. Believe me."

"Anthony, I commend your need to help the less fortunate. You've always been quite responsible in that regard. The years you insisted on spending at legal aid prove it. But really," she continued, her voice tight, "this is hardly the time..."

She began to pace along the length of his desk. "You have a great opportunity here. This Leland business can make you a genuine player in this city. Just think about it. Can you really risk *any* distractions?"

"Mother, I know what I'm doing." He tried to stay calm. Yet he was concerned about Letitia's attitude. True, she always kept abreast of the goings-on at the firm and, to an extent, with his career. This outburst was excessive—even for her. She was angry, but Tony wasn't sure at whom or why.

Pressing her palms on the desk, she leaned forward. "And what does your father have to say about this?"

"He was concerned."

"I should hope so."

He was losing patience. "But I convinced him I can manage my time responsibly. He knows how much I want to continue representing the Somerset tenants and, more importantly, he knows it's my decision.''

Letitia straightened, her face drawn with lines of tension. "Does he really?" She glared down at him for a moment and then turned on her heel and walked out. Tony was stunned. His mother had never walked away from him in his life. He mentally reviewed what had just happened. He may have been a little short with her, but he didn't think he'd said anything rude or malicious. Nothing to warrant her stalking out like that.

Tony went to look for her, hoping she had gone back to his father's office. Finding the door partially opened, he knocked once to announce his presence. His father's silver head was bowed over his desk. "Yes?" he acknowledged without looking up.

Tony scanned the large corner office. "Mother's not here?"

"No, I believe she went to look for you to invite you out to dinner," he replied, finally glancing up. "Didn't she find you?"

"She found me all right." He plopped down on the leather sofa across the room from his father's desk. She must have gone home, he thought. "Dad, she was unusually tense."

"Really? I didn't notice it."

He explained his run-in with Letitia. "I don't know why she's so uptight about the Somerset."

John leaned back in his chair, his hands folded under his chin. "Sounds as if she's more concerned about William Leland."

"Well, yes," Tony agreed. "But why?"

He tossed up his hands. "Sometimes it's hard to tell with your mother. But I shouldn't be too concerned, son. For one thing, she's upset with me for canceling our dinner engagement at the last minute. And for another, she's nervous about her book. It's coming out soon, you know. She's just on edge.''

''That's probably it. Maybe I'll give her a call later.'' Tony got up from the sofa. ''I'd better get back to work.''

''Putting in a long day, too?''

''Yeah. I'm meeting with the CEO of the Hammond Group tomorrow.''

''Good. Any chance you can wrap up an agreement with them soon?''

''I'm going to give it my best shot. But, frankly, Dad, I'm not too optimistic. I think the tenants are in for a long haul.''

''Well, do the best you can.''

''I intend to.''

''Of course.'' His father regarded him thoughtfully. ''Just remember, Leland is still the number one priority.''

Tony held his tongue. He wasn't sure he agreed.

IT WAS A PERFECT fall morning. Susan stood at her living room window, sipping coffee and gazing out at the small park across the street. Trees, drenched with autumn's yellow and orange, swayed with the gentle breeze. At ten o'clock the sun already warmed the day with its golden glow. It was just too nice a Saturday to stay cooped up inside, and since she had nothing else planned, she decided to get dressed and take a long walk. Then the downstairs door buzzed.

''Tony, what on earth—?'' she gasped when he identified himself over the intercom. Quickly she released the outside lock. ''Come on up.''

Delight eclipsed her surprise at Tony's unexpected visit. Although she spoke with him on the phone at least once a day, this would be the first time she'd seen him in two weeks—since the night they'd sat in his car outside the Somerset.

She waited by the door and fussed at her pink bathrobe. Tightening the sash at her waist, she made sure the cotton flannel was smooth and neat around her body. At Tony's solid knock she swung open the door.

The smile on his lips and in his eyes told her, without a doubt, how glad he was to see her. Her heart responded with a little flip-flop.

"I couldn't do it, Susan," he declared, leaning against the doorjamb. "I woke up to this beautiful morning and I just couldn't make myself go to the office. Not again."

She drew him inside and closed the door. "Sounds like you need a mental health day."

"That's why I'm here. I can think of no one better for my mental health than you."

Her skin grew warm with pleasure. "Well, I'll do what I can."

"I was hoping you'd say that." He pulled her closer and slipped his arms around her waist. "How about coming with me for a nice long drive? We can head out toward Leesburg, have lunch and meander from there."

Spending the day with him sure beat a solitary walk in the city. She accepted with enthusiasm, and he sipped at a cup of coffee while she showered and dressed. She did this quickly, not wanting to make him wait too long. Taking a cue from his casual outfit, she pulled on a comfortable pair of navy blue slacks and a maroon Shaker knit sweater. A dab of lipstick, a flick of mascara and she was ready.

Before leaving they agreed not to discuss work. "Even the Somerset case," he added, a trace of frustration underlining his words.

She understood. His talks with the Hammond Group had hit an impasse. The CEO had turned out to be less accommodating than his underlings. Now Tony and Rob Berns were gearing up to fight the issuance of eviction notices, which meant going to court. Any discussion of the Somerset would be counterproductive to the benefits of a mental health day. And he had mentioned before that taking long drives out in the country was one of his favorite ways to unwind.

Once they drove beyond the ever-reaching sprawl of the Washington suburbs, Tony visibly relaxed. "You really do like to drive," she remarked after they turned off the main highway. He answered with a smile of contentment, reaching across the seat for her hand. He squeezed it once, gently, and her pulse quickened. Now on a winding two-lane road, they rolled past houses and farms. Purebred horses and cattle dotted the open expanses of land, reminding them they were in the country of gentlemen farmers and avid horsemen.

In Leesburg they parked and picked up a walking tour map of the historic district. As they strolled along the lovely brick-lined streets, Susan discovered she and Tony shared an interest in Virginia history. While she was well versed in its colonial past, he was more knowledgeable about the area's crucial role in the Civil War.

She couldn't help lingering at the display windows of the town's many expensive antique shops. Finally Tony coaxed her to go into one. "It doesn't hurt to look."

"Looking doesn't. The temptation to buy, however, can be painful." But he didn't seem to hear her as they entered the shop. As it turned out, the selection of English and French furniture was too ritzy for her taste. Nothing really caught her eye. The next shop, however, was where she got into trouble.

It was chock-full of colonial and Federal pieces, and browsing was a pleasure. Then she spotted a bed—a stately mahogany four-poster, circa 1820. She found herself returning to look at it several times. Finally, gritting her teeth, she sneaked a look at the price tag. As she had guessed, it was out of the question. She earned a decent salary—but not that good.

"Nice bed," Tony said, coming up behind her. "Thinking of buying?"

Was he serious? "Not today."

"Why not? You said you had to buy a bed, and you've been ogling this one since we walked in."

He was serious. Well, why wouldn't he be? He could walk into any store anywhere and buy anything he wanted. Fine for him maybe, but he shouldn't assume she could do the same. She lowered her voice. "It's too expensive."

His face fell. He moved to the head of the bed and fingered the tag. "I see," he said, contrite. "I wasn't thinking, Susan. I'm sor—"

"Don't worry. It's no big deal."

"I'll buy it for you. A housewarming gift."

"You will not!"

"But I really want to."

"Well, I don't want you to," she snapped, aware the shop clerk was watching them. "It's too expensive and too personal. And I've already ordered a perfectly good bed." Determined not to be embarrassed, she turned and sauntered out of the shop.

Outside on the sidewalk Tony apologized. "It was damn insensitive of me," he continued, clasping her shoulders between his hands. "I'm really sorry."

She could see how badly he felt. "Forget it, okay? I don't want it to ruin our day."

His eyes held her with their affectionate gleam. A wisp of his golden hair moved in the gentle breeze. He was so heartbreakingly handsome that she could stand there looking at him like this all day.

At last he moved, curving an arm around her shoulders, pulling her against his side. He planted a tender kiss on top of her head, and she wound her right arm behind his back. She liked the feel of his taut muscles against her. He glanced down again and winked. "Let's go have lunch."

They spoke no more about the bed, yet a certain tension about the incident lingered in the air between them. Susan felt it keenly. They were being ever so polite as they hunted for a place to eat. The initial easiness between them was gone, and she wondered if they'd ever get it back.

Because the midday temperature was warm and there wasn't a cloud in the sky, Tony suggested a picnic. "We can drive over to Harper's Ferry, eat and then visit the town. Ever been there?"

"Once—years ago. I'd love to see it again."

Within a half hour they reached the scenic bluffs overlooking the confluence of the Potomac and Shenandoah rivers. All the established picnic areas were busy with weekend visitors. Still, Tony managed to spot a clearing beyond a group of occupied picnic tables. Armed with the plaid blanket he kept in his trunk, they settled on a sloping patch of grass. It was just out of sight of the other picnickers, offering privacy.

"Tell me about the last time you were here," he said after they feasted on the sandwiches and salads they'd bought at a Leesburg deli. He brushed crumbs off his tan trousers and then leaned back on his elbows.

"It's been a while," she revealed, watching him stretch his legs out before him, liking the way he moved. "I was still in college—at Georgetown—and I came with a guy I'd been dating for a couple of years."

He pretended disappointment. "You've been here with another man?"

"Sorry, you're not the first," she teased back. "But if it's any comfort to you, we broke up shortly afterward."

"Really?" Then he chuckled. "Actually, I broke up with my high school girlfriend during an outing here."

"Oh-oh. This doesn't bode well for us."

"Nah. Different time, different circumstances. I was seventeen years old. I was supposed to break up with my high school girlfriend."

"But here?"

"She wanted to discuss the future. We were both seniors, and it was time to choose a college," he explained. "I was home from prep school for spring vacation, so we drove out here for the day. She had been accepted at Radcliffe and I—in typical Brandon tradition—had been accepted at Harvard. Except I was hell-bent on not doing what was expected of me. Nothing my girlfriend could say would change my mind."

"What happened?"

"I told her I was going to Princeton and she would just have to accept it. So she dumped me."

"Because you wouldn't go to Harvard? Were you crushed?"

"Not really," he said with a shrug. "I knew what I was doing. Asserting my independence from my parents was more important at that point than holding on to a girl. You see, all Brandon men go to Harvard—it's practically a birthright. But I wanted something different, to take a new path."

She gave him a sympathetic smile. "That's understandable."

"Not if you're a Brandon. You can't imagine how upset my parents were. It took them years to get over it."

She couldn't imagine doing anything upsetting to a parent. Although her mother, too, had made demands, they'd never seemed unreasonable to Susan. She sensed that Tony's parents had been more difficult.

He turned on his side to face her, his head resting on his bent arm. "Now it's your turn. Tell me about your last trip to Harper's Ferry."

"We came here during a break from exams. Did a little sight-seeing, splurged on a big meal. Afraid it's not very dramatic," she said, lying back on the blanket, hands tucked under her head. The early-afternoon sun warmed her face as she gazed up at the clear blue sky. She could hear the merging currents of the two rivers off in the distance.

"You said you'd been going together for a couple of years."

"That's right. We were both about to graduate and had to decide if we wanted to stay together or not." She felt far removed from that part of her life. Names and places were still clear in her mind, but faces were fuzzy, details blurred.

Tony gestured her to continue. "And?"

"Basically he wanted to get married and I wasn't ready to." Saying goodbye was sad at the time, she remembered. Still, she had never regretted her decision.

"Lucky for me, or we wouldn't be here like this." His hand brushed a lock of hair off her face, then his fingers remained to caress the single strand.

His touch filled her with an electrified awareness. Although she avoided his gaze, she knew he was looking at her, waiting for her to acknowledge the moment. She wanted to, yet found it difficult. Finally she broke the silence with a tumble of nervous words, taking the easy way out.

"You've never told me how you landed at legal aid," she said. "I mean, your parents wanted you to work at the law firm, didn't they?"

Tony sat very still, not saying anything for what seemed like a long time. At last he asked, "You want to hear about that now?"

She nodded, and to her surprise he gave no argument.

"Well, if you asked my folks, they'd say legal aid was the last stand of my youthful rebellion."

"Was it?"

"Maybe," he said with a shrug. "I'd like to think I was motivated by something more noble than that."

She'd like to think so, too. "You're confusing to me, Tony. I know where you come from, I sense what's been expected of you, but the you I know—or think I know—doesn't exactly mesh with that.''

"Hmm. Is that good or bad?''

"Intriguing.''

"I like the idea of being intriguing to you.''

"So tell me, why legal aid?''

"When I was in prep school a teacher took me under his wing and opened my eyes to the real world. From him I learned what a sheltered, almost closed life I led.'' Sighing, he leaned back on his elbows. "It was sort of ironic. Here I was going to school with some of the wealthiest kids in the country and, for the first time in my life, I felt guilty about being rich.''

"This teacher made you feel guilty?''

"Not at all. In fact, he said I shouldn't feel guilty. Instead, he advised me to use my good fortune to give back to those who needed help. Not just money, but my time and talents. I found this notion comforting. It eased my confusion. He encouraged me to get involved with some community service projects, and that was the start. After law school, joining legal aid seemed the next logical step.''

"Seems the man had quite an impact on you.''

"More than I'll probably ever know,'' he admitted. "He was like a second father to me. I was living away from home, didn't see my own father much. Not that I ever did—Dad was always working. So this man's attention meant a great deal to me.''

Never having known her own father, Susan understood something of what Tony meant. "What was his name?''

"Ed Farlow. His son was killed in Vietnam, so I guess I became sort of a surrogate son to him and his wife.''

"Do you keep in touch?''

"We did—visiting back and forth over the years. Then Ed passed away about five years ago, his wife a short time later.''

She heard the sadness in his voice. "You still miss him.''

"When Ed died, I lost my anchor, though it took me a few years to realize it."

Her heart was full of emotions—feelings that were varied yet intertwined. There was so much she still didn't know about Tony, yet she felt closer to him than before. She understood what it was like to feel adrift, not quite fitting in here or there. Maybe they were more alike than she'd thought.

She finally allowed herself to look into his eyes, wanting to tell him how she felt. But words didn't seem to be enough. Without a second thought she began to stroke his arm—wanting to reassure, hoping he'd understand.

His silent, accepting gaze told her he did.

After a few moments, Tony clasped her hand against his sweatered chest. "My experience with Ed isn't something I usually talk about."

"I'm glad you did."

He pressed her hand tighter against him, his eyes steady on hers. "So am I."

Now Tony's gaze made her feel special, as if she was the only person on earth who mattered to him. True or not, it was a heady feeling. His forest-green sweater deepened the color of his eyes to that of lush summer clover. The desire to touch him was strong, so strong that she moved on pure impulse. She seemed to melt toward him until their faces were only inches apart.

He murmured her name in a husky breath, and it was all she needed. Eyes wide open, she lowered her lips to his and kissed him with all the warmth in her heart. This was a bond she wanted with him; this was the connection she needed. Not just empathetic words and reassuring caresses—she wanted to hold and be held by him. It was a need she could no longer deny.

Slowly rolling onto his back with unconscious, fluid movement, Tony curled his arms around her in a tender embrace. Her lids fluttered closed as their kiss deepened.

Gradually the warmth of her feelings fanned a more virulent need deep within her. Enveloped in longing, no longer hostage to thought, she acted solely on emotion. It was a freedom she'd never allowed herself, and she found this one taste exhilarating.

She had no idea how long it was before the kiss drifted to an end. Too soon perhaps. Yet, wrapped in his arms, she felt satisfied. Curious about Tony's reaction, she searched his face.

A lopsided grin curved his mouth. "I've been wanting to do that for a long time."

"I think I have, too," she said softly, and Tony tightened his arms around her.

Suddenly she felt shy. The background noise of chatter and cars pulling in and out of the parking lot came back into her consciousness. She glanced over her shoulder, wondering if anyone had seen their passionate kiss.

"Don't worry. We're fairly far off from the others," he said, guessing what was on her mind. "But maybe we should go into town—while we're still able."

She nodded. Although leaving was his suggestion, she sensed Tony's reluctance as they pulled apart. While they cleaned up their picnic site, her eyes kept wandering his way. She liked him very much; she accepted that. Now she realized, with increasing trepidation, how easy it would be to care for him—deeply.

Chapter Eight

"I want to take you home with me, Susan."

Caught off guard, her gaze froze on the Christmas ornaments she'd been admiring in a shop window.

Tony's invitation wasn't entirely unexpected considering their kiss and the enjoyable afternoon they'd been having in Harper's Ferry. Meandering through the restored mid-nineteenth-century houses and shops, hand in hand, they learned a lot about the historic town. They also stole some quiet moments to talk and learn more about each other.

Now the day was waning, and soon they'd be leaving for Washington. Their lovely time together could end at dusk—or move on into the night.

Apparently her circumspect silence was answer enough for Tony. "I gather you're not ready."

She was relieved, and grateful, for his understanding. "It's too soon," she said, turning to him. "I know it may be hard to believe after—what happened earlier."

Tony sighed. "I believe you. I'm disappointed. But I believe you."

"Sorry." She felt awkward, unsure. Part of her *did* want to go with him.

"It's all right." He put a reassuring hand on her shoulder. "Still, if I can't persuade you to come home with me, how about coming with me to my parents'? They're having neighbors in for drinks, and I told my mother I might drop by for a few minutes." He checked his watch. "If we leave now, we'll get there in time to be fashionably late."

Taken aback by the invitation, her mind reeled with reasons not to go to a little "get-together" at the Brandons' Chevy Chase home. "They're not expecting me."

"It's just a drop-in type thing," he assured her. "And my mother loves it when I bring a woman to these things—expected or unexpected. It shows her friends I'm not a hopeless case. Besides, I'll have a much better time if you come."

"But look at the way I'm dressed." Certainly not to go to a Chevy Chase cocktail party.

"Relax. You look fine. In fact," he said, glancing down at his sweater and pants, "you look better than I do. And I can almost guarantee their next-door neighbor, Ambassador Ring, will be wearing his favorite jeans."

"Their neighbor's an ambassador?" This fueled her apprehension.

"Former. He and his wife are the nicest ones in the bunch. You'll like them."

She was still reluctant.

"We won't stay long. I promise. Afterward, we can go out to eat. Maybe catch a movie." Tony took her hand, and they started down the hill to the parking lot. "Even if you're not coming home with me, I don't want our day to end yet."

His words thrilled her, and her objections dissolved rapidly. Their talk on the bluff still lingered in her mind, and the memory of their kiss was still spinning a certain excitement through her body. There was no question about it. She didn't want their day to be over yet, either.

THE BRANDON HOUSE was as big and as elegant as Susan had expected. Inside, the furnishings were exquisite, the decor well defined. Classic. Everything was expensive. Nothing was ostentatious. It looked like a home, not a museum. And that realization eased her tension a bit.

Even the Brandons' living room, while formal, wasn't intimidating. The sofas and chairs were arranged around the room in comfortable sitting areas, and a gorgeous Aubusson rug added colorful warmth to the dark hardwood floor.

Ten or fifteen people milled around the room, chatting. She was relieved to find that most of them *were* dressed as if they'd just completed a Saturday full of errands and chores. She blended right in. While Tony went to get drinks she stood in a corner observing the crowd. Although feeling better, she decided to wait for him before mingling with the others.

Within seconds a uniformed maid carrying a silver tray approached her. "Canapé, miss?"

She politely refused, and the maid moved on to serve other guests. Her eyes followed the stocky gray-haired woman around the room. No one made eye contact with her, no one said anything to her, no one acknowledged her presence. Yet Susan couldn't take her eyes off her. Unable to grapple with the uncomfortable feelings the Brandons' maid aroused in her, she just kept watching the woman until Tony returned with two glasses of red wine.

"I told my mother you're here. She'll be over in a minute."

Her attention was soon caught by a mature, diminutive blonde winding her way through the crowd. She stopped to chat here and there, as a good hostess would. And Susan swore she could hear something of Tony in the woman's deep, elegant laugh.

"Anthony, there you are," the woman greeted. Her voice sounded like old money—self-assured, aware, knowing. Susan took a quick sip of wine.

Mrs. Brandon gave her a cheerful welcome; she seemed quite interested in the woman her son had brought home. It was all very nice and friendly, and she was beginning to relax. Then Mrs. Brandon asked where she and Tony had met.

"We worked at legal aid together, Mother."

Silent for a moment, Mrs. Brandon's eyes scoured her from head to toe. Yet she smiled all the while. Finally she asked, "You're an attorney, too?"

"No, I'm not," she answered. Yet a perceptible flicker of Mrs. Brandon's eyes moved her to add, "I have a law degree, but I chose not to practice." As soon as she said it, she wished she hadn't. It was something about herself she rarely revealed. Now she felt foolish.

"Chose not to?" Mrs. Brandon echoed, with more than a trace of disbelief.

"I felt my law background could be helpful in a different arena," she explained. She didn't say that by the time she'd finished law school she'd become disillusioned. She'd discovered that the law seemed to move slowly at times, too slowly to help people who needed justice *yesterday*. It had become clear that practicing law wasn't the best approach to the public service work she wanted to do.

"Susan used to manage the legal aid office, Mother," Tony said.

Mrs. Brandon turned to her. "Really? And now?"

"Now I'm a department director at the Senior Citizens' Association."

"I see." Tony's mother gave her another scrutinizing look. "How interesting, dear."

Before more could be said another guest approached and announced he was leaving. Mrs. Brandon left to see him out.

Susan was relieved. She looked at Tony and shrugged. "Did I say something wrong?"

"No, it was me. I believe the magic words were *legal aid.*" He lowered his head closer to her ear. "I told you my parents were upset when I didn't go to Harvard? Well, they were extremely distressed when I didn't join Conners right after law school."

"I see."

His hand cupped her elbow. "It has nothing to do with you."

Maybe not. Still, the appraising look in Mrs. Brandon's pale eyes, the hint of doubt in her voice, made Susan think otherwise. Frankly it put her on edge. Sure, she was nervous. Maybe she was paranoid. Either way she decided to keep out of Mrs. Brandon's way until it was time to leave.

Tony's father extended her a polite welcome but spoke with her and Tony only briefly. He was distracted by the rather animated discussion concerning a new White House crisis, which had erupted between two elderly gentlemen.

She met Ambassador Ring and liked him right off. The ambassador—in jeans—entertained her with a few anecdotes from his days in the foreign service. After a while, her apprehensions receded and she relaxed a little. When Tony was pulled aside by another guest eager to discuss tomorrow's Redskins game, she didn't feel abandoned.

She found an unoccupied sofa in a quiet corner of the massive living room. Thankful to be off her feet, she plunked her wine down on the coffee table and sank back into the thick cushions. She closed her eyes, hoping a few minutes of solitude would extinguish any remaining anxiety.

"There you are, my dear." Mrs. Brandon's distinctive voice rang out. "I've been looking for you."

Because she'd sensed a distinct air of disapproval from Mrs. Brandon earlier, Susan was wary. She sat up straight as Mrs. Brandon took a seat beside her.

"I apologize for leaving you earlier," she said. "I do so enjoy meeting Anthony's new friends."

She managed a weak smile. Although Mrs. Brandon was being pleasant enough, Susan was on her guard. "Except you two used to work together," the older woman added, "so you're really not a *new* friend, exactly."

"No, not exactly." She wished Tony—anyone—would come and join them. Perhaps she was being oversensitive, letting her nervousness get the best of her. But she couldn't help it. She was the outsider in this cozy group of upper-crust neighbors—and with this woman she felt it sharply.

Mrs. Brandon continued. "Now you're with the Senior Citizens' Association—oh, wait—you must be the young lady who brought that Somerset business to Anthony's attention."

Feeling awkward under Mrs. Brandon's level gaze, she picked up her wineglass. "As a matter of fact, I am," she replied. Then she took a long sip of wine.

"Anthony's been working so hard on that. I do hope those people appreciate how fortunate they are to have an attorney of his caliber."

"I'm sure they do," she said uneasily, wondering what, if anything, Mrs. Brandon was driving at. She reached out to the coffee table to put down her glass. "The tenants are aware—" She stopped with a stunned gasp and watched in horror as her glass slipped off the edge of the table, spilling an ugly burgundy blot onto the pastel carpet.

"Oh, no! I—" Without thinking she grabbed her cocktail napkin, got on her knees and started dabbing at the large spot. "I can't believe this. I—"

"Stop! You'll make it worse."

Susan's head jerked up. Mrs. Brandon looked horrified.

"We have someone to take care of that." Her eyes searched the room, and she called for the maid.

Susan stood up. All eyes were on her, or at least it felt that way. How could she have been so clumsy? And here of all places?

"Estelle!" Mrs. Brandon's voice was rough with impatience. "Good God, where is that woman?" Several seconds passed before the Brandons' maid appeared with paper towels and a bottle of club soda in hand.

"For heaven's sake, Estelle, hurry," Mrs. Brandon snapped. "The stain will set."

Susan was shocked by Mrs. Brandon's tone. The maid got down on her hands and knees and began working on the stain. Watching her, Susan felt terrible. "I'm sorry. I've made such a mess."

"Don't worry, ma'am. I've seen worse than this," Estelle murmured over her shoulder. Mrs. Brandon stood over the maid and said nothing.

Susan couldn't stop apologizing. Then Tony came up behind her, urging her not to worry. He slipped an arm around her waist and eased her out to the hallway.

"Your mother must be so annoyed."

"She'll get over it."

"I've probably ruined the rug."

"No, you haven't."

"And the maid...I—"

"Susan, accidents happen. You shouldn't get this upset." He gave her a peck on the cheek. "Forget about it and come back in."

But she couldn't forget about it. And she didn't want to go back to see the maid on her hands and knees trying to sop up the spilt wine.

Taking her hand, he turned toward the living room. "Tony, please." She pulled away from him. "Take me home."

The drive to Susan's apartment passed in uncomfortable silence. Susan wasn't talking, and Tony didn't know what to say. Hell, he didn't know what had happened. She was unduly upset over a harmless accident. It made no sense.

He pulled into the circular drive of her apartment building and switched off the engine. "Feel better now?"

He heard her take a deep breath as she stared ahead at the windshield. "I'm fine for a person who's just made a spectacle of herself in front of your parents and their friends."

"You did nothing of the sort."

"And worse," she continued as if she hadn't heard him, "I made trouble for poor Estelle. Your mother was practically screaming at her."

His mother had been brusque with Mrs. Case, but he'd hardly call it screaming. "Don't worry about Estelle. She's—"

"Don't you dare say she's just the housekeeper!"

Her vehemence shocked him. "I wasn't going to say anything of the kind." He regarded her thoughtfully. "Estelle is like one of the family."

She averted her eyes. "I'm sorry."

Perplexed, he lifted her chin with his fingers and looked into the troubled shadows of her blue eyes. He felt an unexpected pang of affection. "Why don't you tell me what this is all about?"

"Oh, Tony," she murmured, her voice weary, "it's hard to explain." She leaned back in the bucket seat, staring at nothing in particular.

"Susan, I need to know."

She nodded, still staring straight ahead. "When your mother snapped at Estelle, it reminded me of other times I've witnessed a hostess speaking harshly to her housekeeper." She turned to him, her gaze now sharply focused. "Except in those instances the housekeeper was my mother."

"Your mother?"

"*My* mother. That's how she earns her living—cooking and cleaning and serving people like your parents and their guests."

He had had no idea. They really hadn't talked much about their homes or families. He had just assumed Susan came from an average, middle-class family—not that it made any difference to him one way or the other. Yet her revelation explained a lot about her past behavior. Now he was beginning to understand.

"I can see why you're upset." He reached for her hand and cradled it between his own. "Mother shouldn't have spoken that way to Estelle, and I'm sure she'll apologize. But you have to remember that Estelle has worked for my parents for nearly twenty years—she knows my mother gets uptight at times. She also knows how to deal with her."

"Twenty years?"

"You don't think she'd stay that long if she was unhappy? My parents are good to her."

"I'm sure they are."

He squeezed her hand.

"Sorry if I overreacted. But when I saw Estelle in her uniform, I couldn't help thinking of my mother." She looked down at her hands. "She and I were alone. The quality of our life depended on how demanding and stingy or how kind and generous her employers were. It's hard to forget that."

He could see it was still very much a part of her. Compassion and admiration intertwined with the fascination and desire he already felt. "There's so much I want to know about you, Susan."

"Even after this?"

"Because of this." He leaned across the seats to kiss her. Her lips were warm, supple, receptive, yet not really giving. He sensed she was deliberately holding back. But why? Tonight's incident had drawn them together. So why did she always take two steps back for every step they took closer to each other? Filled with longing and frustration, he murmured her name against her lips.

She eased away, taking his face between his hands. Her fingers felt cool against his flushed skin. "I better go."

His initial instinct was to clutch at her hands to keep her from leaving. But he didn't. He wouldn't risk scaring her off. "Are you sure you're all right?" he asked instead.

"Yes, of course." Her hands slipped to her lap. "It's been a long day." She sounded tired as she reached for the door handle, moving even farther away from him. "How about a rain check for that dinner and movie?"

"You've got it. I'll call you this week," he said, his mind scrambling frantically for words to resurrect the promise of those hours in Harper's Ferry. But she slipped away quickly. Alone in the chilly darkness of his car, he watched her enter the building, unable to ignore the sinking feeling in his heart.

SHE WASN'T ALL RIGHT.

As she rode the elevator to her floor, her mind reeled with troubling thoughts. Spilling the wine was bad enough. But telling Tony about her mother and her childhood left her emotions off kilter. While they'd sat in his car she'd been torn between wanting to hold him close and needing to push him away.

What a fiasco. She was relieved to be alone. She needed some peace to sort out the mess in her mind and heart. She put on her bathrobe, heated a can of soup and located a classical music station on the radio. Stretching out on the sofa with a steaming mug of soup in hand, she wanted to let her mind go blank. She tried to give herself up to the soothing strains of music, the warmth of her robe and the aroma of chicken soup.

It was useless. Images of Tony, his mother, Estelle kept flashing in her head. By the time she finished the soup, she half believed that tonight's incident was meant as an omen—a bad one—for Tony and herself.

To keep from driving herself crazy she decided to call her mother. Fay was the only person she could talk to about this.

Fay seemed startled to hear her voice. "Susan! Iris and I were just talking about you. I'm afraid I have some bad news, dear."

Susan's throat tightened with fear. "What's wrong?"

Iris had broken her leg in a bad fall, Fay explained. Given her cousin's advanced age, she'd be laid up for several weeks. "So we won't be able to come down for Thanksgiving as we planned, darlin'. Any chance you can come home?"

She sighed with disappointment. "Don't you remember? I asked several friends to join us for dinner. I can't uninvite them now."

"Maybe they could drive up here for dinner."

"Heavens, no." Her mother's cluttered third-floor walk-up was much too cramped to accommodate more than two or three people.

"And why not?" Fay asked.

"Because—it'd be too much work for you," she hedged, "what with Iris laid up and all. Don't even consider it."

"Well, I won't leave Iris and you can't leave your friends in the lurch on Thanksgiving."

Susan felt a twinge of guilt. "I have to work Friday, but tell Iris I'll come up on Saturday," she promised, still concerned about her cousin's condition.

"Good, we'll have our turkey then," Fay suggested. "But now is everything all right with you? You don't usually call on Saturdays."

Susan told her about Tony and what had happened at his parents' house. "I don't know if I should continue seeing him, Mama."

"In heaven's name why not? Because you spilled wine on his mother's rug?"

"You know it's more than that. It's who he is and what he is, where—"

"He sounds like a lovely young man to me. Very caring," Fay interrupted. "Is he the lawyer for those elderly tenants you talked about?"

"Yes, Mama." She couldn't help smiling. Her mother did have a sixth sense about her.

"I thought so. That other man you're dating . . . what's his name—Phil?"

"Neil. Except we only went out a few times. I don't see him anymore."

"Good, because I was gonna say this Neil fellow didn't sound right for you. Don't ask me how I knew—I just sensed it," she explained. "This Tony, now he sounds just fine."

She was irritated by Fay's unconditional support of a man she'd never even met. "But, Mama, his blood is so blue you can write with it. And I'm not sure we share the same values."

"Then tell me, why do you like the boy so much?"

"I . . . I—"

"Stop sputtering and listen to me." Fay's tone was no longer playful. "I taught you to look for the good in people, and you must see an awful lot of good in Tony to be in such a tizzy over him."

She sighed, knowing every word her mother said was true. "Sometimes I think he's the most wonderful man I've ever met."

"That sounds more like it."

"But you just don't know what his name means in this town," she hastened to add.

"Susan O'Toole, I didn't bring you up to feel inferior to anyone. You're a fine, smart girl, and I'm proud to call you mine."

Susan swallowed hard as a feeling both familiar and undefinable rushed through her. She couldn't say her mother was pushing her, yet she felt a pressure to measure up to some higher, unspoken standard again.

She fought back any resentment, quickly and resolutely. It wouldn't be fair to her mother who, after all, only wanted the best for her.

"Oh, Mama," she sighed, feeling guilty, "I love you so much."

"Of course you do, darlin." Fay's voice softened. "Now I want you to remember something. No matter how different you and Tony may be, something landed you two at the same place at the same time. Fate has its reasons. Don't fight it."

Don't fight it? Was her mother serious?

Susan felt as if she'd been fighting one thing or another all her life. And she wasn't sure now was the time to stop.

Chapter Nine

Sunday morning brunch at the Brandon home was a family tradition Tony adhered to when he could.

Today he wished he had skipped it.

The tension in the dining room was palpable. His parents barely spoke to each other or to him. What in hell was going on between them? he wondered. Looking from his father to his mother and back again, he thought better of asking outright. He didn't need to add to the tension.

After they dined on cheese soufflé and baked ham, his father excused himself from the table. "I'll be in my study," he muttered.

Tony noticed how his mother's eyes followed his father out of the room. Yet her face was an unreadable mask.

"Are you two all right?" he asked finally.

"Of course we are. Why do you ask?"

"Because you and Dad hardly said two words to each other this morning. Did you have a fight or something?"

"Don't be ridiculous," she sniffed, lifting a delicate china cup to her lips.

He didn't think he was being ridiculous. But his mother clearly didn't want to talk about whatever the problem was.

They drank their coffee in silence until Estelle came in from the kitchen, wearing her hat and coat. "Everything is cleaned up and put away, Mrs. Brandon. All you have to do is put these coffee things in the dishwasher. And I sliced up the rest of the ham so you and the Mister can have sandwiches tonight."

"Thank you, Estelle. Have a good time with your sister today."

After Estelle left, Tony reached for the silver coffeepot and offered his mother a refill.

"Tell me, dear, did your friend Susan calm down after you two sneaked away last night?" she asked while he poured.

"She was fine. A little embarrassed, that's all."

"A little?" His mother shook her head. "She seems rather high-strung if you ask me."

"I didn't."

She continued, anyway. "I wonder how well you really know this young woman."

He knew his mother was hinting around for more information on Susan. This wasn't strange in and of itself. Yet he sensed she was motivated by something other than concern or curiosity, which disturbed him. She tended to dismiss, without discussion, people she disapproved of or disliked. And he'd suspected that was how she felt about Susan—until she brought up her name. Well, perhaps she didn't like Susan, but apparently she couldn't ignore her, either.

His mother folded her napkin and placed it next to her cup and saucer. Then she pushed her chair away from the table, impatience lacing every move. "Tell me, Anthony, what do you know about this girl?"

"I beg your pardon?"

"Do you know her well? I mean, how did she get you tangled up with that apartment business?"

"I chose to represent the Somerset tenants—on its merits alone."

She looked skeptical. "She had no influence on your choice whatsoever?"

Now he was losing patience. "What are you getting at, Mother?"

"How involved are you with her?"

"That's none of your business."

She stiffened. "It is my business if your involvement with her is going to derail your commitment to the firm— especially when your father is considering retirement."

"Retirement?" He couldn't believe his ears. "Dad has never mentioned anything about retiring to me."

"It's under consideration." Her voice was tight and low. "Except retirement will be out of the question if he feels your dedication to the firm is less than one hundred percent."

He didn't know how to react to his mother's pronouncement. He was astonished by what she'd said, and concerned by the way she'd said it. Retirement? His dad? A man whose identity was deeply enmeshed with Conners, Brandon and Moffet? And now? When he was only sixty-two? It didn't make sense.

Yet he couldn't ask his mother more about it. She sounded overwrought enough as it was. She'd been snappish and moody for weeks, and he could no longer believe her troubling behavior was due to "nervousness about her new book." No, her edginess about Susan, and the tension between her and his father, had to be connected to this question of retirement. He was convinced of it.

"ALICE FOUND an eviction notice in her mailbox this morning," Susan blurted out as soon as Tony answered his phone. She was outraged about the timing of the evictions.

"Damn! I thought they'd wait at least until after Thanksgiving."

She grimaced. "Guess the Hammond Group doesn't have much heart."

Heart or no heart it was rotten, Tony thought. The tenants knew the evictions were coming, but they weren't expecting them this soon. Thanksgiving was only days away. What kind of holiday could they possibly have now? "How did Alice sound?" he asked.

"Shaky. And I imagine the others are the same."

"Look, can you take some time off to go there and calm things down? I'll get over to court and file for a temporary restraining order to block the evictions."

"This is it, isn't it?"

"'Fraid so," he replied. "Looks like we're instigating a lawsuit against the Hammond Group."

She sighed. She had hoped they could have avoided going to court. "I'm on my way over there. You'll call me as soon as you know anything else?"

"Promise."

By the time she got to the Somerset, a regular coffee klatch had gathered at Alice's apartment. A few people had brought coffee cake and cookies. Alice was busy pouring coffee. Everyone had their pink eviction notices in hand, as if they needed to see them and touch them to prove the reality of what was happening. They'd been ordered to leave their homes within the next four months. Although Tony had warned them it could happen, they still found it hard to accept.

After she relayed what Tony had told her, Susan sat in the living room with Alice. The old woman had calmed down since she'd phoned Susan's office. Tending to her guests had given her something else to do besides worry. "Do you think we'll hear from Tony soon?" she asked.

"Probably not. These things take time," she explained between sips of coffee. "A date will have to be set for the hearing."

"Lordy, who knows when that'll be?" She heaved a sigh of frustration. "Sounds like we're in for a long haul."

Susan nodded, knowing nothing she could say would put the situation in a better light. She regarded Alice with concern. She seemed anxious. Worried, naturally. But she also seemed less emotional about the situation than when Susan first approached her about it weeks ago. In fact, Alice looked more hale and hearty than she had during that first visit. She had gained some weight, and she was sporting a becoming new hairdo. Susan complimented her on it.

"Why, thanks, honey. I decided I needed a change." Alice patted her new white curls. "But I'm not going back to coloring my hair. Too expensive and too much trouble."

Susan smiled. "It's good to see you feeling like your old self again."

"I do feel better, even if we don't know what's going to happen here. At least we're not just sitting around wringing our hands, feeling helpless."

"Helpless you're not."

"Not now. You and Tony had made me see that. And, honey, there's nothing worse than feeling helpless—especially at my age." Alice leaned close as she lowered her voice. "You've energized a lot of other old geezers here, too." She smiled and gently jabbed Susan's ribs with her elbow. "Life's been more interesting around here lately."

Susan laughed. "Oh, really?"

"I'll tell you about it sometime."

"I hope you're still coming to my place for Thanksgiving dinner," Susan reminded. She explained her mother's change of plans for the holiday. "But I'm cooking dinner as promised. My friend Maria and her family are coming, too."

"I wouldn't miss it. I know what a good cook you are." Then she added hesitantly, "Would you mind if I invited

Mr. O'Brien to dinner? I found out he's going to be alone.''

"Of course. No one should be alone on Thanksgiving.''

"Sure you have room?''

"Plenty,'' she assured, realizing that Alice and Mr. O'Brien had become quite friendly over the past few weeks. She was pleased for Alice. It was one more positive thing that had grown out of adversity. Then she thought of Tony and herself. She hoped their relationship would remain positive, as well.

She stayed at Alice's as long as she could. Eventually she had to go back to work. Promising she'd notify them as soon as she heard from Tony, Susan returned to the office. Back at her desk she skipped lunch to catch up with phone calls and paperwork. She thought about Tony, wondering when he'd call with some news. Then she became so busy that she lost track of time. Before she realized it her secretary was saying good-night.

Finally Tony called. "Ten o'clock Monday morning at U.S. District Court. Judge Allen Ferugia.''

She realized she was holding her breath. She exhaled with relief. "Thank goodness.''

"Sorry it took so long. The courthouse was a zoo,'' he explained. "I've already called Alice, and she's notifying the others. She sounded pretty up.''

"After the initial shock of the evictions wore off, they all calmed down. They're ready for a fight.''

"Unfortunately they've got one.'' He paused for a moment. "And how are you?'' His voice was tender and low, making her heart skip a beat.

"Okay—now that you've called.''

"I wish we could get together tonight. I'd really like to see you, except something's come up in New York.''

She felt a stab of disappointment. "Leland?''

"I have to meet with his attorneys. I'll be gone for a few days."

"You're going now? When things at the Somerset are so up in the air?" She knew how this sounded, but she couldn't keep herself from saying it.

"Rob is here if anything comes up between now and Monday—which I greatly doubt. Hammond is sitting tight on this one."

"I know. I guess I'd just feel better if you were here."

"Can I take that to mean you'll miss me?"

The question filled her with a sudden spurt of longing. She would miss him. Still, she found it difficult to admit that to him. "When will you be back?" she asked instead.

"Thursday or Friday."

Instinctively she reverted to levity to mask her deeper feelings. "I'll count the days," she teased.

He chuckled. "A friend of mine is having a party Friday after work. I'd like you to come with me."

"Someone from the office?"

"Yes, one of the partners. Not everyone will be from the firm, though."

Her experience at the Brandons' made her wary. "Let's talk about it when you get back."

Apparently catching her reluctance, Tony didn't answer right away, and she could almost feel the lightheartedness between them evaporate.

"You know, I hate leaving with so much up in the air between us."

Now it was her turn to hesitate as the telephone line fairly crackled with tension. "Tony, I..." What could she say?

"Never mind, Susan. We'll talk about it when I get back."

He rang off without further comment, leaving her feeling sheepish. She should be pleased that he wanted to take her to meet his friends, not reluctant. But the reason she was began long ago with the hand-me-down clothes of her mother's employer's children. It had been reinforced throughout her life—even as recently as his parents' cocktail party.

Intellectually she knew the past shouldn't hold her back from who or what she wanted. But emotionally she still felt like the outsider, at least where Tony's social circle was concerned. It was a powerful feeling to overcome.

SUSAN BUCKLED down at work while Tony was away. She needed to focus her attention on her job after the distractions of the Somerset situation. FDA studies on new geriatric drugs sat on her desk waiting to be analyzed, correspondence to be caught up on, and she still had to work on the speech she'd be giving at a pharmacist's convention that was coming to town the week following Thanksgiving. She stayed late at the office every night that week to work and tried not to think about what Tony might be doing all alone in New York—and why he hadn't called her once.

By Thursday evening she'd written most of her speech and was determined to finish it before the tenants' court hearing on Monday. But finding herself stalled, she decided to read out loud what she'd written so far. In the nearly deserted suite of offices at eight o'clock at night, her voice reverberated with a lonely echo. She read on, however, trying to ignore the eeriness of it all—until the outside door creaked open and she heard footsteps approaching.

Suddenly a golden brown head peeked around her half-opened door. "Working late?"

"Tony!" She let go of her breath with a long gasp of relief.

He was at her side at once, a reassuring hand on her shoulder. "The security guard downstairs usually works the weekend shift in my building. We're *old* pals, so he let me come up. I'm sorry I scared you.''

Delighted to see him, she covered his hand with her own, fighting the urge to caress it with her cheek. "How'd you know I was here?"

"When I couldn't reach you at home, I took a chance. But your switchboard closes early."

"I know." She released his hand. "What do you have there?"

"Dinner—Chinese." He lifted a heavy paper bag into the air, filling her office with appetizing aromas. "I figured if you were working late, you hadn't bothered to eat yet. Am I right?"

She nodded, touched by his thoughtfulness. She couldn't take her eyes off him as he slipped off his overcoat and suit jacket. She was glad to see him, and she could tell he felt the same way about her. Smiling green eyes and a warm, welcoming smile sent her pulse soaring as she watched him roll up his shirtsleeves. Even wearing dark blue suspenders and necktie askew, he looked wonderful. She hadn't seen him since the night of his parents' cocktail party, and only now it hit her how much she missed him.

Tony pulled a small gift-wrapped package from his overcoat pocket. "Here, a memento from the Big Apple."

"You didn't have to bring me anything."

"No. But I wanted to."

Under his watchful eye she slowly tore open the package to find an exquisite silk scarf. She recognized the designer signature. "Tony, it's lovely, but much too—"

"Didn't your mother teach you how to accept gifts gracefully?"

"Thank you," she murmured softly. Then she met his eyes. "Why do you bother with me?"

"Why do I bother? she asks. Hmm, let me see." He sat on the edge of the desk and looked down at her. "She's smart, pretty, a great cook. She's also sweeter than she thinks and sexier than she knows."

"And more trouble than I'm worth."

"Nobody's perfect." Taking her hand, he pulled her to her feet. "Perfect's boring."

"You sounded a little angry when we last talked." She let her hand glide along one blue suspender strap.

Still sitting on her desk, he pulled her closer to him. "Exasperated is the word."

"Not enough to give up on me?"

"What would you have me do Susan? Play it easy? Give up and always think of you as that great woman I never had?"

"Oh, Tony, I—"

"Come here."

Enfolding her in his arms, he brushed her lips with a light kiss, and her mouth tingled. Yearning for more, she pressed against his chest, and he answered with a longer, more satisfying kiss. His tongue tempted her lips until she couldn't refuse to welcome it. She tasted the now-familiar mix of coffee and mint. But soon she was completely lost in the warm sensations churning through her lower body.

When he finally released her, she was breathless. She looked into his eyes, hoping he could see how much his kiss affected her.

"I missed you, Susan."

"I missed you, too."

"Now that's encouraging." He smiled. "So will you come to Mike's party with me tomorrow night?"

She should have answered yes right away. Instead, she turned the question over in her mind yet another time— time enough for her apprehensions to hit her with full force. It was so lovely between them tonight, why follow it with a situation where she'd be uncomfortable as she'd been at his parents'?

Except she couldn't bring herself to admit that to him. "Tony, I have to finish writing this talk for the convention. And I won't have time next week, what with the Somerset hearing and Thanksgiving," she explained. "Would you mind if I passed on this one?"

He squeezed her shoulder. "Do what you have to, Susan."

"Next time, I promise," she said, surprised he was letting it go at that.

He looked at her and nodded, his smile gone. "We should get to this food before it gets cold."

She felt horrible. Not only was she acting cowardly, she was being dishonest. Tony deserved better. Next time, she vowed. Next time she'd go wherever he asked. Next time she would handle it.

TONY FOUND many of the city's top young professionals partying in Mike Stone's Georgetown living room. There were a few journalists, some political appointees, a couple of embassy employees, a doctor here and there. But most of the guests were lawyers. He knew a few of them personally; most others he knew professionally.

Mike, a fellow partner at Conners, looked surprised to see him. "Tony, my man, you made it back from New York in time. I hear things are heating up for Leland over at Justice."

Before he could comment more guests arrived and Mike left to greet them. Tony went into the kitchen, chose a beer from the wide selection of imports and then edged his way into the crowded living room. He had a chance to catch up with some friends he hadn't seen for a while. He always enjoyed comparing notes with colleagues. Almost every person he spoke with remarked on the Leland case: congratulating him for landing it, asking questions about it, inquiring, with much curiosity, about the great man himself.

Obviously people had been talking about the case and about him. The case had gained him a certain notoriety in this circle, and he realized he liked the recognition. He didn't mind the increased respect, either. Although he didn't much cotton to the term, he *was* becoming a player in this city.

"Well, hello, stranger."

Tony recognized the voice and the perfume. He hadn't seen Taylor Peters—willowy and stunning tonight in beige and gold—since that night at the Kennedy Center with Maria and Luis. He hadn't even called her.

Taylor accepted his apologies with a nonchalant graciousness. He sensed that his inattentiveness hadn't bothered her much—which didn't surprise him. Taylor was a sharp woman; she made her own way.

"You must be up to your ears with the Leland suit. Probably working day and night, right?"

"I am busy. Since the last time I saw you, I've also taken on a tenants' rights case over in Rosslyn. It's been a tough one."

"I don't know how you do it, Tony. Imagine squeezing in a case like that now. No wonder no one ever sees you anymore."

Her remarks didn't set well. He wanted to make her understand just how basic and crucial the Somerset situation was. But Taylor, like the others, was full of questions about William Leland and the antitrust suit. He couldn't blame her really. He'd probably be just as curious.

Tony was relieved when Taylor's date arrived to take her off to dinner. By then he needed a moment to himself: to collect his thoughts, to get his bearings. Earlier he had been enjoying himself. Now the charm was beginning to wear off; he wasn't sure why.

He liked many of the people at this party. Yet now, as he stood in their midst, he felt such a loneliness of heart. Something was missing.

Damn, he wished Susan had come with him. He wanted her to meet these friends and colleagues. They were decent people—she would see that. Maybe then she'd understand him a little better. Maybe he wouldn't feel defensive about who he was and what he did. Then maybe she wouldn't need to make up excuses for not coming to gatherings like this.

Out of the corner of his eye he saw Mike approaching, drink in hand. "Tony, a chance to talk at last."

"Great party."

"Thanks, pal." Mike leaned closer. "How've things been going lately? We keep missing each other at the office."

"My schedule's been insane."

"You do look a little ragged. Why don't you make this a long weekend and take Monday off?"

"Are you kidding? I've got a court hearing on the Somerset first thing Monday morning." He gave Mike a dry smile. "Guess what I'll be doing all weekend?"

"I see," Mike remarked with a nod. "How's that one working out, anyway?"

"You know, you're the first person tonight who's bothered to ask."

"Well, I know it's important to you."

"I wish I could figure out just how important."

"What do you mean?" Mike asked, casually leaning his back against the living room wall.

"It was pretty exciting up in New York. Leland Industries is a dynamic place. Coming back to prepare for this hearing is sort of a letdown." He didn't add that he was also let down by Susan's refusal to accompany him tonight.

"Feeling torn, eh?"

"Yeah, can you believe it? After the way I made such an issue of taking on the tenants' case?" He sipped his beer.

"Hey, you're not sorry you took them on, are you?"

With a contemplative sigh he shook his head. "No, not really. I guess I wish I had more support," he answered, still thinking of Susan. "All the way around."

"So that's it." Mike gave him a knowing look. "The firm's still giving you flak about it."

Mike didn't know much about his involvement with Susan, and he didn't feel like getting into it tonight. It was less complicated to let Mike think he was talking solely about the law firm. "Let's just say there's been grumblings from above—especially now that I'm using more of Rob Berns's time."

"I can just bet who's complaining—Mr. 'Out for every buck he can get' Conners. Right?"

Tony chuckled in spite of himself. "Mainly. But my father's managed a broad hint or two."

"So why are you letting them get to you? In a few months you can do pretty much what you please."

"What do you mean?"

"Hey, we've all heard the rumor." Mike pulled himself up straight, his hands in midair as he continued. "You know your dad's about to retire within the year."

"Retire?" Tony couldn't believe it. The only time it had ever been mentioned to him was by his mother, and that had been in passing.

"That's the scuttlebutt around the office, pal. Is it true?"

"If it is, I haven't been told," he snapped, not even trying to hide his ire. "But you know how it is, Mike. The family's always the last to know."

"Well, if it's true, you'll be *the* Brandon at the firm then. With that and the Leland case you're looking ahead at some pretty high times. Conners will have to think twice before giving you flak about the Somerset or anything else."

He scarcely heard a word Mike said as indignation and hurt spun through him. He doubted this was mere rumor. His father must have discussed the possibility of retirement with someone at the firm, and all Tony knew was that it hadn't been him.

"Damn," he spit out in anger. "You'd think he'd say something to me, wouldn't you? After all, I am his only son."

"Take it easy." Mike gave his shoulder a supportive pat. "It may just be a rumor."

"Oh, right," Tony muttered, giving his friend a scornful look.

"Sorry you heard about it like this."

He shrugged. "It's not your fault."

Mike glanced down at Tony's empty beer bottle. "Hey, let me get you another one. I'll be right back."

This was turning out to be a strange evening, Tony thought after Mike left for the kitchen. Now his father's possible retirement was looming over him. No longer was it just a figment of his mother's anxiety—it was actually being talked about at the firm. And, yes, he was mad he had to learn about it via office gossip. Still, he shouldn't have been surprised. His father's not telling him was actually quite in character—so typical of his arm's-length manner of dealing with the family.

If his father's retirement was imminent, he'd have to deal with it. Except he didn't really want to. Not yet, anyway. There was so much else he needed to straighten out, like his relationship with his parents and the types of cases he handled.

Despite the periodic conflicts, working on both the Leland case and the Somerset case had given him a much-needed balance. Yet he felt an emptiness, a need for something more. He didn't think being *the* Brandon at Conners, Brandon and Moffet was going to fill that need.

But he had a good idea what would. He had only to remember how good he'd felt seeing Susan again last night and how lonely he'd felt afterward. And how lonely he was at this moment. Now, standing here in a roomful of people very much like himself, he knew his need for something more had very much to do with Susan O'Toole.

Chapter Ten

Susan pressed hard on Tony's doorbell, scarcely believing she was doing so at eight o'clock on a Saturday morning. Acting on impulse wasn't like her at all. Then again, who wouldn't be behaving a little oddly after a sleepless night spent with guilt and regret?

She jabbed the doorbell again and then rapped loudly on the door, figuring such racket would be the only way to waken Tony this early. She had to talk to him, *needed* to. And if she really had some spunk, she'd have shown up at six.

The third round of ringing and knocking brought a wave of apprehension. What if he wasn't—? Oh, God, please make him be home, she prayed, unwilling to consider the implications if he wasn't. She banged her fist against the door.

At last she heard a muffled voice call out, "All right, all right, I'm coming. Hold on."

Her heart pounded rapidly against her chest as he unbolted the locks from inside. When he finally opened the door, he gasped, "Susan—what on earth?"

His hair was wet and matted against his forehead. A damp white towel around his neck draped over the front of his plaid knee-length robe. His legs were bare, as was his chest. Droplets of water glistened on the wedge of dark blond chest hair exposed by the hastily wrapped robe. She didn't know what she'd expected to find when she tore over here this morning but, naively, it wasn't this. Seeing him like this, fresh from a shower, stirred her in a most elemental way. And the resultant fluttering in her stomach was as unnerving as it was exciting.

"Susan?" Tony repeated, dragging her back to face the matter at hand.

She blinked rapidly to force out how attractive she found him right now. "I'm sorry to come so early, but—" Looking directly into his green eyes, she swallowed hard. "But I *should* have come to the party with you last night."

He just stared back at her for a moment and then waved her inside. Closing the door behind her, he wiped his damp brow with the towel. "Let me dry off and then I'll make coffee. I need some."

Watching him climb back up the stairs, she hadn't a clue as to whether or not he was glad to see her. But what else was new? She *never* knew how things stood with them. They'd been circling around each other for weeks. Each time she and Tony were together the circle got smaller, they got closer. Yet there always remained a distance between them, always something that kept the circle from pulling them together. Her doubts, his parents, Leland, and now his friend's party—they all comprised that distance, a distance she felt strongly.

Too nervous to sit, she paced the short length of Tony's living room. Though small, she guessed it was the largest room in his narrow two-story townhouse. Jittery as she was, she liked it. Sheer size made it feel cozy, and it was simply furnished. It suited Tony.

When he came downstairs, she followed him to the tiny kitchen in the rear of the house. It was so cramped that she had to stand against the windowed back door as Tony prepared coffee in what looked like a very expensive European coffee maker. Once the coffee began to gurgle into the glass carafe, he leaned against the counter's edge. "Well, here we are," he said, folding his arms in front of his chest.

Yes, here they were, Susan thought wryly, sensing the tension in him. If he only knew how difficult this was for her. Forcing herself to meet his gaze, she noticed, for the first time, how drawn-out and pale he looked. Something in her face must have given this thought away, because a dry smile twisted his lips. "Don't tell me I look that bad."

"No, no," she reassured quickly. "Though it must have been some party I missed last night."

"As parties go, this one was pretty low-key. I was home by ten." In response to her questioning look, he added, "I did find out something in a rather distressing manner last night. Thinking about it kept me awake most of the night."

"Want to tell me about it?"

"That depends." His voice was tinged with irony. "It's about my father—and the law firm. Do you want to hear about it?"

"Yes, Tony, I do."

Her quick response seemed to surprise him, and she wondered if he believed her. Turning his back to her, he opened an overhead cabinet and pulled out two coffee mugs. "I found out that my father is retiring—or rumored to be—from the law firm. Not that he's bothered to mention it to me."

She crossed the brief space separating them to stand beside him. "Maybe because it's only a rumor," she said.

Tony explained why he didn't think so, his words full of resentment. She felt badly for him. "I've really tried to be the dutiful son at the firm these past few years," he continued, pouring the now-brewed coffee into the mugs. "I've tried my best to meet his expectations. But, damn, it's always a one-way street with him."

"Take it easy," she murmured, placing her hand on his arm.

He took a deep breath. "Sorry. I probably sound like a ten-year-old complaining that nothing pleases my daddy."

"Maybe he's given you reason to feel that way."

"Maybe he has."

The sadness in his voice struck a chord of empathy and evoked some memories. How often had she felt that her needs took a back seat to the needs of the families for whom her mother worked? How often had she resented Fay's tendency to get wrapped up in their lives? And, of course, she'd always felt guilt-ridden when this happened because Fay was only doing everything possible to support *her*.

She swallowed her first taste of the rich, strong coffee and peered up at Tony. "You know, my mother does that to me sometimes—makes me feel as if I'm just blundering along, I mean. The absolute worst time was when I decided against practicing law."

"Not a popular decision, I take it."

"Not with her, and certainly not with the Harrisons, the people she keeps house for. You see, Blake Harrison offered me a job at his law firm, Miller, Tidwell and Weeks."

Tony recognized the name. "It's an excellent firm."

"I know. They made a generous offer, but it just wasn't right for me." She stared down at her coffee mug. "In any case, my mother was horrified when I turned down Mr. Harrison's help. And both he and his wife had Mama convinced I was making the gravest error of my life."

The notion made Tony smile. "Since your life obviously hasn't gone down the gutter, how does she feel now?"

"Accepted it. What else?"

"Good." He gave her shoulder a squeeze. "I wonder if my parents will ever accept anything I do." But his voice was light as he said this, and she was glad to see his mood had brightened.

"You know what?" she asked, plunking her coffee mug down on the counter. "We should get out of here and do something. Something different—like go on a hike. It's beautiful outside today."

"A hike? That's not why you came here at the crack of dawn, is it?"

"No, but the fresh air will cheer us both up, and heaven knows, I could use the exercise." She put a hand flat against his chest. "Besides, I'd like to spend some time with you. That's all."

"You really want to?" His expression brightened considerably, his eyes gleaming like liquid emeralds.

"I really want to."

Ten minutes later they were driving on the Maryland side of the river, along the Chesapeake and Ohio Canal. Autumn's glow was dwindling, trees had shed most of their leaves and a marked chill filled the air, yet the sky was cloudless and the sun diamond-bright. It was a good morning to be outdoors, and the number of cars in the parking lot near the Billy Goat Trail attested to it.

The trail was aptly named. The hills, boulders and rocky cliffs overlooking the swirling narrows of the Potomac made for a challenging but exciting hike.

"I should have my head examined," Tony grumbled after they climbed over several boulders. "Why did you pick this trail? Hoping I'll fall off a cliff?"

She chuckled. "I chose it because years ago I came here and was scared out of my wits. You see, I have a slight fear of heights."

"Really?" His gaze fell to the drop between the rocks and the river below. He reached for her hand. "No wonder you were scared."

His hand felt warm around hers. The protective gesture touched her heart. "Not only was I scared, but I also barely made it through the trail. I was in pretty lousy shape back then, and the butt of all my friends' jokes that day,'' she explained. ''I vowed never to come back.''

''So why are we here?'' Tony asked between short puffs of breath.

''Guess I felt the urge to try it again. See if I could handle it now.''

''Good for you.'' He was still holding her hand as he followed her up a rocky incline. ''But what about your fear of heights?''

''I refuse to look down, and I'm not getting close to any edges.''

He laughed. ''You know, you're all right.''

''Thank you, sir.''

''And, Susan?''

''Yes?''

Teasing eyes rested on her backside. ''You're not in such lousy shape.''

Feeling herself blush, she smiled and tugged him along. ''Let's keep moving, friend.''

When they were halfway through the trail, they decided to rest. They found a spot near a stone bluff—far enough away from its edge to satisfy her. ''Peace at last,'' Tony said, leaning his back against a large gray boulder. When she sat beside him, he nudged her closer until she rested, snug and comfortable, against his chest.

They sat in companionable silence for quite some time. Feeling such tenderness for him, she began to stroke his arm with a languorous touch. She could love this man, she realized. Maybe she already did.

''Tony, we have to talk.'' Her voice came out in a whisper.

''I know.'' He kissed her hair. ''Are you ready to?''

She sighed. ''I usually get around to the inevitable—in my fashion.''

"In your fashion? I'll have to remember that about you, Susan O'Toole." She couldn't see his face, but he sounded as if he was smiling.

His arms tightened around her. "You've become very special to me, Susan."

"And you to me." She really wanted him to know that. "Every time I'm with you the feeling gets stronger. When it's just the two of us together, I feel the possibilities are endless."

"And when we're not?"

"I lose my nerve. That's why I didn't go to the party with you last night. I wanted to but . . ."

"Oh? You mean it wasn't because you had to work on your speech?" he said with blatantly mock surprise.

He knew. Straightening in his arms, she turned to him.

"You're not a great fibber, Susan," he said. "I advise you not to lie if you ever find yourself on a witness stand."

She shot him a look of exaggerated exasperation. "Lawyers," she harrumphed, turning away, "you're all alike."

Tony laughed. "You may not be such a hot liar, but you sure have evasion down pat."

"All right, all right. I admit my excuse about last night was paltry. And I admit I have qualms. But don't you?" she asked, shifting in his arms until they sat face-to-face.

His face darkened. "My only qualm is how you pull away every time we start to get close. I wanted very much for you to come to that party with me."

"But you didn't say that."

"Was I supposed to push you? Guilt-trip you into it? That's not how I want us to be together."

"Maybe I'm scared of what being together means."

Tony lifted her hands to his lips and kissed them both. His eyes held her gaze. "No one knows what the future holds, Susan. *We'll* never know unless we try. Please try."

Bowing his head, he nuzzled his face against her neck. This caress suffused a creamy warmth through her limbs as she delighted in the sensations of his warm breath and freshly shaven face on her skin.

"It could be risky," she murmured with some difficulty.

"Yes, it could."

"We certainly don't have to rush into anything. We—" His lips moved to her right earlobe, nearly taking her breath away as she struggled to continue. "We could take it one day at a time."

"We could."

"We could take a chance."

He planted a kiss on her cheek before whispering, "We'd be fools not to."

SUSAN WAS RELIEVED to see Tony standing in the corridor just outside the courtroom. After accompanying several nervous tenants to the U.S. District Court in downtown D.C., she had become nervous herself. Seeing him, so commanding in his blue suit, made her confidence resurge. And her attraction.

She hadn't seen him since their hike two days ago. Although they'd been reluctant to part that afternoon, they had both agreed it was for the best. Taking things slowly in their relationship required some physical restraint, since the impulse to make love was strong. But the timing was wrong. They both realized that.

Alice, Tom and the others gathered around Tony and Rob Berns. Everyone spoke in hushed tones, either in deference to their hallowed surroundings or out of nervousness. Standing off to the side, Susan listened as Tony explained the upcoming proceedings to the tenants.

When Rob interjected with a comment of his own, Tony peered over his clients' heads to catch her eye. He acknowledged her with a silent nod of his head. Yet the smile in his green eyes was unmistakable, even through his glasses. It made her feel as if she and Tony were the only two people in the courthouse.

A bailiff pushed open the heavy doors, and all eyes turned to Tony. It was time to go before the judge. The tenants who had come to the hearing—Alice, Tom, Eva, Sally and Lon—filed quietly into the courtroom behind Tony and Rob.

As the tenants found seats in the spectator area, a well-dressed man entered the room. Alice sat down next to Susan. "Hammond's lawyer?" she asked when the man snapped open his briefcase on the defendant's table.

"Must be."

Tom leaned over to Susan. "Looks like a shark."

Alice sniffed. "Tony can handle the likes of him."

The man, dressed in conservative gray, didn't appear that threatening to Susan. He looked like the average, garden-variety Washington lawyer, much like Tony and Rob. But she understood why Tom had perceived him as dangerous. As attorney for the Hammond Group, it was his job to make sure the court didn't put a restraining order on the evictions.

Once U.S. District Court Judge Ferugia entered the courtroom, the proceedings went quickly. Tony and the Hammond attorney presented brief arguments outlining their requests. Then, after reviewing the class-action suit filed by the Somerset tenants, Judge Ferugia decided to grant a temporary injunction against the Hammond Group.

A confused Alice turned to Susan. "That's it? It's over?"

Susan couldn't help smiling. "That's it for now. The judge still has to hear the suit later on."

"Alice, don't you get it?" Tom asked, jostling her elbow. "We won this round. He blocked the evictions."

"Well, I thought he did. But it was so quick! My heavens, I can't believe it."

Tom gave Alice a victory hug. "That's the way I like 'em, quick and painless." Susan had never seen Tom O'Brien so animated. That and Alice's joy doubled her pleasure over the hearing's outcome.

As the fact of victory sank in, the tenants were all laughing and hugging. Finally a friendly guard bustled them back out to the corridor so that the next case could begin. When Tony and Rob joined them, they got their share of hugs and thanks, too. Susan could tell Tony was pleased with the hearing's outcome. It was written all over his handsome face.

Although Tony was enjoying this moment considerably, his professional caution reared its practical head. He looked at the aged faces of his clients, now happier than he'd ever seen them. They deserved to be jubilant. Hell, *he* was thrilled. But it wasn't over, and he had to be sure they understood that.

"Folks, before you bring the good news back to the other tenants I'd like to say a few words." All eyes turned to him as everyone quieted down. "I'm not saying this to put a damper on your celebration, but it would be remiss of me not to emphasize that this injunction is only temporary—until we come back to court. We have a lot of hard work ahead."

He scanned their faces again. Not one was crestfallen. These people were fighters, bless them. "Now that we've gotten that piece of business out of the way—go home, have a party, and a happy Thanksgiving, too."

He watched them straggle away, chattering and laughing. Rob went with them to make sure they found their way to the Metro stop. Finally he was alone with Susan, which was where he had wanted to be for the past two days. God, she looked good. She was wearing the trim red suit he liked so much. He fancied she had worn it because she knew this. His eyes dipped to her legs. Black pumps made them look longer, sexier.

When he put his arm around her shoulders, she wrapped her arm around his waist. He liked the way it felt—relaxed, special. "Did I do the right thing," he began as they walked down the hall, "reminding them the injunction was only temporary?"

"You had to. Besides, it didn't seem to faze them."

"You're right, it didn't," he agreed, feeling reassured.

"Alice invited us to drop by after work. I think they're going to celebrate all afternoon."

"How about a celebration of our own tonight? After we stop by Alice's."

"Great. I'll cook up something really special—"

"No." He shook his head. "I know you love to cook, but this is my treat. You're going to relax and enjoy."

"Mmm. Sounds nice."

He hugged her to his side. She was special, very special, and he wanted to plan something that would show her that. "What's your favorite kind of food?"

"I like everything—ribs, Greek, Mexican, Italian, French—you name it."

"Hard to please, aren't you?" he quipped as an idea struck him. If it could be worked out, he knew it would be perfect.

IT WASN'T EASY getting away from the little party at Alice's. The spirit of victory had lasted well through the afternoon and early evening. When he and Susan arrived, they were treated like guests of honor. Everyone wanted to talk to them.

"So where are we going?" Susan asked when they finally managed to slip away. "I'm starving."

Unlocking his car door, he beamed at her across the roof. "A favorite place of mine. You'll see when we get there."

She muttered something about not liking surprises, yet he could tell her curiosity was aroused. But she didn't mention it again during the brief ride back into the city. As he cruised along the streets of Foggy Bottom, searching for a place to park, she turned to him with a speculative eye. "I see we're in your neighborhood. Are we dining at *your* house tonight?"

"I don't cook, remember? And if we were, would I be hunting for a parking space?"

He wondered if she would have objected to dinner at his place. He'd thought about having a meal brought in and spending the evening together at his townhouse. He would have liked nothing better than to have her all to himself in such an intimate setting. Yet he was concerned that might be rushing things, pressing Susan. The one thing he didn't want to do now was scare her away.

He found a space near Washington Circle, a block away from the restaurant. The evening air was mild, and the stars were tiny whispers of light in the dark sky. Taking her by the hand, he led her down Pennsylvania Avenue to the narrow three-story building that housed Guido's.

She stared at the restaurant's darkened front entrance. "Tony, it's closed. See—" she pointed at the sign on the door "—closed Mondays."

"Today's Monday?" He pretended to check the date on his watch. "Funny, they took my reservation."

She cast a doubtful glance his way.

The front door was locked tight. "Must be a mistake," he declared as he started rapping on it.

"For heaven's sake, Tony."

They heard the door being unlocked from inside. "Signor Brandon," a man greeted as he opened the door, "we've been waiting."

"Good evening, Guido. We're not late, are we?"

"Not at all. Everything is just right," he assured in his light but smooth accent. "Signorina O'Toole, welcome."

Apparently puzzled by this turn of events, Susan stood gaping at the tall, dark-haired man. Tony introduced her to the restaurant's owner and then escorted her inside.

"Your table is waiting," Guido advised. They followed him through the small rustic dining room, which was completely devoid of customers. The lighting was muted, a fire glowed in the brick fireplace, and the tables were covered with brown and cream linens. The place looked welcoming. He gave Susan a sidelong glance. Her eyes were wide as they absorbed the surroundings.

Guido stopped at a square table close to the fireplace. Autumn flowers in golds, oranges and yellows and two lit candles topped the table as he had requested. Guido took their coats, and Tony held a chair out to an amazed Susan.

"Tony, this is wonderful. How did you manage it?" Her hand waved at the empty dining room.

"Guido and I've had business dealings in the past. He was nice enough to agree to open for us tonight."

"You hired the entire restaurant just for us?"

He reached across the table for her hand. "You said you liked it best when it was just the two of us." He hesitated for a moment. "You don't mind?"

"Of course not. It's a lovely idea." She gave his hand a squeeze. "Makes me feel special."

He gazed at her in silence. In the candlelight her eyes sparkled like enormous royal sapphires. Dancing flames in the fireplace warmed the deep hue of her red suit. Her face glowed.

His body stirred with a longing that was as disturbing as it was delightful. He wanted to make love to Susan, and had wanted to for weeks. But he hadn't arranged all this as a prelude to seduction. He took seriously her fears and uncertainties. He respected her request for time. Susan—as sweet and maddening as she was—meant so much to him. The restaurant, the candlelight, the flowers—everything tonight was to show her how much he cared.

Guido returned with a bottle of Asti Spumante stashed in a bucket of ice. After pouring the sparkling wine with an elegant flourish, he left them to toast their day in court.

Grinning, Susan shifted comfortably in her chair. "The wine is heaven. And whatever they're cooking smells wonderful."

Seeing Susan content was an experience to savor. Her fine features softened. Her angular body seemed to grow more supple as she relaxed.

"What's that big smile about?" she asked.

"You. The more I get to know you, the more I like you." He lifted his glass to her. "Here's to you, Susan. The day you came back into my life was a turning point for me."

"What?"

"I realized that in court today."

"Tony, all I gave you was a hard time."

Shushing her, he tapped his fluted glass against hers. "To you." They drank together, gazing at each other over the rims of the crystal glasses.

She put her glass down. "You give me too much credit. You're the one who ultimately decided to represent the tenants."

"But you challenged me—in ways you may not realize. I felt so alive when Judge Ferugia ruled in favor of the tenants today. It's been a long time since I've used my profession to make such a basic difference in *anybody's* life."

Winning that injunction for the Somerset had given him back a piece of himself, an integral piece that had been drifting aimlessly through the rarefied halls of Conners, Brandon and Moffet. He couldn't help feeling gratified. The pieces of his life were starting to come together.

Guido returned with a waiter. While he poured more wine, the waiter served them each a steaming plate of risotto. Tony and Susan ate, talked and held hands through several more courses and another selection of wine. Before dessert was served a young man dressed in a tuxedo and carrying a violin came out of the kitchen. With a closemouthed smile, he nodded and lifted the instrument to his shoulder.

Susan listened to the sweet, tender strains of the violin, then turned to him, wide-eyed. "Did you arrange for him, too?" she whispered with disbelief.

"Guido's nephew," he said, bending his head closer to her ear. "He's the only violinist we could find on such short notice. I hope he's all right."

She looked at him as if he were crazy. "He's doing beautifully." She watched the young violinist as he stationed himself by the fireplace, his playing always smooth, even when he moved.

Tony watched her. If he thought she'd been glowing before, she was radiant now. He noticed, though, that her gaze had taken on a glassy sheen. Tears? he wondered. Couldn't be. Not Susan O'Toole. Before long, however, a tiny teardrop welled up in the corner of her eye.

Somewhat surprised, he reached out to reassure her. When he touched her shoulder, she turned to him full-face, revealing her glistening navy blue eyes. His thoughts reeled with tenderness. She did, indeed, have the eyes of an angel, but he would never again suggest she possessed a heart of stone. She was very real. And very vulnerable.

He wanted to hold her, so he asked her to dance. She hesitated; he insisted. There was enough space between the tables and the fireplace for them to dance, unhindered. Enfolding her in his arms, he felt her self-consciousness. He held her against his chest, his cheek resting on her hair. As they moved together with the music, her back became less rigid and her body gradually yielded to their closeness.

"Okay now?" he whispered. She nodded, and her shiny hair felt like silk against his face. His arms slipped down her back to encircle her waist. In response, she curled her arms around his shoulders, pressing her body even closer. His muscles tightened and his pulse soared.

Guido's nephew began playing the classic song "Fascination." Leaning her head back, Susan smiled in amazement. "I can't believe it. This is just like the movies."

"Too corny?"

"Uh-uh. I love it."

"Why, Susan O'Toole, you do have a sentimental streak in you."

"You don't have to act so surprised." Still smiling, she laid her head back on his shoulder.

They didn't really dance; they swayed. He relished the feel of Susan in his arms, her body lithe, her perfume now familiar and cherished. His senses drank her in. She was all that existed for him at this moment. For the first time in his life he understood what it meant to feel like the only two people on earth.

The song ended. Although the violinist continued with another, Susan stood still, but she didn't pull away. When she finally looked up at him, her eyes were luminous, revealing. Possibly, they revealed more than she wanted to.

"You've made this evening so beautiful—so romantic," she murmured. "No one has ever—I've never..." She struggled for the right words.

He was moved by her attempt, but he wouldn't help her. Suddenly he didn't want to hear the rest. He didn't want to know how she felt. What he wanted was space, fresh air, distance. He *needed* distance from her. Otherwise...he just didn't know.

Dropping his arms from her waist, he turned away. "Let's get out of here."

Chapter Eleven

Susan was in a daze. Even outside, with the cool night air washing over her, she wasn't sure what was happening—to Tony or to herself.

She gave him a sidelong glance as he straightened his overcoat. His face seemed stern, his gaze flat. Had she said something wrong inside? She replayed the last minutes in her head. She'd been about to tell him what his thoughtful and romantic planning of their "celebration" meant to her. It was all so lovely and new to her, and she wasn't used to expressing those kinds of feelings. Self-consciousness had made the words even more difficult to say. Had she turned him off somehow?

Pained by the thought, she reached out to him. "Tony?" Her hand rested on his coat sleeve.

Their eyes met. One of his hands covered hers. "Let's walk for a while."

They walked to the end of the lengthy block in silence and crossed, with the traffic signal, to Washington Circle. The sound of light but steady traffic hummed around them, and an occasional pedestrian passed by. She and Tony stood side by side, but they didn't touch.

Although she was confused by his behavior, she felt a certain empathy for him. He was torn about something; she could see that. And she knew *that* feeling well.

Yet tonight her own feelings were absolute. For once she had no qualifying buts. Despite their abrupt departure from the restaurant, the desire to reveal these feelings remained strong. Tony had done something so special for her; she refused to allow fear to hold her back. Maybe her tongue would fumble all over itself. Maybe she wouldn't make a whole lot of sense. But maybe what she had to say would ease whatever was on his mind.

"You didn't let me finish what I was saying," she said. "Back at Guido's, I mean."

He sighed in dismay. "I'm not sure what got into me. Sorry."

"Don't you want to know what it was?"

He was slow to answer; he seemed to be mulling the question over. For one awful second her confidence faltered. Then she caught his eye and held it. His face softened. "Of course I do."

The gentleness in his voice made beginning easier. "When I said everything tonight was so romantic, you have to understand how your care and thoughtfulness moved me." She realized she was listening to herself, scrutinizing every word. If she kept that up, she'd never make herself understood. It was time to throw caution to the wind, to speak—for once in her life—from her heart, not her head.

She started over. "I haven't had a lot of hearts-and-flowers-type romance in my life, Tony." She gazed straight ahead as they strolled on the circle's outer sidewalk. "None of the men I've known really considered me in that light, and I didn't think it was important. Maybe because I never thought of myself as a hearts-and-flowers kind of girl."

He looped his arm through hers as they walked, and her heart lightened considerably. "Tonight you gave me that kind of romance—with Guido's, the violinist, the flowers, even the food and wine you chose. And it's not the

impressiveness of it all, or the expense of it that matters.''
She stopped walking and turned to him. ''You *thought* of
me in that way. That's what touches me so.''

''Susan, I—''

''No, please.'' She pressed her palms against his chest.
''I have to finish now or it won't come out right.''

He nodded, and she felt his arms slip around her back.
His touch encouraged her.

''The thought you gave to tonight, the care you took, the
way you held me when we danced...'' She felt her voice
fade into an emotional whisper. ''You made me feel feminine. And cherished in a way I've never felt before.''

She gazed up at him, her heart unabashedly expectant.

''That's why the tears over the violin music?'' She nodded, and he pulled her closer. ''Susan, you are special to
me. I've told you that.''

''I guess tonight finally drove it home.''

''You deserved everything, and more.'' He pressed his
forehead against hers. ''I didn't start out this evening with
any ulterior motives in my mind—at least not con-
sciously. But now...''

She pulled back to search his gaze. Even with the dim
shadows cast by the streetlights, his eyes were easier to read
now. Their intensity sent thrilling warning chills down her
spine.

''Susan, the minute we started dancing I wanted you.
More than anything, I wanted to take you home and make
love to you.'' He shook his head. ''Taking things slow, like
you asked, was the last thing on my mind.''

She could feel a subtle tension in his arms and shoulders, and her heartbeat quickened. ''Is that why you
practically bolted out of the restaurant?''

''I had to get a handle on my feelings—cool off. You
thought it was so romantic, and all I could think of was
taking you to bed.''

"And now?" she asked, realizing how he answered mattered a great deal.

"My feelings haven't changed. If anything, I want you more. I know it wasn't easy for you to say the things you did just now. But you did, and that makes me feel special."

"Oh, you are. You've got to know that." She curved her arms under his arms, pressing close to his chest.

"Susan," he said, his gaze as imploring as his voice, "I don't want to let you go."

"Then don't."

She felt breathless as he responded with wide-eyed silence. For what seemed like an endless moment he studied her face—as if he wanted to be sure she'd meant what he'd heard. At last he murmured, "Let's go home."

With his arm hooked around her waist as they walked, she felt as if she were being swept away by excitement and anticipation. As they moved briskly across Washington Circle, she realized they weren't going back for his car. Instead, they were heading down New Hampshire Avenue—toward his house.

The night fell into a dreamlike quiet. Not another living soul was about. As the neighborhood streets narrowed, she could hear their quick footsteps tapping on the brick sidewalks. Within minutes they reached his house, and when he unlocked the front door, her heart began to pound.

He drew her inside and into his arms.

His kiss was long, urgent and unlike any other before it. A warm need stirred deep down in her belly, intensifying, along with the kiss, into a burning ache. Finally breaking apart, she felt as if every nerve in her body was raw and crying out for more of his touch.

He helped her off with her coat, folding it, and his own, over the back of an upholstered club chair. A single table lamp lit the small front living room, casting a flicker of warmth through the lonely darkness.

"Would you like a glass of wine? Cognac?"

"No." Her throat felt tight.

A hint of uncertainty shadowed his face. "Susan, are you sure you want this?"

"Yes." There was no turning back now. She didn't want to.

His hand clasped her forearm. "Come upstairs."

He led her to the staircase. But a remaining shred of common sense made her hesitate on the first step. "Tony, I... don't have any protection."

Bending down from the step above, he kissed her forehead and then murmured, "I do."

At the top of the stairs he let go of her to move away in the dark. He switched on the night table lamp, illuminating the compactness of his bedroom. Standing by the wide bed, he held out his arm.

She walked into his arms, and they closed tight around her. Cupping her head between his hands, he leaned it back gently for another impassioned kiss. She welcomed the languid probing of his tongue even as her knees weakened beneath her. He pressed against her breasts, and she could feel his muscles tense. She was so lost in sensation that she couldn't maintain a coherent thought. When his sure hands began caressing her back, she felt herself sinking deeper with little hope of reemerging. Moaning, she tore her mouth away.

It was one thing to express passion, but losing yourself in it—leaving yourself vulnerable, risking exposure—was something else again. Her desire faltered just enough to permit her head to distance itself from her body's pleasure.

Although she had remained in his arms, Tony apparently sensed her withdrawal. He held her away from him, his expression wary. But when he spoke, his voice was low, tender. "Don't be afraid."

Her heart was in her throat. He knew her well—frailties and all.

"Please don't hold back, Susan. Not tonight."

Don't hold back. That was exactly what she was doing and had been doing most of her life. Now it was no longer possible, no longer desirable to do so. She had already opened the door a crack by revealing what this evening had meant to her. Now that door couldn't be slammed shut. She couldn't hide the longings of her heart and body any longer. The realization made her tremble.

Tony's arms reclaimed her, and he murmured in her ear, "Trust me, Susan."

"I do." She held his face in her hands to kiss him with all the hunger in her soul. As the kiss slowly tapered off, she slid his suit jacket off his shoulders. She felt his eyes on her as she slipped one suspender down his arm and then the other.

With his eyes never leaving hers, his hands smoothed the red wool of her suit top, curving over her breasts. "I do love this on you," he said, undoing the first shiny black button. "But I'm going to love taking it off you even more."

When they were completely undressed, his eyes gazed over her body from head to toe. Anticipation fluttered in her stomach as he held her to him again. "You're lovely, you know." He nuzzled her neck, his body rigid as it rubbed against her breasts.

Pulling away without letting go, he reached over to push aside the bed covers. Together they eased down on the smooth white sheets. He lifted his head slightly above hers, and their eyes locked. "I've wanted you—and this—so much," he said, his voice languid and low. For a long time he stroked the rounds and hollows of her body with tantalizing care. She felt exquisite.

He smiled at her. And that smile, as loving as the look in his eyes, as ardent as his caresses, touched a chord deep inside her. It moved her beyond sensation into the realm where tenderness, passion and caring converged into an unstoppable force. The resulting emotions showered over her like a cleansing rain. Now she couldn't hold these feelings in check if she wanted to.

Her hands reached out to him, gliding over his silky skin, relishing the hard, masculine feel of his well-defined muscles. His body trembled under her touch, and this thrilled her. She wanted to pleasure him, as her own pleasure was undeniable. She returned each kiss, each caress with increasing fervor until a feverish heat radiated from her head to her toes. "Tony, please," she moaned, her voice unrecognizable.

His hand slid to her thighs, his touch exciting as it added to the pressure building deep within her. She gave herself up to the feeling and to Tony. She knew she was leaving herself vulnerable, her heart and body exposed. Yet all those years of holding back, of trying to maintain control, had made her lose sight of her softness, her feminine desires. She had never felt like this before because she couldn't or wouldn't allow it. Now with Tony she could. Now she felt free.

With this new sense of freedom desire flared—full-blown, intense, without restraint. She clung to him as his body covered hers. "Sweetheart," he rasped as he began to move against her. She had never felt so womanly as when she drew him inside her. She welcomed his warmth and weight, and they moved together in a rhythm that was exhilarating and intense. The world closed around them. She was only conscious of their minds and bodies spiraling together toward the brink of ecstasy.

Release was both searing and sweet as her body shuddered under his. She felt such *joy*. And love. Love for this man who had taken her so far physically, emotionally. Cradled in his arms, she could feel his heart pounding, hear his ragged breathing.

Her hand skimmed over the sheen of his damp skin. Tony snatched it, lifting it to his lips. Then, lacing his fingers through hers, he held it against his chest. His breathing was nearly even now; his heartbeat had calmed.

"You look happy," he said, a noticeable twinkle in his eye.

She let out a long breath. "I am." And grateful and triumphant and satisfied, she thought. But she didn't know how to sort all those feelings into a coherent statement. She snuggled close, knowing that she only wanted to be with him.

"I love you, Susan." As his gaze intensified, so did the emotion in his voice. "I really love you."

Her eyes were drawn to his. The words came so easily to him, yet she knew he meant them, and they filled her with a glorious exhilaration. She wished with all her heart that she could express her feelings with equal ease. Slipping her hand from his grasp, she instead cupped his cheek and lowered her mouth to his. She kissed him with the intensity of a love she was too overwhelmed to put into words.

Hours later the gray dawn peeped through the cracks of the window blinds. A single bird chirped loudly. Susan awakened, but her eyes were slow to open.

"Good morning, sleepyhead," he said in a gentle tone suited to the hour.

She felt herself wrapped in his arms, just as she'd been all night. She sighed with satisfaction as her eyelids fluttered open. "Haven't you slept?"

"Some. Mostly I've been watching you."

"Oh, dear. You'll be a sight at the office today." Of course, to her, he'd look wonderful even with dark circles under his eyes.

"I wish I could forget about the office and stay here and make love to you all day."

"Sounds nice." She brushed her hand along his cheek, his morning beard rough against her palm. "I wish I could stay, too. But people have begun to clear out for Thanksgiving. My staff is already down to the bare bones.''

"You and I are too dedicated.'' His chin nuzzled the top of her head.

"Speaking of Thanksgiving, would you like to come for dinner?'' She explained about her plans with Alice and Tom and Maria's family. "I'd thought about asking you before, but I wasn't sure..."

"I know. I'd been thinking of inviting you to my folks. After what happened the last time, however, I figured you'd just as soon pass on it.''

Which was exactly how she felt. She appreciated him realizing it.

"Isn't your mother coming down?'' he asked.

She told him about Iris's fall and why her mother wouldn't be coming. She almost mentioned that she was driving to Baltimore on Saturday, but thought better of it. "I gather you're expected at your parents','' she said instead.

He nodded. "As much as I'd love to be with you, I don't feel I can let them down. Things between them have been strained lately. I wouldn't feel right leaving them alone.'' He cuddled her to him. "I'll be thinking of you, though. Every minute.''

SUSAN WAS VERY MUCH on Tony's mind on Thanksgiving Day as he imagined what sharing this holiday with her would be like. In his thoughts he envisioned the way she would look, the food she'd cook, the table she'd set, the guests she'd greet. Damn, he wished he was there.

As Estelle served her fabulous turkey with oyster dressing, Tony couldn't help wondering how Susan's Thanksgiving dinner was progressing. It had to be livelier than this one at his parents' house.

The people seated at the long, rectangular dinner table had been in attendance at every Brandon Thanksgiving since he was a boy. Seated to his left was old Ned Whitney, his mother's uncle. At eighty food was his greatest pleasure. Although as thin as a rail, he had the appetite of a teenage boy. Every year he devoured Estelle's turkey, and every year he threatened to steal her away from the Brandons.

To Uncle Ned's right was Henry Brandon, his father's first cousin. A confirmed bachelor, Henry dined at the house weekly. He was a quiet, private man. Tony had known him all his life, yet he felt he hardly knew him.

Across the table sat his father's younger brother, James, and his wife, Alicia. Uncle James was a good sort, always kind to him. But he and Alicia were, much to their great sorrow, childless. Because of this they'd kept their distance from the family through the years. As he got older, Tony had sensed Alicia looked upon him, the only Brandon child, as an affront to her barrenness.

His mother, regal yet rigid as she presided over the family feast, sat at one end of the table. At the opposite end sat his father, an affable host and serious about his role as the family's patriarch of sorts.

Taken on the whole they were a pretty dour bunch. And he had never realized until today what a lonely group of people they were—even his parents. Still, they were his family and he loved them. He just didn't want to end up brittle and colorless like them.

They ate in silence. Tony tried to start a conversation with Uncle Ned, but the old man didn't want to be distracted from his meal. He glanced over at his mother, but she didn't look in the mood for conversation. Knowing her, he suspected whatever was troubling her was of her own making. He was concerned about her nonetheless.

Before dessert, while Estelle was still clearing away the dinner dishes, his mother attempted to fill the lull between courses. Unexpectedly she focused on Cousin Henry.

"Now, Henry, you must tell us about your last trip. Golfing in Scotland, wasn't it?"

"Why, yes, yes, it was." He seemed surprised that anyone would bother to ask about his vacation. "Quite a pleasant respite."

When it was clear that was all Henry had to say, his mother turned to Ned. "Henry took early retirement from his accounting firm, Uncle Ned. Since then he's been traveling a great deal. Doesn't he look wonderful? So rested."

Uncle Ned, who was probably more interested in Estelle's pumpkin pie at the moment, shot a glance at Henry. "You look good, Henry."

When his mother urged Henry to comment further on the joys of retirement, Tony cringed. He looked over at his father. His face was a blank, but his pale blue eyes had the steely look of disapproval Tony knew well.

"I'm so looking forward to John's retirement," she continued. "I'm already collecting travel brochures. In fact, I may make a world cruise the setting of my next book."

"Letitia—"

"John, you're retiring?" a shocked Uncle James interrupted. "Don't you think you should have advised me?" Because his father had been a founding partner, James maintained a financial interest in the firm.

"Don't do it, John," Uncle Ned piped in. "I've been retired fifteen years and I've hated every damn day of it."

"James, Ned, please," John said, the palms of his hands splayed flat on the table. "My retirement isn't imminent. Nothing's been decided." Then he directed a cold stare straight across the table. "Letitia, we shouldn't mention this matter in front of others when it's only under the vaguest consideration."

Her eyes flared in anger, but she said nothing. The resulting tension was stifling. As far as Tony was concerned, the meal wasn't over a moment too soon. He was just grateful Susan hadn't come, after all; he'd hate subjecting her to this.

After the guests left, Tony found his father in the study. He was determined to get to the bottom of this retirement business. "What is it, son?" John asked, sounding annoyed at being disturbed.

Tony ignored this and plunked himself down on the other leather wing chair. "I want to know what's going on between you and mother. And what is this talk about retirement?"

He closed his eyes and shook his head. "That's all your mother's idea. As I said, it's scarcely a consideration."

"Aw, come on, Dad." He was irked by his father's brush-off. "There's more to it than that. People at the firm are talking about it, for God's sake."

He frowned. "I did discuss the possibility with Mac Conners before a meeting. His secretary was hovering around. She must have—damn! I should have been more circumspect."

"Why don't you discuss it with me, Dad?"

"Tony, I—"

"I'm not just another partner in your law firm. I'm your son. Confide in me for once."

His father seemed taken aback by his candor. Tony was somewhat taken aback himself. John stared down at his hands. "Perhaps I have been remiss."

Looking uncomfortable as he spoke, John explained how the impending release of Letitia's first novel had galvanized her into making plans for the future. The murder mystery had bestseller potential, and she wanted to write more. "She insists she's ready for a new role in life," John added, "one that's no longer restricted by our commitments to the law firm."

Tony could empathize with his mother. Being Mrs. John Brandon entailed involvement in numerous time-consuming social and community activities. It was practically a full-time job, and she devoted herself to it for the good of the firm and her family. Just as she'd been raised to do.

His father was lost in thought. Sitting in the blue leather chair, with the stark light from the table lamp glaring on every line and wrinkle on his face, he looked *old*. Tony's throat tightened with emotion.

"How do you feel about retirement, Dad?" he asked after a time.

"Now? Well, it's very inconvenient as far as the firm is concerned."

He exhaled sharply. "Forget about the firm for once. Tell me how *you* feel."

The edge in Tony's voice seemed to shock his father. "It's not easy for me to express these things to you, son," he finally admitted.

"I understand—we don't talk about personal things nearly enough. But try. It might help."

John sighed. "Of course, I'm flattered that she wants me to help with her career."

"But?"

"But I'm not ready to give up my life's work," he revealed. "And, frankly, I don't think I'm ready to be alone with your mother."

THE SATISFIED FACES sitting around her table assured Susan that the dinner was a success. Everyone had seconds; some were on thirds. She could relax now.

"What a cook," Tom O'Brien noted as he mopped up the gravy on his plate with a bread roll. "Absolutely tops."

Alice gave him a blistering look. "Did you say tops?"

"Hah-hah. After you, of course, dearie." He reached out to give Alice's folded hands a squeeze. Alice's eyes softened, leading Susan to wonder just how often she cooked for the man.

Everyone helped clear the table for dessert, except for Maria's son, Roberto, who had been sullen the entire afternoon. Home on a short vacation from boarding school, he apparently hadn't wanted to come with his parents today. Roberto wasn't happy and made no effort to hide it. He even rebuffed Alice's and Tom's well-meaning overtures.

Susan went over to the living room sofa where Roberto had plopped himself down after dinner. He was watching football on TV. "Dessert's ready, Roberto." He didn't look up. "Alice baked apple and pumpkin pies. They look great."

"Don't like pie," he said, still staring at the television.

"There's ice cream. You can eat in here if you like."

"No thanks," he said, deigning to glance up for a second. When he looked away again, Susan figured it was pointless to persuade the boy further. She didn't know much about adolescent boys, but for his mother's sake, she hoped Roberto was just going through a phase. She knew Maria treasured the boy and held high hopes for him.

Alice stood at the table slicing the pie, and Susan was about to pour coffee when there was a knock on her door. Perplexed as to who it could be, she handed the coffeepot to Maria. Peering through the door's peephole, she was surprised to see Tony standing in the hallway. She swung the door open. "Don't tell me—you smelled the coffee brewing," she said, her eyes drinking him in. She hadn't seen him since they'd made love at his house.

He smiled, the corners of his eyes crinkling. "No. I just really missed you today."

The look in his eyes made her flush. Aware that Roberto was sprawled on the couch directly behind her, she brushed a kiss across his cheek. "You're just in time for Alice's pies," she said, her voice husky with restrained emotion.

"You're still eating?"

"Turkey took longer than I'd figured." She took his overcoat. "By the way, how'd you get into the building without buzzing my intercom?"

"Snuck in behind the couple ahead of me."

Shaking her head, she hooked her arm through his. "So much for security."

Tony stopped to greet Roberto. She was amazed that the boy actually smiled and shook hands.

Everyone gave Tony a warm welcome. Alice sliced him some pie, Maria poured him coffee, Tom pulled up an extra chair. And Luis patted him on the shoulder. "What's with the coat and tie?" he asked.

Laughing, Tony discarded those articles with relish and dug into Alice's apple pie. Susan sat back with her coffee, absorbing the warm camaraderie between her good friends. If she couldn't be with her mother today, these people surely made up for it. The conversation, jokes, laughter gave her a sense of family. For them she was truly grateful.

Her eyes settled on Tony. Nothing could describe how pleased she was to have him here, lazing about her table like this. Her mind drifted back to the other night, to the feel, taste and sound of him. Her pulse quickened.

Tony looked up and caught her staring. A secretive smile shadowed his lips, and she sensed he knew she'd been thinking about their lovemaking. Tiny throbs radiated from the core of her belly as he held her gaze with his gleaming green eyes. For the first time in her life she knew how it felt to yearn, really yearn, for a man.

After the guests left and she was alone with him, she felt jittery. She didn't know how to handle the excitement in her blood or the tension in her mind. She wanted him, but she didn't know how to ask.

So she busied herself with clearing and straightening. Feeling his eyes on her as she bustled about, she waited for him to comment. Instead, he helped her return the dining room table to its original position against the wall. "By the way, what was Roberto's problem?" he asked as he tucked the chairs beneath the table.

"He didn't want to come. Maria said some kids from his old neighborhood found out he was home from school and they've been after him. Last night they wanted him to go out, but Luis wouldn't allow it. Seems he's been sulking ever since."

Tony shook his head. "I've known that kid most of his life and I've never seen him as sullen as he was tonight. Too bad. He's a really bright boy."

"He must be if he's going to a school like Oakridge."

"Hope he gets his act together." He followed her into the kitchen.

There she was confronted with piles of dirty dishes, pots and pans. "Oh, yes," she began, turning to find him leaning against the door frame. "I forgot to thank you for turning down all those gracious offers to help with the dishes."

A sly grin curved his lips as he reached out for her. "I had to do that," he said. "Otherwise they'd be here all night and we'd never be alone. I didn't have the patience." He encircled his arms around her waist.

Pressed against him, she could feel the extent of his impatience. "Are you going to wash all those?" she asked, although her own impatience made talking difficult.

"Anything," he breathed. "I'll do anything you ask. Tomorrow." He bent his head and found her lips. His kiss was sweet comfort for her longing, and she reveled in it.

He came up for air. "I love you," he murmured against her cheek. "Sweetheart, how I love you."

Her heart felt near to bursting. Curling her arms around his shoulders, she held him tight.

In time, however, his embrace loosened and he stepped back from her. A lock of golden brown hair had fallen low across his forehead. His eyes were questioning. "Is it really so hard for you to say you love me?"

Chapter Twelve

"You must know I do."

"Then why not say it?"

"Are words that important to you?"

"Only when you deliberately evade them."

She hadn't been conscious of her evasive responses until he pointed it out. Why was she doing it now? She did love him. She felt him waiting for an answer; he wouldn't permit any more evasions.

"It's hard to explain. My love for you keeps getting tangled with feelings and fears I've had for a long time," she explained. "Saying how I feel puts it all—my all—on the line. I guess I'm afraid I won't measure up." She looked at him, hoping she'd made some sense.

"Come here, Susan." He pulled her into a comforting embrace and held her. Just held her. It was what she needed.

After several minutes, he finally spoke. "The kitchen's a hell of a place to have a conversation like this. Come on." He led her to the sofa in the living room. Leaning back against the cushions, he cradled her to his side. "Is this better?"

"Much."

His fingers played in her hair. "I'm in love with you, and I think you feel the same way about me." He paused. "I'm hoping we'll be together for a long time."

Before this moment she hadn't dared think about them in long-range terms. Now she realized the reason: she wanted it very much.

"We may have a future together," he continued. "Given time."

Susan realized she wanted that, too. Still, fear kept nagging her heart. "I only hope I can live up to the expectations."

"Whose expectations?"

"Yours. Your family's."

"Susan, I want you just the way you are."

"Is that good enough for your parents? Surely they never expected you to become involved with the daughter of a maid."

"Not only is that remark unfair to my parents, but it's unfair to you. For God's sake, what are you ashamed of? I love you, and that's all that should matter—not what my parents do or don't think."

She wasn't sure she agreed with him. His parents were a part of his life, and if her relationship with him was to survive, she'd have to learn to deal with them. For her this was a daunting prospect.

She stroked his arm. "I want things to work out for us."

"It will. I've a lot of faith in you."

Hearing this meant a great deal to her because it meant he'd be there for her. If she had his support as well as his desire, their relationship might have a chance. She touched his cheek, her fingers gently caressing his skin as her heart welled with pride and affection.

"You may drive me to distraction at times, but you're one exciting woman." His hand covered her fingers and guided them downward. His lips seeking hers, he began a long, delightful kiss. Her intense yearning from before re-surged anew.

Her hands felt the ragged movement of his chest as he ended the kiss. "Susan," he half breathed, half murmured, "I want you to make love to me."

His gaze warmed her blood. She nodded her consent and stood to take him to her bedroom, pausing at the threshold to turn to him. "I love you, Tony," she whispered. Then she led him inside.

THE TELEPHONE was ringing. Startled out of a contented sleep, Susan opened her eyes to complete darkness. She felt Tony's arms still wrapped around her as he began to stir. Her bedside clock read 1:00 a.m. as she fumbled for the phone.

It was Maria Lopez.

"I'm sorry, Susan, but I'm trying to find Tony." She sounded frantic. "Is he there?"

She handed the receiver to a groggy Tony and then switched on the light. Concern clouded his face as he listened to Maria. "I'm leaving for the station right away," he said. "I'll meet you there."

He handed the receiver back to her. "My God, what's happened?" she cried.

"Roberto's been arrested." He bolted from the bed.

"But he was just here a few hours ago."

"Apparently he sneaked out after Maria and Luis went to bed." He tugged on his pants. "I'm going down to help bail him out."

"I'm coming with you."

The next hours were tense. Susan waited with Maria and Luis while Tony met with a police sergeant and Roberto. "He was with two boys from the old neighborhood. I knew they were trouble," Maria told her. "After we left your place, we had a big argument about school. He doesn't want to go back to Oakridge.'' She shook her head, unable to continue.

Luis squeezed her hand. ''He deliberately defied us. One of the older boys has a car, so Berto arranged to be picked up after we were asleep,'' he explained. ''A cop stopped them for running a red light and sensed something fishy. Lo and behold, he discovers a stash of stolen electronics in the trunk.''

''You don't think Roberto...?''

Before Luis could reply Tony finally returned. His news wasn't good. ''He just won't deny involvement in the robbery, and his 'friends' aren't letting him off the hook, either.''

Devastated, Maria began to cry. Luis comforted her as Tony advised that Roberto was being released in their custody. ''He'll be charged in juvenile court, and they'll want assurances he'll be living at Oakridge until trial.''

''If they don't kick him out for this,'' Luis muttered.

''I'll call the school and explain the situation,'' Tony offered. ''I think I can smooth things over on that end.''

Driving Susan home after Roberto's release, Tony was quiet. He looked troubled. ''You did the best you could for him,'' she said.

''I guess so.'' he said. ''You know, this isn't his first brush with the law—although it's the most serious one.''

''Maria had intimated there had been problems.''

''Basically he's a good kid, just easily influenced. But after my mother helped get him into Oakridge, we thought he'd straighten out.''

''Your mother got him in?''

''She graduated from there long before it went coed. Now she's on the board.''

She didn't know why she was surprised Mrs. Brandon had used her pull to help Roberto. After all, he was a child of one of her husband's employees. Still, it didn't fit in with the image Susan had of her.

"It was good of your mother to intercede," she said, and she meant it. "But Oakridge may be part of Roberto's problem right now."

"What do you mean?"

"If his experience at boarding school is anything like mine was, I'd say he's feeling a little lost these days."

"How so?"

"It's like being an alien from another planet—everything seems strange, you feel out of sync, lonely. Then you go back home and you don't really fit in anymore. Eventually you adjust, but you always feel like some sort of hybrid."

"Is that how you felt?"

She nodded. "It's hard to handle at that age. I imagine it's even more difficult for Roberto. He has a culture gap thrown into the bargain."

Tony didn't comment; he seemed to be lost in thought as he drove down Constitution Avenue. Sitting at a red light near the Ellipse, Susan glanced through the window at the White House lights glimmering in the distance. As her eyes skimmed back across the Ellipse, she noticed the dark shadow of the giant evergreen tree.

"I guess they'll be lighting the National tree soon," she mused out loud.

Tony glanced back at the Ellipse. "I can't remember when I last came down for it."

"I've never been," she said as the light turned green. But Tony drove off in silence, clearly distracted by Roberto's problems.

FOR SUSAN the following weeks were hectic, stressful *and* happy. Pleased by the way her new job situation was jelling, she didn't mind the frazzled pace at times. Her talk at the pharmacists' convention met with success, initiating more invitations to address groups and conventions. Increasing demands and challenges enlivened her workday.

Although life for the Somerset tenants was quiet at the moment, the unknown still lurked ahead for her elderly friends. The waiting was hard. Yet the legal machinery continued to grind ahead. Lawyers for the Hammond Group were busy filing legal papers refuting discrimination claims against the developer. Their motion to have the suit dismissed was scheduled to be heard in court shortly before Christmas. Tony and Rob were preparing for it in earnest.

As for Roberto, Maria had told her they were trying to make it through one day at a time. He had returned to Oakridge until trial, and the school had arranged for him to meet regularly with a staff psychologist. It troubled Susan to see the toll the incident had taken on her friend. Gone was Maria's easy laughter. Her face had become pinched with worry, and she seemed to be tired all the time.

Yet despite the trouble and stress, an ember of happiness glowed quietly within Susan. For now she had Tony. Although their jobs made their days hectic, their nights alone together were sweet indeed. When she was with him, the exciting newness of their love had the power to lift her above daily concerns. With him her recurrent fears about the relationship would fade almost completely away. Almost.

But the arrival of the holiday party season brought an evening she'd been dreading: the Brandons' annual open house for the law firm's partners. It would mark her first return to the Brandons' since the night she'd spilled wine on their rug, and the first since she and Tony had become lovers.

She fought nervousness for weeks, even as she spent her rare free lunch hours doing one of her least favorite activities—shopping for party clothes. Before, she had maybe one big Christmas party to attend a year. Tony's calendar listed several, and he wanted her by his side at each one.

She was touched by his sentiments, but uncertainty about what to wear to these events was making her a wreck.

For tonight's open house she'd decided to play it safe and conservative in deep blue silk with only a hint of holiday glitter at the neck and waist. "What do you think?" she asked when Tony came to pick her up. She turned around before him.

He whistled his approval.

"That's not what I meant."

"No?"

"I want to know if it's appropriate."

"Oh, I see." He put his arms around her. "Other than being the best-looking woman there, you'll fit in just fine."

She laid her head on his chest. This man did have a way about him. Her stomach might still be in knots, but her heart was reassured.

"Where's your coat?" he asked.

"You want to leave now? It's still early."

He went to the front closet. "We have to make a stop first."

"Where?"

"That's a surprise. Which coat?"

"The black wool," she replied. "Tony, I'm not crazy about surprises." Especially on a night like this, she ruminated to herself.

He slipped the coat over her shoulders. "Now wait a minute. Tell me you didn't like my last surprise."

Recalling Guido's and what had happened afterwards, she spun around and met his glimmering eyes. "Okay, take me on another mystery ride."

Driving downtown in heavier than usual rush-hour traffic, Susan noticed the large number of people walking on the sidewalks—all headed in the same direction. Only then did she remember the notice she'd read in this morning's paper. "The President's lighting the National

Christmas tree tonight," she said, turning to Tony. "Is that your surprise?"

"Bingo."

At last he found a parking space just big enough to squeeze his car into. Then, arm in arm, they joined the crowds heading for the Ellipse.

The grounds were lit up like a—well, like a virtual Christmas tree—with TV lights, stage lights, streetlights. The giant spruce was surrounded by smaller decorated trees, one from each state, Tony explained. Christmas music blared from loudspeakers, children oohed and ahed, groups of friends laughed.

"This is great," she said, getting into the spirit of things. "I've never been to one of these."

"So you told me."

She remembered; it was the night of Roberto's arrest. She was surprised that Tony had remembered—he'd been so distracted then.

"I thought this might get your mind off the open house for a few minutes. Help you relax."

Although she had made a point not to mention her nervousness about his parents' open house, she should have realized he'd sense it. Bringing her here was such a considerate, loving gesture on his part. Right now she actually believed she was the luckiest woman in town.

A choir standing on the temporary stage beyond the tree began singing carols. She and Tony joined in on "Joy to the World." More entertainment followed, and he held her tight against his side, shielding her from the mid-December wind. A little after five the First Family took the stage, and the President delivered a seasonal message of peace and goodwill. Finally, with a press of a button, the tree—the National tree—glittered and glowed in the late-afternoon dark.

Susan did feel better as they drove to the Brandon house in Chevy Chase. Buoyed by the fun of the tree lighting, she resolved to make the most of her second meeting with Tony's parents.

The evening began on a promising note when Tony's father extended her a cordial welcome. "I'm glad Tony brought you back," Mr. Brandon added, much to her surprise.

The living room was lushly decorated with holly and evergreen boughs trimmed in plaid satin. Dozens of red and white poinsettias topped tables and filled corners. Over the loud chatter Susan could just hear the delicate sound of traditional Christmas strings piped over the stereo system. A waiter in bright white shirt, black bow tie and slacks greeted them with champagne, and soon after a waitress wearing similar attire came by with a tray of canapés. Tony helped himself, but she refrained. Although she was feeling easier about the evening in general, she didn't think she could swallow a bite.

"See, I told you you'd be the best-looking lady here," Tony murmured before they started to mingle with the other guests.

Susan wasn't sure about that. There were many very attractive women of varying ages around the room. Some were wearing very expensive designer outfits. But she felt her dress was suitable; she blended right in.

The people Tony introduced her to were, on the whole, quite friendly. Her current job, as well as her background as a consumer advocate, sparked the interest of several guests, and as the evening progressed, she found herself in the center of more than one discussion.

At one point Tony politely edged her away from one of these conversations. "Seems everyone finds you fascinating, sweetheart. Of course, I'm not surprised," he said, guiding her to the opposite end of the room. "A good friend of mine wants to meet you."

Susan understood why Michael Stone was one of Tony's better friends at the firm. She learned that, like Tony, Mike was one of the younger partners, single and a native Washingtonian. He also had an easygoing charm that wasn't apparent in the other partners she had met. She liked him and his date, Janine, a lawyer with the Justice Department.

"Heard you wangled a meeting with Bret Lawton," Janine was saying, and Susan recognized the name as that of an assistant attorney general.

"Hoping to smooth things out on Leland's purchase of Central Satellite Systems?" Mike asked.

"Hoping to speed up the process, if nothing else," Tony replied. "Both parties are anxious to complete the sale."

Mike patted him on the shoulder. "Good luck, pal, 'cause you're going to need it." His voice had a warning ring to it. "You've got a hell of a lot riding on it."

"I know, I know." Tony's anxious tone made Susan uneasy.

She'd long ago gathered that having Leland on the client list was a big deal for the law firm. And she knew Tony was excited to be representing him, that it was a professional boost. Yet she had never really realized how much handling Leland *meant* to him personally. It was disquieting to think that facilitating a business deal for one of the richest men in the world had become crucial to Tony.

Or was she overreacting again?

After Mike and Janine moved on, Susan was still trying to shake this disturbing notion. When she spotted Tony's mother approaching, all thoughts scattered from her mind. The knots resettled in her stomach with a vengeance.

"Anthony, dear." Mrs. Brandon clutched his hands and held her cheek out for a kiss.

"Mother, where have you been all this time?"

"Elaine Bolton had me cornered and I had a devil of a time getting away. Then there was something of a crisis with the caterer. Lord, I wish Estelle had agreed to stay tonight and keep her eye on them." She sighed as if it all was such a trial. "Every year it's something with this party." Then her eyes fell on Susan.

"You remember Susan O'Toole, Mother," Tony said as his arm closed around her.

"Of course I do." Mrs. Brandon smiled but failed to add a "lovely to see you again."

Susan got the distinct feeling that Mrs. Brandon wasn't too pleased to see her. And she knew she wasn't being paranoid this time.

Mrs. Brandon turned to Tony. "Your father told me William Leland will be in town next week. Shall I arrange a dinner?"

"I wouldn't. He'll only be flying down for a few hours, and I'm not even sure which day he's coming. It'll probably be a last-minute decision on his part."

"Keep me advised if his plans change," she said. "Oh, yes, don't forget. I'll be autographing books downtown next Friday. My publisher's throwing a PR luncheon just before it, and I do want you and your father to be there."

"Next Friday? But the Somerset hearing is that day." He looked at Susan. "Isn't it?"

She nodded slowly, taking little comfort in the fact that Tony's mother was no longer ignoring her. Now she felt the full force of Mrs. Brandon's disapproving stare.

"I see. Well, Anthony, I hope you'll be able to drop by the autographing for a few minutes, anyway."

"I'll try, Mother. I'm sorry about the conflict. It can't be helped—"

Mrs. Brandon stopped him with a wave of her hand. "No need to explain. I *am* a lawyer's wife, after all." Her tone sounded forced. "Ah, I see Mac Conners has finally arrived. I must say hello."

Watching her walk off, Susan turned to Tony. "Your mother doesn't like me," she said, feeling rather matter-of-fact about it.

"She was rude to you, Susan." He lifted her chin with his fingers and peered into her eyes. "I apologize for her from the bottom of my heart."

"It's not your fault."

"My mother doesn't seem to like anybody these days, including my father and me," he explained. "She's having some problems."

Susan tried to understand, but the promise of the evening had already soured. She could hold her own with Tony's peers, but his family? Frankly they intimidated her. How could she ever fit in with them? She remembered all too well why she used to avoid visiting the homes of her prep school classmates.

Driving home with Tony, she kept this fear to herself. He had worries enough. Besides, loving him the way she did, she had no choice but to hang in and hope the situation would work out. She was prepared to do what she could to achieve that end.

She wasn't prepared, however, for what Tony suggested as they crossed the river back into Virginia. "I know this is probably an untimely idea, in light of my mother's behavior tonight, but I've been thinking about it for a couple of days now," he said, reaching across the car seat for her hand. "What do you think about you and your mother spending Christmas Day with my family?"

Susan didn't know quite what to say.

"Look, I know it sounds crazy," Tony said in answer to her silence. "But it is the holidays, and I'd like for our families to get together. It would be just the five of us—not a crowd to distract my parents from getting to know you."

"Which might make matters worse."

"I disagree." He squeezed her hand. "But you have every right to be hesitant. I know I'm asking a lot, except I really think it's worth a shot."

"How do you know your mother will want to invite us?"

"Don't worry. She'll invite you."

She glanced over at him. "This means a lot to you."

"Means a lot to both of us."

He was right. Still, knowing this didn't alleviate her doubts. "I'm just not sure about your mother, Tony. Why don't we see how the next week or so goes? Okay?"

"If it makes you feel better." He squeezed her hand again, but he sounded disappointed.

Her spirits sank. She wanted to please him. And now, more than ever, she wanted his parents to like her—for his sake, if not her own.

WAITING ANXIOUSLY outside Judge Ferugia's courtroom, Susan finally caught sight of Rob Berns rushing down the hall. He was almost out of breath by the time he reached her. "Sorry to cut it so close," he gasped. "Everyone inside already?"

"Yes. But where's Tony?"

"He's been delayed, Susan. He'll be here as soon as he can."

"Delayed?" She was stunned.

Rob pulled open the heavy door. "Some emergency came up on another case. It couldn't be helped." Backing into the courtroom, he added, "I'll explain to the others before the judge comes in."

The door closed behind Rob, leaving her virtually alone out in the vast hallway. The echo of hurried footsteps forced her to look up, hoping to see Tony. It was a stranger in a blue suit with a briefcase tucked under his arm. Another lawyer no doubt.

After one more hopeful look down the hall, she shook her head. Tony wasn't going to make it. She didn't know why, but her thoughts began to darken.

Inside, the judge had begun to hear the Hammond Group's motion for dismissal. Still dazed, she slipped into the back row. She tried to concentrate on what was being said, but her eyes were drawn to the clock on the wall. It was amazing how slowly the red second hand ticked past the huge black digits. Yet still no Tony.

She tried to refocus her attention on the proceedings. Rob looked so young standing there in front of the courtroom, although she sensed he was holding his own. Every once in a while, however, he'd glance back at the courtroom door, looking worried, seeming restless. She, too, kept stealing glances at the door, *willing* Tony to appear.

He did eventually, taking a seat next to Rob's at the plaintiffs' table. Listening attentively, he jotted some notes on a pad. He didn't speak, however, allowing Rob to finish what he'd begun.

When Judge Ferugia announced his decision, her entire body tensed. As she listened, it gradually dawned on her that he was going to side with the developer. Ruling that the tenants hadn't specifically affirmed that the Hammond Group had discriminated intentionally against the elderly, the judge dismissed the lawsuit.

She felt numb. The courtroom took on an eerie stillness as the judge and lawyers seemed to move and talk in slow motion. She had no idea what was being said, not that it mattered now, anyway. Her gaze was drawn to the group of tenants behind the plaintiffs' table. She couldn't see their faces, but they sat so painfully still.

When the judge left the courtroom, she moved closer to Alice and Tom. Tony was talking to the group, saying he'd file a second suit immediately—something about denial of rights to housing. But she could tell by their faces that they were too stunned to absorb a word he said.

One of the Hammond attorneys took Tony aside for a few words. Gradually the tenants, gathering coats and purses, began to file out of the courtroom. Tom had donned his coat and held Alice's. "Come on, dearie, it's time to go home."

Alice didn't move. "It's over, isn't it, Susan?" she said without glancing up.

She clasped the old woman's thin hand. "No, not yet. There's still time to work something out."

"Not much, I'd say. This was a real blow." Alice turned her pale eyes to Susan, her hand trembling. "I had such hopes."

"Alice, I'm sorry we lost, but . . ." Her voice felt shaky; she couldn't continue. She felt she'd failed her friend miserably.

Taking Alice's free hand, Tom knelt low beside her. "Now, dearie, how many times have you yelled at me to fight for my home? 'Don't just sit back feeling sorry for yourself, Tommy,' you're always saying."

"Well, I've got a big mouth."

"Right, you do," Tom said. "And it taught me not to give up. So I'm not about to let you do the same."

Alice lifted her eyes to Tom's. "You're a good soul, Tom O'Brien."

"Right again, smart lady." Without releasing Alice's hand Tom straightened. "We'll see this through to the end—just like you're always saying. And, if worse comes to worse, we'll find somewhere else to live. I know we will."

Alice shook her head. "That won't be easy."

"Aw, come on, dearie, look who's being Miss Doom-and-Gloom now."

This drew a chuckle from Alice. "All right, all right. That's enough," she said, getting to her feet. She took her coat and turned to Susan. "We'll be going now. Thank you for everything, honey. I mean it."

"Alice, I'm so sorry this happened."

"Don't go being sorry. It's not your fault. It's not anybody's fault."

Still, she felt terrible—and responsible. She wished she knew a way to make everything come out right. Watching

Alice and Tom leave the courtroom, she felt her throat tighten with emotion. They were so dear to her. It pained her to think of the uncertainty they faced.

"Susan."

She heard Tony but couldn't bring herself to turn around and face him.

He came up close behind her. "Are Alice and Tom all right?"

"I don't know." She shook her head, staring at the courtroom door.

"Susan?" He put his hand on her shoulder.

She shrank from him. "How could you let this happen, Tony?" She spun around to confront him, disappointment and disbelief drowning her heart. "You promised you wouldn't let them down!"

Chapter Thirteen

His mind reeled from the blow of Susan's words. Feeling as if he'd been dealt a one-two punch—first the dismissal and now this—Tony glared at her, speechless.

"How could you—how dare you show up late for this hearing?"

"Didn't Rob tell you?"

"Sure he told me—some emergency on another case. What happened?" she asked, her eyes flaring. "Did William Leland finally decide to descend upon Washington? Or did Justice put up another roadblock to that precious purchase of his?"

"That's enough," he warned, aware that a guard and a clerk still remained in the courtroom.

He grabbed her wrist and tugged her out to the hall. She protested, but he paid no attention. What he really wanted to do was give her a good shaking. He understood why she'd turned on him like this. But that didn't condone her behavior. It only ignited *his* anger.

He led her across the hall into a glass cubicle used for private client-lawyer conferences. The door clanged shut behind them. He leaned against it, staring straight into her distressed eyes. "When are you ever going to trust me? You know I wouldn't be late for this hearing unless it was absolutely necessary."

"I *thought* I knew that. Maybe that's why I'm so disappointed." Averting her eyes, she moved away from him. "Of course, we may differ on the definition of 'absolutely necessary.' Somehow any trouble Leland may have doesn't cut it when these people are in danger of losing their homes."

Her words hurt, hurt more, perhaps, than the lawsuit dismissal. Of course she was disappointed about the hearing's outcome, but no more than he was. Surely she must realize what a loss this was for him, too? Yet she gave no indication she did—she only blamed. And this left him feeling isolated from her and afraid for their future. He felt as if he'd plunged into a bottomless hole, suspended in the interminable darkness of her anger and mistrust.

Weary, he sat at the small wooden table. "Now that you've jumped to your conclusions, would you care to hear where I was?"

She didn't answer.

"I was at the police station with Jorge Oliva, one of the kids arrested with Roberto. He gave evidence, proving Roberto had no knowledge of the robbery."

Susan's eyes widened. "But how...?"

"I've been calling this Oliva kid every night for weeks, trying to convince him to come forward with the truth," he explained. "He finally agreed to go to the police this morning—but only if I went with him. If I didn't, no deal. He was frightened."

"So you went."

"What other choice did I have? The kid was real shaky. I didn't want to wait and risk his changing his mind."

"The charges were dropped?"

He nodded, noting her relief.

"Why didn't you tell me this sooner?"

"Because it shouldn't make a difference. You should've trusted my judgment."

"I'm sorry." She sank into the other chair, her voice uneven. "It's just when I saw you had sent Rob to the hearing alone—"

"Rob knew this case backward and forward. He and I have gone over it again and again, anticipating exceptions, objections, any problems we could think of. Rob did everything I would have done, as well as I could have done it."

"It's no one's fault," she murmured, remembering Alice's remark.

"What it comes down to is the judge didn't buy our argument. Now we have to make a better one."

She still avoided looking at him. Reaching across the table, he touched her hand. "It hurts to think how little faith you have in me."

Silently she lifted her gaze.

"I've tried so hard to strike a balance, to make this work," he continued. "I've never felt so torn in my life. Every time I turn it feels as if you or my parents are waiting—just waiting—for me to slip up. And today you were so sure I had."

Tears sprang to her eyes. "I never meant to pressure you like that."

The tears began streaming down her cheek, and soon she was trembling from the effort to swallow back her sobs. He had never seen her cry like this before; it took all his self-control to keep from pulling her into his arms to comfort her. But he held back, knowing that holding her would resolve very little.

"Why are you so quick to think the worst, Susan?"

"Oh, God. You don't know how many times I've asked myself the same thing." Her voice was shaky as she brushed her wet cheeks with the back of hand.

"Come up with any answers?"

"Only one that I keep coming back to."

"Which is?"

She avoided looking at him by staring down at her hands. "I can't forget how you quit the legal aid office," she said almost defensively. "You left us high and dry then. Who's to say it won't happen again?"

"After everything, that's still it?" Frustrated, he glared across the table at her bowed head. "Susan, will you please look at me?"

She did as he asked. "What's so hard to believe? Makes perfect sense to me," she said, no longer defensive.

He seemed surprised by her adamance. "I knew you resented the way I left. But that was over four years ago. I never expected you to still be this upset about it."

She felt the flush of anger on her face. "You probably never gave legal aid a second thought after you left." She looked straight into his bewildered green eyes. "But for me, taking over as manager of that office was an important step. I had such hopes of turning it around. But before I had a chance you upped and quit, and within a few months the university shut the office down."

"You blame me for the shutdown?"

"You couldn't have quit at a worse time."

"I admit I handled my resignation badly—my father was pressuring me."

"Oh, yes. Didn't he dangle some juicy antitrust case in front of you? And you jumped."

His shoulders stiffened. "Yes, yes, I did. And you know why?" he asked roughly. "Because I was sick and tired of banging my head against a brick wall at legal aid. Winning some minor cases, getting nowhere with the cases that really mattered because we lacked manpower, time, resources. We never had enough money to do things properly, nor the clout."

"Money and power. Your law firm certainly has plenty of both." Past inadequacies came to mind. If her managing skills had been sharper back then, maybe she could have compensated for the bureau's low resources.

"I wanted to make a name for myself in this city. Is that such a crime?" he asked. "As for the money—sure I like it. But it's not the driving force in my life."

"I didn't think it was."

"Well, thanks for that pat on the back." Leaning his hands on top of the table, he got to his feet. "But I really resent the way you're making my resignation from the legal aid office into some sort of moral issue—four years after the fact yet! Come on, Susan, life goes on."

She sank lower in her chair, feeling foolish. Tony's anger was justified. What right did she have to judge him? The legal aid office was dissolved on her watch, not his.

"It might please you to know that I felt pretty guilty about the entire episode," he added with disgust.

"It doesn't." Weary, she leaned her arms on the table, her head resting between her hands. "I did resent you terribly for resigning when you did. Still, I should've been able to make the office thrive with or without you. I should've been up to the task but, as it turned out, I wasn't."

The ensuing silence made her aware of Tony's stillness. What was he thinking? She sensed the tension between them easing somewhat, but she couldn't bring herself to look at him. Finally he touched her shoulder with a light hand.

"So you see," she continued, her voice wavering, "I blame myself. Guess I always have."

"That office was in trouble before you ever got there. You knew when you signed on that the federal government was cutting back its funding."

"Yes, but the university was still pouring money into it."

Tony shook his head. "The university wasn't going to continue supporting the office as a full-time proposition once the Feds cut out. Surely you must have realized that?"

"I did and I didn't," she admitted. "I was too idealistic to see reality. I honestly thought I could turn it around. I wanted to so badly." She shrugged. "Pretty foolish, wasn't I?"

"Maybe a bit." He gave her a kind smile. "The writing was on the wall for that place. It wasn't your fault that it folded."

"Guess I never really got over it, though. Which is probably why I've been carrying around this resentment of you all these years. I'm sorry."

"Put the past away, Susan, once and for all." Lowering himself on his haunches in front of her, he took her hands in his. "Accept me for who I am now."

"That's what confuses me."

He sighed and thought for a moment. "Remember when I told you how much satisfaction I got out of helping the tenants? Well, I find another kind of satisfaction in working for William Leland. Leland has a right to legal representation, too. And I'm not prepared to drop him in favor of a client deemed more worthy or needy. Maybe that's what you would like, Susan, but I can't do it."

She shook her head as one more tear trailed down her cheek. "I don't want you to. And I hate that this has happened. I'm just so terribly sorry."

Feeling her hands tremble, he squeezed them tight. "I know, honey, I know."

She took several deep breaths and tried to smile. "I'll try to be more understanding—I will."

"That's all I ask." Taking heart, he lifted one hand to caress her damp cheek. "I'm going to go over to the Somerset tonight. Think you'll be up to coming with me?"

"Absolutely."

"That's my girl."

Leaning over to give her a kiss, he wasn't sure how much had been settled. He wished he felt better about things than he did. Yet he realized that, if nothing else, the occasional skirmish did clear the air.

ALTHOUGH SUSAN had been shaken by their confrontation at the courthouse, she realized it had, ultimately, drawn Tony and her closer. Over the next several days they spent as much time together as possible. And this renewed closeness strengthened her desire to make this Christmas a joyous one for Tony.

On the night of the law firm's formal Christmas dinner dance at the Marriott, she wasn't even nervous. She had taken the afternoon off from work to get her hair done and to take her dear sweet time getting ready. It had been worth it. She felt relaxed and pretty. This time she felt confident about the suitability and attractiveness of her new strapless black velvet gown.

When Tony came to pick her up, he let out a long, low whistle. But she was pretty dazzled herself by his black tuxedo, crisp white shirt and slicked-back hair. "Wow, you look like something out of a magazine."

"You look like something out of a dream." The twinkle in his eyes set her pulse spinning.

The dancing was in full swing when they arrived. She never realized how large a firm Conners, Brandon and Moffet was until she saw the vast number of employees making merry in the hotel ballroom. If nothing else, it would be easy to lose oneself in this crowd.

While Tony checked their coats, she went to comb her windblown hair in the nearby powder room. When she came out, she couldn't find him. She peered into the ballroom entrance, thinking he might be standing near the door. He wasn't. Returning to the narrow corridor leading back to the coat and rest rooms, she heard his voice. Before she turned the corner his voice—and someone else's—became clearer.

"It was bad enough you missed the luncheon entirely," Mrs. Brandon was saying. "But you could've at least spared a few minutes to come down to the bookstore. Was that asking too much?"

"Mother, I've already explained it to you. I wanted to get there. It was just impossible. I'll try to be there next time."

"Next time," Mrs. Brandon scoffed. "Really, Anthony, you haven't been yourself for months. You've been way too distracted lately."

Surmising that Mrs. Brandon considered her one of Tony's distractions, Susan decided she didn't want to hear another word. She started to walk away, but Tony's raised voice stopped her.

"This isn't the time nor the place to get into your gripes about me—"

"Anthony!"

"But tomorrow, I promise, I'll be at the house," he said. "You and I are going to sit down and have a very long talk—about everything."

As Mrs. Brandon continued to complain, Susan hurried away. She shouldn't have listened; yet, in a way, she was glad she had. Now she realized that Mrs. Brandon was basically one unhappy woman, and Susan found herself feeling sorry for her. On the other hand, she was relieved to hear Tony patiently put down his mother's little tantrum. He hadn't allowed himself to be manipulated.

She realized, however, that Mrs. Brandon's behavior was uncomfortably similar to the way she herself had acted after the suit dismissal last week. She, too, had been trying to manipulate him with guilt about the Somerset. She felt ashamed. How could she have been so unfair to Tony? So disloyal?

When he found her by the ballroom entrance, he led her onto the floor for a slow dance. She was happy to be the woman in his arms. And grateful, too—grateful that he was the kind of man who could understand and forgive the rigidity that she so desperately wanted to overcome.

He held her close, not saying a word. Their bodies moved together in time with the music, and as the orchestra played on, she felt transported beyond time and place. Every sensation was a spark of magic: the pleasurable weight of his hand on her back, the soft friction of his silk and wool against her black velvet, the gentle warmth of his breath on her temple. Even his fluid dance steps made her feel as if a silken cloud had lifted them far above the crowded ballroom. If only they could dance this way and stay together like this all night. They would never tire, and the magic between them would protect them with its shimmering shield.

But in the real world of the ballroom below, orchestras took scheduled breaks, and silken clouds drifted irrevocably back to earth. Still, as they strolled off the dance floor, Tony held her close to his side, and when she gazed into his eyes, she knew he had felt the magic, as well.

"Save the next dance for me," he murmured in her ear.

"You can count on it."

Then her stomach rumbled loudly. She looked up at Tony, aghast. He was smiling. "Hungry, Susan?"

"Not very ladylike, was it?" she said. "But I haven't eaten a thing since a cup of yogurt at lunch."

"Come on." He led her to the long buffet tables set up near the end of the enormous room. She couldn't believe the food spread out before them. Platters were loaded with beef, salmon and shrimp. Exotic desserts filled one entire table. Waiters carted around magnums of champagne. Clearly the law firm had spared no expense.

As she and Tony filled their plates, Susan couldn't help thinking about her own office's Christmas party. It was held at the end of the workday, and everyone lent a hand in setting up the food in her boss's conference room. Homemade goodies, punch and jug wines comprised the bill of fare. Good jokes, gag gifts, a little office gossip and a tape of Christmas music made up the entertainment. She had loved it. But it was worlds apart from this fete, that was for sure.

Mac Conners invited them to join him and several other partners at their table. Although everyone was pleasant, Susan was somewhat intimidated. Several of the wives wore jewels that took her breath away, and casual mentions of people and places she often read about in the paper filled the conversation. The situation aroused her old insecurities, leaving her shaky.

Her appetite now gone, she put down her fork and sat quietly, acting as if the table talk had captured her complete interest. In actuality her mind struggled with the unwelcomed feelings of the past. She told herself it was ridiculous to feel like the poor, out-of-place scholarship student. Tony's presence at her side was what really mattered, she reasoned. But this time her emotions refused to buckle under to reason.

Eventually Tony left to get them dessert, and as soon as he did, Mrs. Brandon appeared at the table. Lightly dropping a hand on Susan's shoulder, she gave a sweet greeting to the others seated at the table. "I'm afraid I must steal this lovely young woman from you for a few minutes," she announced to Susan's astonishment. "There's someone I very much want her to meet."

Mrs. Brandon took her hand and quickly whisked her through a side door into a long narrow service hallway. It was dimly lit and deserted. Susan knew at once that Tony's mother had no intention of introducing her to anyone.

More irritated than apprehensive, she finally found her tongue. "Mrs. Brandon, what's the meaning of this?" She glared at the older woman, whose well made-up face seemed sallow under the fluorescent lighting, her body a little too thin in a creamy lace gown.

"I apologize for the subterfuge, Susan. But I want to talk to you and I could think of no other way to get you away from Anthony."

Susan's guard was up. "You mean whatever it is you have to say, you don't want him to know about."

"Wonderful, we understand each other."

Her dry smile chilled Susan's spine. "Mrs. Brandon, I don't think—"

"Now dear, I'll make this quick. I have just one question." Mrs. Brandon paused, giving her an assessing look. "Have you given any thought whatsoever to the influence you're exerting on Anthony's career?"

"I beg your pardon?" She didn't know what to say. Mrs. Brandon's tone made her feel as if she'd been stung with a poison dart.

"My son has always had a rebellious streak. If we said black, he'd say white. We'd tell him to walk and he'd run."

Susan sensed what Mrs. Brandon was getting at. "And tell him to work for the firm, and he joined legal aid?"

"Exactly. And he still has something of the rebel in him. Which I'm sure is why he's entangled himself in a time-consuming pro bono case when his father prefers he direct his energy on William Leland."

"Then why do you think I'm influencing him?"

"Because of who and what you are. Anthony has a need to do the so-called right thing," Mrs. Brandon explained. "Someone like yourself simply, ah, *nourishes* that need."

"What's your point, Mrs. Brandon?"

The older woman's face lost its contrived sweetness. "The point is that you should consider the possibility that you're really nothing more than a social conscience to Anthony."

Susan was incredulous. "I don't know what you want from me, Mrs. Brandon."

"Not a thing, my dear, not a thing," she insisted. "I'm trying to do you a kindness actually. By warning you that your relationship may not be based on what you think."

A kindness? Susan stared at Tony's mother, and the pity she'd felt earlier intensified. No longer did Mrs. Brandon have the power to intimidate her.

But she was annoyed.

"You know, I don't think you have a clue as to the kind of man your son is," she asserted, forcing herself to remain calm. "I could never make Tony do anything he didn't want to do. Nor would I try. And as far as our relationship goes, you obviously don't have an inkling of what it's about."

"Maybe, maybe not," Mrs. Brandon replied, her poise as solid as steel. "But allow me one more question."

Susan didn't think she could bear this another minute. "Yes?"

"Knowing that the firm is Anthony's legacy, why would you want to get trapped into a life-style that even *I'm* trying to liberate myself from? Think about it." With that Mrs. Brandon swept out, leaving Susan alone in the dismal hallway.

She was in a daze. What on earth had just happened here? God, it had been like a scene from her own worst nightmare. Although she'd kept her wits about her and stayed calm, she'd been unnerved by the encounter. Who wouldn't have been?

Worse, the confrontation made her wonder. Did she somehow serve as Tony's moral conscience? And, if so, would he eventually come to resent her? Or, if they married, would their lives inevitably become like his parents'?

It galled her that Letitia Brandon had managed to leave such questions in her mind.

When she made her way back to the ballroom, Tony greeted her with concern. "They told me you were with my mother."

"That's right."

"Are you okay? She didn't give you a hard time, did she?"

She had already decided against telling Tony what had happened. Frankly, she didn't want to think about it anymore. "Everything's fine."

"Are you sure?" he asked, a skeptical look in his eye.

Before she could answer the music started up again, and Susan jumped at the chance to change the subject. "I believe I saved you this dance."

But this dance was different from the first. She couldn't get that floaty, magical feeling back no matter how hard she tried. Instead, she found herself fighting confusion.

Part of her wanted nothing more than to get away from Letitia Brandon and this party and all it represented. Tony's mother had practically told her that she didn't belong here. Well, maybe she was right.

Yet she couldn't convince herself that she didn't belong with Tony. Nothing in Mrs. Brandon's argument could blur the fact that she and Tony wanted to be together. Nothing. And realizing that, what could she do? What choices did she have? As the questions whirled through her mind over and over, Tony pulled her just a little bit closer against him. She realized then that there were no choices. All had been decided earlier when they danced on that silken cloud.

At the song's end she and Tony made a second attempt to get dessert. As they headed toward the food tables, they heard Maria's lilting voice calling to them.

Their friend hurried across the room with Luis following just a few steps behind. "We've been looking all over for you two," she said.

Susan was pleased to see the change in her friend. Wearing a striking dark red silk dress, her wavy brown hair loose and flowing to her shoulders, Maria glowed.

Tony gave Maria's shoulder a friendly tap. "You haven't told Susan your good news yet, have you?"

Susan looked from Maria to Luis and back again. They had such foolish grins on their faces. "What news?"

Before they answered Tony intervened. "Why don't I get us all dessert while you tell her?" he offered. "Maria, Luis? Dessert?"

"I'll have some of that chocolate mousse, if there's any left," Maria answered.

Luis looked at her. "But you just ate dessert, honey."

"Well, I'm still a little hungry."

"Chocolate mousse it is," Tony said, giving the three of them a sly wink before heading off.

Exasperated, Susan turned to the couple. "Stop torturing me and tell me what's going on."

Maria's brown eyes widened. "So much, I don't know where to start."

"Of course, you know the charges have been dropped against Berto," Luis said. "That's the most important thing."

Maria nodded in agreement. "We can't thank Tony enough for keeping after the Oliva boy. Otherwise, who knows?" She shrugged. "But Tony's always been a good friend to Roberto and me."

"He cares about you both very much." Susan patted Maria's arm. "And how is Roberto now? Is he home for Christmas vacation?"

"No. We're driving up to Connecticut after work tomorrow to spend the holidays with him there," Luis told her. "We thought that might be the best thing."

"Therapy seems to be helping," Maria added. "He's stopped griping about Oakridge and has agreed to stick it out till the end of the school year. Then we'll see."

"That is good news."

Luis held up his hand. "Ah, there's more."

Susan sensed their excitement. "Tell me."

"Luis and I are going to have a baby."

Thrilled, Susan gave them both big hugs, offering her congratulations. She wanted to hear all about it.

"We found out the day the charges were dropped," Maria revealed. "A few days before Luis insisted I go in for a checkup."

"She was tired and dragged out all the time. I was concerned about depression."

"We were so caught up in Roberto's problems that it never occurred to us that I might be pregnant. What a shock!"

"A good shock," Luis continued. "It's due a few weeks after Maria graduates from law school. Talk about perfect timing."

It was easy to be drawn into her friends' excitement. No two people deserved happiness more. Yet Susan couldn't help feeling a pang of envy. Maria and Luis were very close; they shared so much. There was no question they were meant for each other. And now they were going to have a baby. She wanted to have a baby of her own some day. Yet she despaired of finding a man *meant* for her as Luis was for Maria. At this point she wasn't sure she and Tony were up to that kind of lifelong commitment.

Tony returned with the desserts, and the four of them ate and chatted happily about the Lopezes' good news. Later on Mike Stone and his girlfriend, Janine, joined them. When a yawning Maria announced it was time for her and Luis to leave, Mike and Janine stayed on for one last drink with Tony and herself.

"Susan, I read about the Somerset tenants in the *Post* the other day," Janine told her. "And there was a brief spot about it on Channel Four. Do you think the coverage will help?"

"We hope the publicity will put pressure on the developer. But it's still too early to tell."

Following the lawsuit's dismissal, she and Tony had phoned every contact they had in the media. They had done this when the Somerset situation first arose, but the results were mixed. Now that the courts had decided against the tenants and the eviction clock was ticking again, the story had become more dramatic *and* more appealing to the media.

When the orchestra announced the last song of the evening, Mike and Janine initiated the farewells. "We've made reservations at St. Kitts for the long Presidents' Day weekend," Mike said before leaving. "Why don't you two think about joining us?"

Tony's eyes lit up. "Sounds like fun. We'll talk it over and let you know."

The idea of a midwinter jaunt to the Caribbean sounded heavenly to her. Yet her niggling practicality quickly brought her down to earth. In truth she couldn't afford a trip like that right now. She was still paying off her credit cards for the move from Baltimore and for the new furniture in her apartment. Not to mention the money she gave her mother every month. More debt was out of the question. Yes, she knew Tony would offer to pay her way. She also knew she couldn't and wouldn't accept.

The two of them would indeed talk the matter over, and Tony wasn't going to like her answer. Suddenly she felt weary.

Tony clutched her hand. "One last dance?"

"Would you mind if we just went home? It's been a big night."

"Of course not," he said, his expression thoughtful. "I'll get our coats and meet you outside the ballroom door." He kissed her cheek.

Making her way through the dwindling crowd, Susan was glad to be going home. True, the party had had its high spots, and she *had* made it through the evening without running into Mrs. Brandon again. Still, she couldn't see herself attending this type of gala on a regular basis.

"Susan?"

Rob Berns fell into step beside her. "I wanted to say something to you earlier tonight about the Somerset hearing," he said. "But there were always two or three other people around."

She sensed he was about to apologize for the suit dismissal. "You've done a terrific job on the case all along, Rob."

"Apparently not terrific enough."

"No one thinks that. I know the tenants don't."

His lips twitched with a slight smile. "Alice McGraw sent a kind note. Tom O'Brien called at the office to thank me."

"See? And you and Tony will have another crack when you file the second lawsuit."

"Maybe." He shrugged. "If it gets that far."

Puzzled, she stopped and turned to him. "You don't think Hammond's going to make a decent settlement without one, do you?"

Looking uneasy, Rob hesitated. "Possibly not, but—didn't Tony tell you?"

"Tell me what?"

He gave a despairing sigh. "I've put my foot in it, haven't I?"

"Probably. But tell me, anyway."

"Tony's getting a lot of pressure from the big guys to settle this case—soon."

"Soon? But why?"

"It could drag on for some time," he explained. "And it's already getting expensive, what with Tony's time and my involvement."

"I see." Boy, did she ever see. "By the big guys—do you mean Tony's father?"

"Mostly Conners and Bolton are pushing it. But I gather John Brandon has had a word or two to say about it."

She didn't know what to say. All she could do was shake her head.

"Susan, Tony's not buying this. He's trying to change their minds. I'm sure he'll resist it as long as possible."

Rob's comments offered little comfort. She was numb, anyway. This had been one incredible night. Her emotions had zigzagged so many times over the past few hours that she couldn't figure out how upset she was.

Minutes later, as she and Tony headed to the hotel parking garage together, she tried not to jump to any conclusions, nor to make any snap judgments. She'd tried hard to grow beyond that. Still, why hadn't Tony told her about the pressure the law firm was putting on him about the Somerset case? They were in this thing together. They were supposed to trust each other.

She might not be jumping to conclusions, but she couldn't help racking her brain with the question "why?"

Tony drove out onto Pennsylvania Avenue. "Your place or mine?" he asked.

It was a normal question, one which had been asked a dozen times over the past few weeks and one she'd always been happy to answer. Yet this wasn't what she'd call a normal evening. Now she needed time to herself.

"I'm awfully tired, Tony. Would you mind just taking me home? I'm ready to call it a night." She tried hard to keep the awkwardness she was feeling out of her voice.

He shot her a wary glance, anyway. "Are you feeling all right?"

"Fine. Just tired."

"Sure my mother didn't say something to put you off?"

"I'm sure," she said, too weary to get into that. Mrs. Brandon's warnings rang in her ears. She knew discussing it with Tony would just make matters worse. But if she didn't, wouldn't it make her as guilty of omission as Tony?

Tony turned to another subject. "What do you think about going to St. Kitts in February?"

Another great topic. "I don't know, Tony."

"It'll be fun. You'll love the island."

"Probably I would. But I can't think that far ahead right now," she snapped. "I don't even know what to do about Christmas!"

Tony stared at her, his eyes uncomprehending. He pulled the car over to the side of the street. "Okay, Susan, tell me what's going on."

Desperate to keep her frayed emotions in check, she refused to look at him. "I've decided it would be best if Mama and I didn't spend Christmas with your family, Tony. In fact, I'm thinking of going home to Baltimore instead."

"What?"

"I need to get away for a few days."

"From me?"

"From you and—everything." She dared to glance at him. He looked as if he'd been slapped in the face. Pain quivered in her chest, feeling almost as if her heart were crumbling.

"For God's sake, what happened to you tonight? You were perfectly happy when we left your apartment."

With a brittle laugh she shook her head. "What didn't happen tonight?"

His eyes narrowed and his voice took on a defensive tone. "Why don't you just pick one thing to start with? I'm sure we can take it from there."

He wanted her to pick one, did he? No contest there, she thought, not knowing if she was being driven by resentment or hurt or both. She did know she couldn't keep whatever it was inside her any longer. "Okay. I'll start by asking you a question." She looked him straight in the eye. "Why haven't you told me about the quick settlement your bosses want on the Somerset case?"

Chapter Fourteen

"You know."

"By accident. Rob didn't know it was supposed to be a secret."

"It's not. And nothing's been decided yet." He closed his eyes. He should have told her; he knew that. Bringing himself to do it had been something else again.

"Then why didn't you say something?"

He opened his eyes to look at her, wondering if she really didn't have a clue about why he had kept quiet. Her blue eyes revealed nothing, her impassive face even less. Her guard was up. He could tell. He also felt the distance she was putting between them already, and that hurt. It hurt because he wanted them to be beyond that. It also irritated the hell out of him.

"I wanted to tell you—several times. But with all the things going on between us I thought this was one bit of news our relationship could do without."

"Our relationship?" she cried. "What about the Somerset? What about the tenants?"

Her look of shocked disbelief was the last straw. Irritation grew into frustration, and he needed to vent it badly. "I don't want to hear it anymore, Susan. This is about us—not the tenants, not William Leland, not my parents.

Us—you and me. Can't you see that we're what matters here?" he implored. "Or don't you want to?"

"Right now I'm so confused that I don't know what I want."

"How can you be confused about us after all we've been through?"

"I didn't think I was until tonight."

"Because of what Rob said?" His anger was rising in spite of himself. "You want to know why I didn't say anything about it? Because, Susan, I just couldn't face another round of proving myself to you."

"That's how I make you feel?"

"Sometimes." Despite his anger it pained him to say so.

"Then maybe we need time apart."

"I don't think that's an answer."

"It's the best I can do." She turned to him, her eyes full of anguish. "If I'm ever going to figure out what it is I do want, I've got to put some distance between us."

"Sounds like running away to me."

"Don't you see, Tony? When it's just you and me together, alone, life is beautiful. The minute we step outside into the world reality comes along and smacks us in the face."

He had never perceived their relationship that way. It was hard to accept that she did. "Perhaps your expectations are unrealistic."

She just stared at him, saying finally, "I've got to go."

How could he convey the depth of his feelings for her? He had tried in so many ways, so many times over the past few weeks. The quiet dinners, the cozy nights alone at home, trying to get their families together at Christmas, all the cajoling and reassuring... Apparently that wasn't enough for Susan.

It was a bitter pill for him to swallow.

"Are you walking out on me because of my last name? Your last name? The law firm? The Somerset?"

"Tony, stop."

"Damn it, Susan. What will it take to prove to you that we're meant for each other?"

"I'm not sure that we are." Her voice was devoid of emotion, her eyes were ice-blue steel.

How could she sound so matter-of-fact about this? Although she was sitting only an arm's length away—close enough to touch—he felt as if a vast distance already separated them. The love that had taken months of careful, tender weaving had been ripped open by its very first endurance test. Perhaps the threads had been too weak from the start.

The gaping hole that remained chilled his heart.

"If you really need time to sort things out, take it by all means. I'll wait," he said, peering at her from across the car. "But not indefinitely."

"SORRY I'm going to miss another chance to meet your mother, honey," Alice told her over a cup of tea.

Susan had dropped by Alice's to exchange Christmas gifts before leaving for Union Station and the noon train to Baltimore. A sleet storm and icy temperatures had made a frozen mess of the roads, and Susan had decided against driving home on her car's aging tires.

Alice had knitted her a lovely maroon scarf and matching gloves for her Christmas present. She gave Alice a new set of blue towels to replace the almost threadbare ones she'd noticed hanging in the bathroom.

"Will Tony be going up with you?"

Susan shook her head, trying hard to hide her distress. "Not this time."

Alice's large, cool hand covered hers. "The course of true love never runs smoothly, honey."

So much for hiding her feelings, she mused. She used to be so good at it...before Tony. Still, for Alice's sake she tried to put on a brighter face. "Things may work out yet."

"Of course they will. You and Tony are good people."
Patting Susan's hand, she added, "Besides, if it's not one
thing it's another. You just have to hang in there with your
fella. Take it from me." She gave Susan a meaningful look.
"You see, Tom and I have sort of an understanding between us."

Alice's news didn't come as a big surprise. Susan already had suspected a growing romantic relationship between her and Tom O'Brien. Nothing had ever been said,
but she'd seen how the two of them acted together. Subtle
yet tender gestures and gentle teasing had been the give-
aways.

"And do you know where Mr. O'Brien is right now?"
Alice continued. "Meeting his two sons and their wives at
National Airport. They're here to spend the holidays."

"How nice for Tom." But a glint of uncertainty flickered in Alice's eyes. "Isn't it?"

"Sure it is. Except they know about the evictions here.
And Tom's worried they'll try to persuade him to go back
to Arizona with them."

"They can try, but that doesn't mean he has to."

Alice didn't look convinced. "And another thing—those
boys may be surprised to find out their dad has a lady
friend. Honestly, Susan, I don't think the old fool's told
them about me."

"Oh, dear."

"That's for sure," she muttered. "Like I said, if it's not
one thing it's another."

Alice's apprehension was increasing noticeably. "Do
you want me to wait until Tom gets back?" she asked.

"You're a doll for offering, but I won't hear of it.
You've got a train to catch."

Alice insisted that she was fine as Susan pulled on her
coat to leave. They hugged warmly, wishing each other
Merry Christmas. "Now remember what I said about

hanging in with your fella," Alice said, standing at her apartment door. "Tony's a good one."

These parting words nagged at her all the way back to her own apartment. She knew Tony was a fine man; that was what made the situation so sad. When she got home and saw the lone wrapped package under the tabletop tree, she felt even worse. The package was Tony's gift from her—a heavy two-volume tome on the Civil War, books he'd been wanting to read for some time.

She decided to call and tell him she'd deliver his gift when she returned after Christmas. After all, she'd gone to such lengths to get the books, searching local stores for weeks until she'd found them. Naturally she wanted to make sure he received them.

"He's in court this morning, Susan," his secretary advised. "But I expect him back any minute. I'll have him call you."

"No, don't," she responded hastily, realizing this call hadn't been such a good idea, after all. She'd go running right back to him if she heard his voice right now. "I mean, I'm leaving town now and I can't be reached. Don't bother him with a message. I'll call him tomorrow."

Later, as the train moved out of the station, she felt as if she were finally making her escape from confusion and doubt. Yet she couldn't prevent her eyes from searching the platform until it gradually disappeared from view. In case... just in case.

It was snowing hard in Baltimore when the taxi dropped her off in front of the apartment building. Iris and Fay's apartment was a third-floor walk-up in a neighborhood that had seen better days. Yuppie gentrification hadn't yet reached Edison Street, and a fresh blanket of wet snow couldn't mask its shabbiness. Whenever she questioned the neighborhood's safeness, Iris insisted she had never had a problem in over thirty years. Fay always backed her up.

Inside the apartment, though, it was warm, clean and cozy. Iris's old furniture of dark wood and faded upholstery topped with hand-crocheted doilies along with Fay's collection of knickknacks and endless framed photographs brought back plenty of memories of her growing-up years—some happy, some not. But her mother's welcoming embrace sparked the warmest memory she possessed—that of always being loved and wanted.

"Fay, let go of that girl. Give someone else a chance to get a good look at her," Cousin Iris called from where she was ensconced in a blue vinyl recliner, her injured leg on a tattered ottoman.

Susan bent down to kiss her old cousin's cheek. She noticed that Iris's cast was covered with signatures. Maybe she really did still know everybody in the neighborhood, Susan mused. "How do I look, Iris?" She did a playful twirl.

"Pretty as ever—no, prettier!" Iris declared, eyeing her up and down. "Something down in Washington sure agrees with you, Suz. Or should I say someone?" Iris gave Fay a knowing look.

Fay hooked her arm around Susan's. "Now, Iris, let's give the girl a chance to catch her breath. We'll all have a nice long talk over supper."

Talk they did, over supper and throughout the next day. She told her mother about the people she worked with as they baked Christmas cookies together. During several hands of gin rummy, Iris appraised her of the neighborhood gossip. As they all decorated the tree, both her mother and Iris were full of questions about her friends at the Somerset. And they were more than a little curious about Tony.

She was deliberately circumspect in what she said about him. She feared saying too much and alerting their concern. But her mother didn't let her get away with it.

"So why haven't we met this young man yet?" Fay inquired after she helped Iris to the bedroom for her afternoon nap. "Did you invite him for Christmas dinner like I asked?"

No, she hadn't. Just as she hadn't told her mother about Tony's invitation to join his family on Christmas. She felt sheepish about it now, but during the past few weeks she'd held off from mentioning each invitation to Tony and Fay. She'd felt paralyzed in a way, unable to act, unable to connect the two most important parts of her life. She'd held off until the questions had become moot. Although for the life of her, she couldn't explain why.

Holding a glass ornament in midair, Fay peered over a tree branch. "Well? Is Tony coming?"

"No, Mama, he couldn't get away." She realized how lame this sounded and half expected Fay to call her on it.

Instead, Fay hooked the glittery ball on a lower branch. "I imagine his parents expect him at home."

"Exactly." Avoiding her mother's gaze, she dug into the box of ornaments on the floor. She despised herself for lying.

When they finished decorating the tree, her mother glanced at the old glass clock on the fireplace mantle. "Oh, heavens, look at the time. Mr. H. will be here in a few minutes."

Susan looked at her mother. "What?"

"Mr. H. is picking me up. You'll put away all these boxes, won't you, Suz?"

"You're going to the Harrisons' tonight?"

"Didn't I tell you Mrs. H. called while you were out shopping? I must have forgotten in all the excitement with the tree," her mother said.

Forgotten, ha! Susan thought wryly. Clearly she wasn't the only O'Toole who knew how to skirt around the truth. "Mama, are you going to work at the Harrisons' tonight?"

"Only for a few hours, dear. Long enough to serve dinner and clear away."

"It's Christmas Eve, for God's sake."

"Try to understand, Suz. The two girls have shown up with both their boyfriends—unannounced, and the sister-in-law from Pittsburgh is back. Mrs. H. is desperate. Not only did the poor thing beg me to work, but she offered me triple rate."

"But what about *your* daughter?" she shot back. Her mother had touched a nerve, a nerve Susan didn't even know was raw. "For as long as I can remember you'd go running over there anytime Mrs. Harrison wiggled her little finger." She felt the resentment rising in her throat. "Why now? You don't have to do it for the money anymore."

"I'll be back in plenty of time to go to Mass tonight." Indignation flashed across Fay's gray eyes. "The money is my business."

"I can give you any extra money you need, Mama. Besides, you're supposed to be working less—not more."

"That was your idea, not mine."

Fay's remark felt like a slap in the face. "You agreed it was best to cut back on your hours—and Mrs. Harrison knows it. She's taking advantage of you, playing on your sympathy, dragging you away from home on Christmas Eve. She shows no respect for you at all."

"Oh, Mrs. Harrison respects me just fine. But, young lady," she added with a stern wag of her finger, "I'm not so sure *you* do, what with all this fuss you're making over such a measly matter."

"Mama! How can you say that?"

"I mean it, Suz, and it's gotten worse since you moved to Washington. What with all this talk of moving down there with you and cutting back on work. And every time Mrs. H. asks me to do a little extra, you get up in arms."

"I just want to make things easier for you."

"I know, honey, I know. But if I didn't work, what would I do? Play gin with Iris all day? I'd go nuts."

Bewildered, Susan sat on the carpeted floor and began gathering up the empty ornament boxes. "You could develop some new interests."

"Cooking and cleaning is all I know, and I like doing it." She bent down to help Susan. "I like working in Mrs. H.'s modern kitchen, cooking those fancy recipes of hers. And I get a kick out of knowing that I can run that big old house of hers ten times better than she or anyone else can."

"You do?" She had never looked at it that way.

"Know what else?" Fay added, her eyes shining impishly. "Mrs. H. knows it, and I like that, too."

Smiling in spite of herself, Susan stood and helped her mother up from the floor. A heavy, impatient knock sounded at the door.

"Heavens, that's sure to be Mr. H. I told him I'd be waiting out in front." Fay rushed to the hall closet for her coat. "He wasn't too happy about driving down here, but I said if they wanted me tonight, it meant no bus and no cab."

"Good for you, Mama."

Smiling, she covered her head with a flimsy nylon print scarf. "Just remember, you and I have nothing to be ashamed of."

"I'm not ashamed of anything."

"No?" She cast a skeptical eye on Susan as she tied the scarf beneath her chin. "Then why didn't you invite your Anthony Brandon *the second* to Christmas dinner?"

Susan tried hard to dismiss this parting remark. It was bad enough that her mother had seen through her lie about Tony, but accusing her of being ashamed really stung. Ashamed? She looked around the cluttered apartment. Of this? Of her mother? Ridiculous, she told herself. Fay had it all wrong.

Didn't she?

By the time she went to bed that night, she'd managed to put the notion out of her mind. Still, sleep eluded her, and it wasn't the lumpy living room couch that kept her awake tonight. She missed Tony. It was as simple and as complicated as that. Missing him, however, didn't make up for her fears about the viability of their relationship. Loving him didn't take away the risks.

She couldn't bear the possibility that she'd feel like an outsider in certain aspects of his life: his family, the law firm. The prospect that they'd be continually at odds about professional choices and decisions was daunting. It had hurt them enough already as it was. The night of the dinner dance she could practically *feel* their mutual trust and respect unraveling.

But early Christmas morning she woke up with Tony on her mind. She hadn't dreamt about him, yet she was filled with a sense of him. She could almost hear the rich timbre of his voice, smell his light citrusy scent, feel his tender touch. And her body ached with emptiness. Yet she didn't know what to do.

It was still dark as she rose from her makeshift bed on the couch and pulled on her flannel robe. She padded carefully, and quietly, through the cluttered living room. Fay and Iris, asleep in the bedroom, hadn't gone to bed until after midnight Mass at St. Mike's. She didn't want to disturb them this early.

After plugging in the Christmas lights, she sat beneath the tree. The multicolored lights gave the darkened living room a magical glow, just as they had when she was a little girl. How she had loved gazing at the Christmas tree in the dark. Images of past holidays filled her thoughts: her mother waking her on Christmas mornings with hugs and kisses and news that Santa indeed had remembered her; the last lovely Christmas with Gramps O'Toole; the year Iris had cashed a savings bond and given her the money to participate in a sixth-grade class trip to Washington.

These memories vibrated with a life that carried them clear and sharp over the years. Poor as they'd been, the O'Toole Christmases were rich with the spirit of love. When Tony described the holidays of his youth, she remembered thinking how sterile and lonely they'd sounded. Yet by not bringing him home she'd lost the chance to share her family's treasure with him.

And why? Because, God help her, her mother was right. *She was ashamed.*

The truth had finally seeped through her subconscious. Good old compassionate, open-minded, do-gooder Susan couldn't see the hypocrisy she was guilty of until her mother had laid it before her eyes. Now it stared back at her with painful clarity.

Worse, it wasn't the walk-up flat she was ashamed of, nor the shabby furniture, nor Iris's unschooled speech. No. No, the fuss she'd made over her mother's working at the Harrisons' on Christmas Eve really said it all. She didn't like the idea of *her* mother going off to serve someone else's family on one of the most special nights of the year— even if she wanted to. She *was* ashamed that the mother of an educated, well-paid woman still peeled potatoes and cleaned toilets for a living.

And even though Tony knew that her mother was a housekeeper, bringing him here would have presented him with the reality. In the back of her mind she knew there was a chance Fay might go popping off to the Harrisons' at any given moment. How would that have looked to Tony?

When she realized how unfair that was to Tony and Fay, a deeper shame burdened her heart. She'd never felt so wretched.

She gazed at the ornaments her mother and Iris had saved over the years. They weren't elegant or fancy by any means. As a child, her particular favorites were the white plastic angels with painted yellow hair and painted gold wings. She'd thought they were beautiful.

Susan touched one of the old angels dangling from a lower branch. The plastic was yellowing, the gold paint scratched and worn in places, but the memories it evoked—of wonderment, of hope—were flawless and bright. Just as all their Christmases had been.

Fay and Iris may not have had much money when she was growing up, but they'd always managed to make Christmas special for her. Her happy, vivid memories proved that. She'd been truly loved and cherished; she had belonged with them.

Belonged.

Susan was staring at the glittering tree when the notion hit. Suddenly she knew why she'd been off kilter—restless—since returning to Baltimore. Although she loved being with her mother and Iris, the feeling of being home, of belonging, had been missing during this visit. Now she understood the reason why: she and Tony were apart.

She missed him, yes. But, more importantly, she realized how connected she was to him. The link between them—though precarious at times—was powerful. She knew, deep in her soul, that this was true, like it or not. And it frightened her.

She glanced out one of the front windows. Winter morning gray had soaked up the darkness. The luminous face on the mantel clock read quarter to seven. Still early. Yet the urge to speak to Tony burned inside her. He wouldn't be awake at this hour on Christmas morning. But she was anxious to hear his voice, to make contact. He'd be annoyed. Then she thought of how he kept his arms around her while they slept. Maybe he wouldn't be annoyed, after all.

Returning to the couch, she pulled the black telephone set off the end table to rest on her lap. Used to touch-tone speed, her impatient fingers seemed to take forever to ring up Tony's number on the phone's rotary dial. Each long click between digits fed her nervousness. She worried about what to say to him. What did she want to say? she asked herself over and over until she heard Tony's groggy hello.

"Tony, it's me. Sorry to wake you up."

"What time—?"

"Almost seven."

"Are you all right?" Concern overcame grogginess.

"Yes. I . . . Merry Christmas." Why had she called like this? What did she want to say to him?

"Merry Christmas to you."

It felt good to hear his voice; she had needed to hear it. "I miss you," she blurted out.

"Good."

She flinched at his serves-you-right tone. "You're still angry with me."

"For leaving—yes. But I miss you like crazy."

"Good," she said as her pulse quickened.

"Has going away helped you sort things out?"

Had it? But in asking herself this she realized the fog of confusion hadn't lifted completely. Tony was waiting for an answer. She had to tell him the truth. "I'm not sure. I guess I'm still afraid about us."

"Damn it, Susan, come home. We have to work this out together."

Home. When he said that, all she could think of was his parents' big house and their perfectly attired guests who talked about things she couldn't care less about while being waited on by unobtrusive servants. Thinking that way was just as unfair to Tony as the way she'd felt about his coming home with her. She hated herself for it, but she couldn't stop.

"I promised my mother I'd stay until New Year's."

She heard his exasperated sigh. "Staying away makes it that much harder."

"Tony, this is already very hard. I'm just not ready." She was muffing the whole thing badly. She shouldn't have called.

"I'm sorry. I don't want to pressure you. Take the time you need. I'll be here when you come back."

When she hung up, she realized her mother was standing in the doorway leading to the bedroom. She looked worried.

"Mama! How long have you been there?"

"Long enough to hear everything isn't as hunky-dory as you've been claiming." Fay sat beside her. "Which I suspected, anyway."

"But you never said a word."

"I was hoping you'd say something," she explained. "Then maybe I could help you."

"You already have. You were right about why I didn't invite Tony here." Her voice trembled slightly. "I'm sorry, Mama. I've been such a jerk."

"Not my girl. Not ever." Fay curved an arm around her shoulders. "You're just a little mixed up."

"A little? Oh, Mama, you just don't know."

"At least now I have some idea of what's going on. And it strikes me that hanging around here till New Year's isn't real smart, Suz."

"Gee, thanks, Ma." She rubbed her forehead against her hand.

"Besides, I'm in the mood for a quick little trip to Washington. In fact, Iris and I were talking about it before we went to bed last night."

"You were?"

"Iris is well enough to do without me for a few days. And Ellie Pickard from downstairs has offered to stay with her while I'm gone. Of course, she can't come until her company leaves in the middle of the week, but that'll give me time to get the apartment ready for her."

She listened to her mother's ramblings with disbelief. "You've planned this already, haven't you?"

Fay shrugged. "I just think it's about time I met this Tony Brandon of yours."

THIS COULD HAVE BEEN the best Christmas of his life. Instead, it was turning out to be the worst. Tony stared at the sophisticated silver ornaments on his parents' eight-foot tree. After the three of them exchanged gifts, his mother had closeted herself in her bedroom and his father had taken refuge in his study. He was left to his own devices in the living room.

And Susan was in Baltimore. She'd only been gone a couple of days, yet it seemed like an eternity. She was on his mind ninety-five percent of the time until he could practically see her, smell her, taste her. If he closed his eyes, he could feel how the curves and hollows of her body fitted against his own. . . .

Still, there was a distinct possibility that when Susan returned things wouldn't be the same between them. At first the notion would tear him apart and he'd be ready to jump into his car and drive up to her mother's. But reality would set in and the questions would start. If they really valued each other, why the doubts? The mistrust? If they loved each other as much as they claimed, why all the problems?

Susan's call early in the morning had given him a brief flash of hope. But it had become evident that nothing had changed, and it had left him feeling even more unsettled. As a result, questions about their relationship had turned into questions about himself.

Her second-guessing of his commitment to the Somerset tenants had disturbed him from the beginning. Yet, secretly, he feared there might exist a kernel of truth in her doubt. How long was he willing to represent them when intriguing new cases beckoned? He had been so adamant about sticking with the tenants until the bitter end. He had told his father, Mac and Carter as much just last week. But representing William Leland had been exciting, challenging; the lure of more work like that was irresistible. Did that mean no more pro bono cases?

It had been difficult representing the tenants. He had little trouble with the amount of time and effort required to do the job. It was the juggling of everyone's interests— the clients', the firm's, his parents', Susan's, his own—that sapped his energy. It was a balancing act he could do without.

Something had to give. But what? So much was at stake, personally and professionally. He had to find a way to fulfill his ambitions and still be his own man. He hoped he'd be the man Susan wanted, as well. He loved her, but he wouldn't sell himself short to prove it.

"Ah, there you are, son." His father glanced his way briefly when he entered the room. He stopped to check the fire in the fireplace. The flames were petering out. "Where's your mother?" he asked as he stoked the hot embers with the brass poker.

"Upstairs in her room. Napping probably."

"I see. We both deserted you." He shook his head with regret. "How about a drink? Now, I know you young men don't drink as much these days," he continued, heading toward the liquor cabinet. "Nobody really does anymore, do they? Probably wise."

Tony sensed his talk of drinking habits was his father's awkward attempt at making light conversation—as if he didn't know what else to talk to his son about. During the past few years, most of their conversations had revolved around the law firm.

"I can get you a beer from the kitchen if you'd prefer," John offered.

"Whatever you're having will be fine, Dad." He watched John pour two fingers of Scotch—neat. "Maybe

I'll have soda with mine," Tony added quickly, joining him at the liquor cabinet.

Dressed in casual sweater and slacks, feet in leather slippers, his father didn't appear as imposing as he did at the office. When Tony thought of his dad, he usually visualized him sitting behind his heavy desk, wearing a conservative suit, his silver hair impeccably groomed. It was a funny way to think of one's own father. Funny and sad.

Yet, as far as fathers and sons went, they had missed out on a lot. Family had always come second to the law firm, and Tony thought he'd accepted the fact long ago. But deep in his heart he knew it was why he had eventually joined the firm. Finally he would get his father's attention. Then he'd prove himself.

Now that didn't seem important anymore. John Brandon, kingpin of Conners, Brandon and Moffet, wasn't mixing him a drink on Christmas Day. His "old man" was. For all his faults the man was his one-and-only father; he loved him. That was all that mattered. He didn't have to do a sales job on his worth to prove one damn thing.

Accepting the Scotch and soda, he followed John to the sofa in front of the fireplace. They sat in silence, gazing at the flames. Finally, after some thought, Tony turned to John. "Dad, I need your help... with the Somerset."

John looked startled. "You do?"

He nodded. "I'm torn about negotiating a settlement. At first I thought, absolutely no way. Yet the more I look at the big picture..."

"Actually, I've been thinking about that situation a great deal."

"You have?" It was his turn to be startled.

"Ever since the suit was dismissed. I know what a blow that was to you," he explained. "But I hesitated to interfere. You're so independent. You rarely ask my advice. I didn't think it would be welcomed."

He had no idea his father felt that way. "I'm asking now, Dad."

Taking a second sip of Scotch, John then plunked the half-filled glass down on the end table. "To begin with, Mac Conners spoke to me about it again yesterday. And from the firm's standpoint, I can't say I disagree with his position. What we have to do is work out a settlement where both sides win."

"A cash settlement isn't going to do it for these folks, Dad. They need housing."

"I understand that. The recent press about the situation hasn't been very favorable to Hammond, has it?"

"They're not pleased."

"Good. And, of course, you've been following up with all the proper authorities."

Tony nodded. "The tenants have written reams of letters to their senators and congressman. Susan's been cultivating contacts in the county government. And I've been talking to people in Richmond and on the Hill." Then he added dryly, "For all the good it's done us."

His father looked thoughtful. "Maybe we ought to get those people talking to each other."

"I wish that was as easy as it sounds."

"It's not. I know. But tomorrow morning you and I are going to make some well-thought-out phone calls. I'll start with a fellow over at HUD who should be more than happy to help me out. We'll get this ball rolling."

Tony was amazed by his father's confidence as, together, they outlined a strategy. Clearly John had been thinking about the situation for some time, and he could have kicked himself for not going to him sooner.

"I'm going to call Susan later and run these ideas by her," he said after they finished brainstorming. "I think she'll be pleased."

John got up to fix himself another drink. "She seems like a fine young woman. Very involved."

"Very." He couldn't suppress a wry smile. "But that's what makes Susan Susan." It was one of the things he loved about her, even if it did drive him crazy at times.

He wanted to talk more about Susan, but after John settled back with his second Scotch, he looked as if his thoughts were a million miles away. Disappointment took the edge off Tony's earlier excitement. He should have known. His father's involving himself with the Somerset case was one thing; opening himself up to his son's personal life was quite another.

He studied his father's profile. The man looked distracted, even troubled, and Tony wondered if he should bring up his mother. He'd never seen his father looking so forlorn, and the tension between his parents this morning had been horrendous. Although John had been reticent about discussing the situation with him in the past, Tony felt he should press.

"What about you and Mother? It was pretty icy around the tree this morning."

John's face fell, and he sat stock-still.

"I'm worried about you two," Tony continued. "You haven't resolved this retirement business, and Mother's more and more withdrawn each time I see her. How long can this go on?"

"It can't, obviously."

"Meaning?"

John shook his head. "I don't think it's a good time to discuss this, Tony."

"Dad, come on."

"Look, this isn't the kind of news I want to break to my son on Christmas Day. It's still all up in the air."

It was clear his father wanted to leave it at that, but this time Tony wasn't going to let him off the hook. "Tell me, anyway, Dad."

Taking his time to answer, John drained the remainder of his Scotch in one long swallow. His saddened eyes drifted to Tony. "God help me, it's even hard to tell a grown-up son something like this."

He put his hand on his father's arm. "Go ahead."

"Your mother and I are considering a trial separation."

He couldn't understand why this came as such a shock. He knew they were having troubles. But a separation was the last thing he'd expected. "It's actually come to that?"

"It's been extremely difficult for us to sort out what we each want at this stage of our lives."

"What about a marriage counselor?"

"Your mother and I aren't the type of people to air our problems in front of a stranger."

Tony decided it would be a waste of time to disagree; they wouldn't even confide in him, their only child. It was a bitter pill to swallow. "Can't you at least meet each other halfway?"

"You simply don't understand the complications."

He glared at his father, no longer able to hold the lid on his exasperation. "Maybe I would understand if you'd talk to me once in a while. Just getting you to tell me what's going on around here is like pulling teeth."

His father stared down at the drink in his hands, looking rather dazed, and Tony regretted his sudden outburst of anger. "Sorry, Dad. I shouldn't have—"

John raised his hand to stop him. "No, you're right." Then he looked up at him with chastised eyes. "If your mother and I sat down and talked, could we rectify things?" he asked. "Do you think it's possible? At this late stage?"

"I guess it depends on how much you want it."

Before his father could respond the telephone rang. "I better get that before it wakes your mother," he mumbled hastily, escaping out to the main hall to answer the phone.

He returned within seconds. "The call's for you. It's Susan."

Chapter Fifteen

As Susan stepped down from the train, she thought she heard someone calling her name. She quickly scanned the crowded platform but recognized no one. Turning to help her mother, she swore she heard her name again.

"Sounds like someone's calling you, Suz," her mother said when she was firmly settled on the platform.

"It's a pretty common name, Mama."

"Susan!"

The voice was closer now and very familiar. She spun around, her eyes combing the throng of disembarking passengers. Then she spotted him, weaving briskly through the crowd, his trench coat open and flapping behind him like charcoal-gray wings. When he waved, she swallowed hard. Seeing him this way, after several days apart, filled her with an unexpected mélange of feelings. Relief, curiosity, pleasure, fear. Fay craned her neck for a better look. "Is that him? The good-looking one in the glasses?"

Susan could only nod, for her lips were trembling. She bit down hard to make them stop. But the closer Tony came the more difficult it was to control her feelings. She had missed him deeply.

Smiling as he approached, Tony didn't say a word. He wrapped his arms around her in a light embrace, gently kissing her lips and cheek. She realized his restraint was out of deference to her mother, and she appreciated it. Yet she was too happy to see him to let go of him. "You didn't have to meet us here tonight. I told you that."

His arms stayed around her as his smile reached his green eyes. "When you said you were coming back early, I knew I had to be here."

Off to the side Fay cleared her throat loudly.

Susan introduced her mother to Tony and they hit it right off. As she knew they would. After collecting their bags and packing them into his car, Tony drove them around the mall in order to show Fay the national monuments in their evening grandeur. Then he took them out for dinner.

She sat back and listened as Tony and her mother got better acquainted at the restaurant. It did her heart good to see the two people she loved best get along so well. She only wished she had that kind of rapport with Tony's parents. Not wanting to spoil the mood, she quickly brushed aside that troubling thought. Tomorrow would be soon enough to tackle problems; tonight she would bask in the warmth of this homecoming.

While waiting for coffee and dessert, Tony asked Fay how long she'd be visiting. "Two days. I'll be leaving on New Year's Eve," she said.

"So soon?" He sounded disappointed.

"'Fraid so, dear. I've got to get back to my cousin Iris. She's a bit frail these days," Fay explained. "But Susan and I thought it might be nice to have your parents for lunch before I leave. If the invitation's not too last-minute for them, that is."

The New Year's Eve day luncheon was her mother's idea. Susan had been reluctant, but Fay insisted it was a good way to start over with Tony's parents. Although she saw the wisdom in it, she was apprehensive. "Do you think they'll come?" Susan asked Tony.

He reached across the table to give her hand a reassuring squeeze. "I'll talk to them."

By the time they arrived at her apartment, Fay was ready to turn in. Tony waited while she helped her mother get settled in the bedroom, and when she came back into the living room, he drew her into his arms.

His kiss was a hungry one, making it clear how much he missed her. It seemed so long since they had held each other with such passion, such urgency. Her desire for him had been overwhelmed by her troubled heart. Now, back in his arms, the yearning and longing resurged deep inside her. Her own hunger sparked, she pressed against him, her limbs as weak as Jell-O, her body throbbing. She moaned against his mouth and finally broke away. "Tony...not now." She was breathless.

"I know, I know," he murmured, his arms reclaiming her. But now he just held her until both their bodies had calmed. Then he led her to the sofa and they sat cuddled close together.

"I like your mother." He rested his chin on top of her head.

"It was her idea to come back a few days early."

"In that case I like her even more," he added. "Although it would be nice to think you came back because you missed me. Like, in absence makes the heart grow fonder?"

"Oh, it does. But—"

"But it doesn't change our basic problem."

"Tony, let's not get into that now. Can't we enjoy being together this way for one night at least?"

"Sounds good to me." He planted a kiss on her hair.

Blocking out tomorrow's demons, she lifted her eyes to his. "I still have your Christmas present."

She got the package and placed it in his lap. He tore open the wrapping, and his face shone with delight. Carefully he leafed through the two books. "We talked about these ages ago. I can't believe you remembered."

Tony's pleased look and demonstrative thanks made the weeks of searching well worth it.

"I have a present for you, too," he said. "But I left it at home."

"You can bring it tomorrow."

He gave his head a sly shake. "I don't think so. I'd rather wait until we're alone—really alone. Maybe after your mother leaves."

"Why?"

"You'll see."

"Sure, now that you've got your present, you make me wait days for mine. What a pal," she teased, although she was intrigued by his mysterious air.

"Sorry." Tony patted her shoulder. "I have some good news I've been saving for you, though."

Her head shot up. "Is it the Somerset? Has something developed already?" She'd been excited about the prospective new plan since Tony had told her about it on Christmas afternoon.

Grinning broadly, he nodded. "Nothing's definite until all the papers are signed and sealed, but it's looking good, Susan, all the way around."

"Then you were right? Hammond did want to deal?"

"Better believe it. This plan even makes them look good. They're willing to sell twelve to fifteen apartments to the local housing authority."

"What about the money, though?"

"A federal subsidy is ninety-nine percent guaranteed. The state has to kick in some funds, but that looks promising, as well," Tony added. "Dad and I are going down to Richmond next week to firm things up."

"And then the county will be able to buy the apartments and rent them back to the present tenants at moderate rates, right?"

"That's how it's supposed to work."

"No more lawsuits, no evictions, no exorbitant rents?" She shook her head in amazement. "It's happening so fast."

"Well, it'll take several weeks to finalize everything. But as my father says, mountains move—if you get the right people talking to each other."

"Your father's been such a big help. I'll have to thank him."

"You can—when he comes here for lunch."

Again she felt a twinge of apprehension. "He'll want to come, won't he?"

"I think so—if he knows it's important to me," he said. "Since Christmas, Dad and I have been communicating a little better. Nothing earth-shattering, but it's a start."

"I'm glad for your sake."

Nodding, he pulled her close against him. "But I should warn you, the situation between my parents is touch-and-go, although Dad did take the rest of the week off to spend time with Mother. I gather they're doing some serious talking."

She sensed his worry. "I hope they work it out."

"Me, too." His arms tightened around her as she tucked her head on his shoulder. "In any case, my mother will come if Dad can convince her to."

She sat quietly in his arms and considered how much more relaxed she'd feel without Tony's mother at their luncheon. On the other hand, she'd feel terrible if Mrs. Brandon snubbed the invitation altogether.

SUSAN GAZED at the table with satisfaction. It looked lovely. The glassware sparkled and her white china was elegant in its simplicity, and the floral arrangement Tony had sent made a wonderful centerpiece. Her mother's seafood curry tasted delectable, and even the rice ring came out perfectly. After years of cooking for the well-to-do,

Fay certainly knew how to prepare a proper luncheon. Everything would turn out just fine. Or so Susan kept telling herself.

When Tony arrived with both parents, she still had the jitters. Yet she was relieved that Mrs. Brandon was with them—for Tony's sake more than her own. It meant his parents must be making some headway with their problems, and she knew how important that was to him.

As soon as Tony introduced his parents, her mother took over with poise and charm. But that was Fay, equal to anybody. No one had ever kept her down. Suddenly Susan's mood eased as she realized she'd survive the afternoon.

Despite her mother's efforts, the first few minutes were uncomfortably quiet, as if no one really knew what to say to one another. When they sat down to eat, Tony held her hand under the table during the initial nerve-racking minutes. Susan loved him dearly for that; she always would.

He proposed a toast to the New Year, and as they sipped their wine, he added, "I'm glad we've all gotten together at last."

Susan looked across the table at the Brandons. "Mama and I are so pleased you could join us."

Mr. Brandon nodded her way, but Mrs. Brandon made no eye contact with her. Instead she turned to Fay. "Your curry is very good, Mrs. O'Toole, and the table looks lovely."

"Why, thank you. And call me Fay, please."

An awkward, silent pause ensued until John Brandon spoke up. "And we're John and Letitia," he offered quickly. "And I agree, this is fabulous."

"Thank you, John. I'm glad you like it." Fay gave him her warmest Irish smile, which proved irresistible to Mr. Brandon, who smiled right back. The ice between them had broken.

"Actually, this curry is ten times better than Estelle's." He sounded more relaxed now as he turned to his wife. "Don't you think so, darling?"

"Oh, yes," Letitia agreed without looking up from the table. Another tense silence followed, and Susan couldn't help feeling angry at Tony's mother. They were all trying so hard to be kind to her, to put her at ease, yet she sat there quiet and stiff. Susan didn't particularly like being ignored in her own home, but it really irked her that Letitia wasn't making more of an effort for Tony's sake. Didn't she realize how much this get-together meant to him?

Then Tony patted her knee beneath the table. "Susan's a pretty good cook herself, Dad," he said, finally cracking this last uncomfortable silence.

John eyed her kindly. "I'm sure you are. And I'm given to understand you're also quite a talented and capable young woman."

"That she is," Fay piped in before Susan could murmur her thanks.

"You must be very proud of her, Fay," John answered.

"I am, but probably no prouder than you are of your son."

"You're right, Fay." Mr. Brandon looked across the table at Tony. "Although I'm quite lax about telling him so."

Tony met his father's gaze and smiled. Susan knew he'd been waiting a long time to hear that, and it filled her heart with happiness to see the look in his eyes. No matter what else happened—or didn't happen—today this moment alone made the gathering a success.

After the Brandons left, Susan helped Fay finish packing for the train back to Baltimore. "I think it all went rather well, Suz," Fay claimed as she folded a blouse into her suitcase. "John turned out to be a really nice man—once he warmed up a bit. And I could tell he likes you."

"I think so, too." She fetched her mother's two dresses from the bedroom closet. "Too bad Mrs. Brandon doesn't feel that way."

Fay gave her a thoughtful look. "You know, I think she was doing the best she could under the circumstances. She's surely one unhappy lady, and who are we to know why? My feeling is that it has little to do with you."

"You're probably right. It would just be easier if I felt she liked me."

"These things have a way of working themselves out." Fay took the dresses from her. "I never told you this, but your Grandmother O'Toole—God rest her soul—didn't cotton much to me until you were born. Then, suddenly, I was like a long-lost daughter."

"Is that true?"

"Cross my heart." She folded the last dress and placed it carefully on top of the other. "So forget about Mrs. Brandon. Marry the boy. Make a life together. The rest will fall into place."

Susan felt her skin grow warm. "Despite the difference between us?"

"Differences? I didn't see any."

She felt flustered. "Well, he hasn't even asked."

"He will." Fay snapped the locks on her suitcase. "And when he does, do yourself a favor, darlin'—don't fight it."

DRIVING AWAY from Union Station, Tony held Susan's hand. "I hope your mother comes back soon. She's great."

"Thanks." Susan gave his hand a squeeze. "This has been a good day, hasn't it?"

"Sure has. And it's not over yet."

Her eyes fluttered with confusion.

"It's New Year's Eve, remember?"

"Oh, gosh, with all the excitement I nearly forgot."

"Are you in the mood for a big blowout type party?" he asked, hoping she'd say no.

"Not really. Do you mind?"

"Are you kidding? I've been waiting for days to get you alone."

She blushed. "Well, you've got me if you want me."

That was all he needed to hear. He turned left on Pennsylvania Avenue and headed for his place, thanking the stars that she wanted the same thing.

Once they were settled in at his house, Susan remarked on how nice it looked. "Cleaning lady came this morning," he explained, taking her into his arms for a long, leisurely kiss. It was so good to touch her, to feel her soft curves press against him. How many times during the past week had he wondered if he'd ever hold her like this again? God, how he missed her, missed this. He was hungry for the feel of her, the smell of her, the taste of her.

But he put the brakes on his body and his mind. The entire evening was still ahead of them, and he had so much he wanted to say to her. He forced himself to come up for air. "I've got champagne in the fridge," he said, breathless. "And a dinner from Guido's we can heat up in the microwave."

Susan pulled back, a mocking glint in her otherwise heavenly blue eyes. "A spotless house, chilled champagne and a dinner just waiting to be heated? Seems you're well prepared," she noted wryly. "But what if I'd opted for the big blowout?"

"I'd change your mind."

Grinning one of the sexiest grins he'd ever seen, she hugged him tightly. "I love you," she declared with an incautious ease that warmed his heart. His hopes for the evening soared.

While he heated Guido's zucchini soup and veal marsala in his tiny galley kitchen, Susan built a fire in the living room fireplace. "Something smells wonderful," she called out to him.

"Wait until you see it," he added as he carried plates and glassware out to the dining room table. "Although I'm still stuffed from lunch. Your mother is some cook."

"Hey, I helped, too, you know." She rose from the fireplace, grinning. "But Mama did a great job, didn't she? And I can't get over your father—I've never seen him so outgoing. He and Mama got along rather well."

"You seem surprised."

"I am."

"Maybe he's been doing some serious soul-searching about his personal life these past few days."

She took the silverware from him and helped him set the table. "I'm even more surprised that he got involved with the Somerset situation, especially after all this time."

"That was partly my fault. He thought I didn't want him butting in. I, on the other hand, didn't think he approved of my taking the case."

When the timer on the microwave oven buzzed, Susan followed him into the kitchen.

"It's a misunderstanding that I think underscores the biggest difference between him and myself," he continued as he placed the hot veal in a serving dish. "He's a man who revels in the pursuit of power—he relishes the politics of it. I, on the other hand, do not."

"Not even after seeing how he used his connections to turn around the situation at the Somerset?"

"Let's just say I accept its usefulness." Leaning against the counter, he gave her a thoughtful look. He wanted to explain this carefully. "I think power, used correctly, can accomplish more for the little guy than all the public interest groups in town. Like it or not, Susan, influence and connections are what make Washington spin."

"But most people don't have that kind of connection to power, nor the influence. Where does that leave them?"

"To people like you and me—and my father—who'll get out there and help them." He handed her a basket of warm, crusty bread. "You can see for yourself how Dad used the connections he's cultivated over the years to help the Somerset tenants. Now Alice and the others will keep their apartments and the Hammond Group will still redevelop the building. How can you argue with that?"

"It's hard to," she said, shaking her head. Yet she still sounded doubtful.

"Sweetheart, it's basically a matter of compromise. Most good solutions are."

She didn't respond, but he sensed she was mulling the idea over in her mind. He felt it best to let it go at that. Dwelling on the Somerset and the politics of power was the last thing he had in mind for this New Year's Eve.

Following a leisurely dinner, they lazed in front of the fire enfolded in each other's arms, sharing their thoughts. When they were alone together like this, they really were on top of the world. He had to admit Susan had been right about that all along.

As midnight drew closer, he brought out the champagne and switched on his favorite classic rock radio station. Old romantic songs from his school days poured through the stereo speakers. "Perfect," he whispered. Susan smiled, and he pulled her into his arms.

Her hair felt soft against his cheek, her scent filled his senses with a heady excitement. He felt so close to her right now, physically, emotionally. And he was thankful—very thankful—for the meaning she'd given to his work and to his life.

When Susan left town at Christmas, his days had seemed painfully empty. For years before their fateful meeting on the Metro he had allowed himself to be content with the status quo. But Susan had made him come alive. True, their relationship had a roller-coaster beginning, but the strenuous ride had fortified their bond. They were still together and, hopefully, ready for whatever new bumps might come their way.

This was turning out to be the best New Year's Eve of his life, and he wanted it to be the most memorable of their lives. "I've been doing some soul-searching of my own," he murmured into her ear as they moved slowly to a romantic song.

With her arms draped against his chest she lifted her head to meet his gaze. "Tell me." Her voice was soft, encouraging.

"As far as work goes, I know now that my need to serve the community is still strong. Yet I have to reconcile that need with my desire to handle the kind of high-visibility cases I've been working on at the firm."

"Like Leland's."

"Especially Leland's," he replied. "It looks as if Justice is going to approve the Central Satellite purchase. Now Leland's already lining up more work to send my way."

"You may not believe this, but I am pleased for you."

"Thank you." He gazed into her deep blue eyes, wanting nothing more than to lose himself in them. Instead, he kissed her forehead and made himself continue.

"So, as you see, I want to have my cake and eat it, too. And I think I can."

"How?"

"By committing a set percentage of my work load to pro bono cases while continuing on with my established clients. It'll mean passing on some of the new, juicier cases coming into the firm. But being a hotshot isn't that important to me now."

"I'm wondering if it ever really was," she said.

"It held its charm." Then he shrugged. "But I feel good about this new decision. It's a balance I can live with. The question is, can you?"

He felt her body flinch against his chest. "Me?" she whispered just as the DJ on the radio began the one-minute countdown to midnight.

"Susan, one thing I've learned this week is that you're more important to me than my career, or anything else for that matter." He was forced to speak louder as the radio countdown grew louder. "Our future together is worth pursuing, worth all the compromises it takes to make it work. I believe that from the bottom of my heart."

The DJ cried out Happy New Year, which was echoed by a raucous chorus of cheers in the background. A big band rendition of "Auld Lang Syne" followed.

He clutched her to him as the song blared around them. "Susan, you know how much I love you. Marry me."

Chapter Sixteen

Her mouth suddenly felt very dry.

"Will you?" He kept her close against him.

His touch reassured her, and she was finally able to look into his eyes. They were full of love—love for her. There was no other way to describe them. Their expression touched her soul in a way the endearments, the embraces, the kisses of the past months never had. Yes, she knew Tony loved her. Except now...now she *felt* this love. And for some irrational reason she felt like crying.

"It just seems so soon." Bowing her head, she blinked back these unshed tears. "My mother said you would ask."

"Smart lady. I see a lot of her in you."

"Maybe I'm not as smart. I told her we still had our differences."

"Susan." His fingers gently lifted her chin as his eyes sought hers. "The changes in my career—they're the best I can do."

"Oh, Tony, I think they're wonderful. Really. And I pray they work out for you."

His eyes darkened with dismay. "You love me, don't you?"

"Very much," she insisted. "But now we're talking marriage, and I'm not sure I'm equipped to be the kind of wife—"

"Kind of wife?" His voice hardened as he pulled back from her. "What's that supposed to mean?"

She remembered Mrs. Brandon's words of warning at the dinner dance. "The partners' wives I've met so far are nice women, but they seem so wrapped up in promoting their husbands' careers," she explained. "And they're very conscious of the image they project—wearing the right clothes, choosing the 'in' designer to decorate their homes, sending their kids to elite schools, raising funds for the symphony. I can't do that, Tony. I can't be the kind of wife your mother is to your father."

"Who says you have to be? If I wanted that kind of wife, I wouldn't have fallen in love with you, Susan O'Toole." He shook his head. "This is my life, my career. I've no intention of reliving my father's."

She believed him. Yet something still held her back. Was it the voice of reason or just plain fear? She cradled his hands between her own. "I need time, Tony. Time to think this through. Please?"

"That's not exactly the answer I was hoping for. Although it's better than a flat-out no." He raised her hands to his lips and kissed them. "Will you promise me one thing?"

"Anything."

"Promise me you won't fight what's really in your heart."

SUSAN WAS STILL in a daze the following afternoon. Tony's marriage proposal had changed her world. No matter what she decided, her life would never be the same. Even though her love was genuine, the commitment was daunting. Marriage meant forging two lives together into one. Marriage meant forever. Yet her mother had warned against fighting it, and Tony had asked her not to. Could she be her own worst enemy?

She looked forward to the Somerset tenants' impromptu New Year's Day party as a respite from this perplexity. Alice had mentioned plans for the get-together at the neighborhood senior citizens' center when she dropped by the apartment to meet Fay. The tenants viewed it as something of a victory celebration because, at last, they felt confident they'd be keeping their homes.

When she and Tony arrived at the center, Tom O'Brien was the first to spot them. He gave her an affectionate hug and Tony a hearty handshake. "It's good to see you two kids together again. Alice'll be tickled." He took their coats. "Go ahead into the rec room. Everyone's there."

The recreation room was humming with the chatter and laughter of friends and families of the tenants. "Looks like the whole world's here," Tony said, a protective arm keeping her close to his side as they plunged into the crowd. Several tenants greeted them warmly with kisses, hugs and heartfelt thanks. A few of the ladies became teary-eyed when they spoke of their relief and happiness. Susan choked up a little herself each time they did.

Eventually they made their way to the back of the room where refreshment tables were set up. While she surveyed the cookies and pastries donated by a local bakery, Tony went to get her a glass of punch.

"Susan." Tony gestured to the huge sheet cake sitting between two punch bowls. "Take a look at this."

She read the inscription on the red, green and white frosted cake: There's No Place Like Home.

He looked at her. "How about that?"

"Oh, Tony," she sighed as the sentiment behind the inscription hit her square in the heart. She leaned against him, and his arm curved around her shoulders in support.

"They wouldn't be celebrating today if it hadn't been for you," he murmured softly.

"And you."

"There's no end to what we can accomplish together."

They stood arm in arm like that for quite some time. With Tony by her side she felt centered, complete. It wasn't a feeling she was used to. In fact, she felt as if she'd been searching for it all her life. Could it be that if she didn't embrace Tony as part of her life, she'd forever feel like an outsider looking in? She wondered.

"Tony, Susan, I've been hunting all over for you." Alice stood before them, jubilant and beaming in what looked like a brand-new forest-green dress. She threw her arms around them both. "Doesn't this crowd beat all?"

"It's great," Susan said.

Alice clung to her arm. "We can't ever thank you two enough."

"You're the ones who hung tough even at the bleakest point," Tony reminded her. "You didn't give up hope."

"Sure felt like it at—oh, my gosh, I forgot! Tony, your pop just got here. I told him I'd find you and send you over," Alice revealed.

Susan turned to Tony. "I didn't know he was coming."

His shoulders lifted in surprise. "Neither did I."

"God bless that man. He's the guest of the hour—right after the two of you," Alice said. "Of course *we* invited him. Heck, we even invited Hammond's lawyers."

She told Tony his father was waiting at the main entrance with Tom O'Brien. "I'll go get him," Tony said, giving Susan a peck on the cheek.

"I see you've patched things up," Alice remarked after Tony disappeared into the crowd.

"We're working on it. And you and Tom? I take it you survived his family's visit."

"Survive is the word for it. I have to tell you the news about the settlement made all the difference." Alice shrugged. "Don't get me wrong. His sons are nice enough boys. They're just naturally concerned for their pop."

"It's understandable."

Alice nodded, and then she burst into a wide grin. "But honey, let me tell you my news. As soon as the dust settles around the Somerset, Tom and I are moving in together. Now what do you think about that?"

Susan couldn't help her look of astonishment. "I think it's great . . . if that's what you want?"

"Actually, it's a compromise. Tom thinks we should get married. But, darn it, Susan, marrying at our age? I'm not sure it'll work."

She understood all too well how Alice felt. "So you're simply going to live together?"

"Temporarily, anyway. If the living arrangement works and we can swing it financially, I promised Tom I'd marry him. Now his boys aren't crazy about the idea," she added, "but he says they'll just have to learn to live with it."

When Tony returned with his father, Alice excused herself to help Eva refill the punch bowls. She made sure they promised to stay for the cake cutting.

Mr. Brandon seemed pleased to see her, and for Susan the feeling was mutual. Tony's pleasure at his father's presence was written all over his face. It occurred to her that his happiness was lifting her spirits even higher. It was a heady feeling.

"For heaven's sake," Tony declared, peering over his father's shoulder. "They really did invite Hammond's attorneys. Fred Dowling and Joel Epstein are right over there. We should say hello."

"You go ahead," Mr. Brandon urged as he picked up a paper plate from the table. He glanced at the cookies and pastries. "We'll catch up with you in a moment."

"I trust your lovely mother arrived home safely last night," John said to Susan, placing several cookies on his plate. "It was a pleasure meeting her—a pleasure for both my wife and me."

He caught her startled reaction. Smoothly he edged her away from the refreshment table. "I apologize for her absence today. Although we're both trying to make adjustments in our lives, she still was uncomfortable about coming here today."

"Mr. Brandon, you don't have to explain."

"Oh, yes, I do. Letitia knows full well how important you are to Tony, and yet I sense she hasn't been entirely fair to you. Of course, you would never admit that, would you?"

Not knowing how to answer, she looked down at her half-empty cup of punch.

"I hope you'll be patient, Susan. Letitia is a good woman at heart. Honestly. She raised Tony with little help from me, I'm ashamed to say. And he didn't turn out too badly, did he?" he added with a slight smile.

Yet regret crossed his face as he continued. "I realize now that her recent behavior has been partly my fault, and I'm taking steps to rectify the situation."

"I'm glad to hear it."

"For my marriage's sake I've decided on semiretirement. It seems a workable solution." Then he touched her arm. "I assure you my plans will in no way affect Tony's recent decisions regarding his career. He knows what he wants, and he's determined. The law firm will never dictate his life as it has mine."

Mr. Brandon left her to find Tony and the Hammond attorneys. Watching him wend his way across the recreation room, making himself quite at home among the other guests, Susan considered how people bend, change, grow. She'd thought she had changed a great deal before returning to Washington to live. And, indeed, she had.

But she had changed even more *since* then. The events of the past few months had taught her that change and personal growth were never-ending. To grow and thrive she had to be flexible, she had to give people the benefit of the doubt. Tony wasn't the same discontented lawyer she had resented so much four years ago. Tom O'Brien was no longer the dour pessimist she had first encountered at the tenants' meeting. Nor was Mr. Brandon still the aloof figurehead of Tony's lonely family.

As for Mrs. Brandon, perhaps the two of them would never be friends. She certainly wouldn't be the first woman with a difficult mother-in-law. Of course, as Tony's wife, she'd try to win her over. But if she couldn't, then Mrs. Brandon—like Tom's sons—would just have to learn to adjust.

As Tony's wife?

Before this moment she hadn't allowed herself to think in those terms. Suddenly the cloud of uncertainty that had been befuddling her for far too long lifted from her heart. She loved Tony. He loved her. They belonged with each other. And happiness was hers for the asking. There was no reason to fight anymore.

She searched the room for him. Was it her imagination, or had the crowd grown larger? Where was he? Finally she heard his rich laughter floating above the crowd. With her heart pounding wildly she found her way to him.

Tony's green eyes twinkled with welcome when she approached. He held his hand out to her. "Can we talk?" she murmured in his ear. He excused himself from the two Hammond lawyers and followed her into the long corridor.

"What's this about?" he asked. "Or don't I want to know?"

"I certainly hope you do." She led him outside to a bench in front of the building. It was chillier outside than she had thought. She tried not to shiver because she didn't want him insisting they go back inside. Not even to get their coats.

"Here, take this." Tony took off his tweed sport jacket and slipped it over her shoulders.

"But—"

"See, I'm wearing this vest. It'll do."

The brown V-neck sweater vest he wore over a shirt didn't look that warm. So she sat close against him, hoping their joint body heat would warm them.

"Actually, this is kind of nice," he said, rubbing her back.

She smiled, her heart light as she looked into his eyes. She liked him, liked him a lot. A man like Anthony Brandon II came along maybe once in a lifetime. She'd never find another man like him and she didn't want to. Tony was part of her now, and she loved him deeply.

Every nerve in her body came to life as excitement rushed through her veins. She held his free hand, her eyes locked on his. "Will you marry me?"

He let out a long breath. "Are you sure?"

"I've quit fighting fate. I want to be happy. I want to make you happy."

His gaze intensified. "I want you."

She no longer felt the cold because she was melting deep inside. "Is that a yes?"

"Yes."

He bent his head to kiss her, and his eyes opened wide, never wavering. Her pulse quickened when their lips touched at last. It was the most exquisite kiss of her life, a kiss deep with longing and full of promise for the years ahead. It was a kiss they were both reluctant to end.

"Oh, Susan," he murmured, slightly out of breath. "I'll do my damnedest to make you happy."

"I know. We're going to have a fine life together."

His hand fumbled at her side, and she realized he was trying to get at his jacket pocket. "What are you after?"

"This." He produced a tiny box, beautifully wrapped. "Your Christmas present."

The box was so small that she could guess what was in it. She felt weak in the knees.

"Aren't you going to open it?"

She pulled at the wrapping with nervous fingers. It seemed to take her forever. When she finally lifted the box's velvet lid, she couldn't speak. She could only stare at the elegant diamond ring inside it.

"Well?"

"It's beautiful," she gasped.

"I've had it for weeks now. But you're difficult to pin down."

"Tony, I'm sorry." She sighed. "I always seem to take the hard way."

"That's part of your charm, love." He took her hand. "Besides, now this has more meaning." He removed the ring from the box. "I'm so proud that you want to be my wife," he said, slipping it onto her finger.

She looked from Tony to the ring and back again, her heart nearly bursting with joy and love.

Tony's mouth cracked a broad grin. "You know, I never imagined I'd be doing this in front of a senior citizens' center."

"I don't know," she mused. "In our case it seems to be appropriate."

He gently toyed with the ring on her finger. "Let's get married soon."

"How soon?"

"In about a month?"

Her mouth fell open. "That's too soon. I've always thought long engagements were kind of romantic."

"How long?"

"Just a year. We could have a Christmas wedding. My mother and father were married on Christmas Day."

"*Just* a year? I don't want to wait that long."

"What'll we do?"

"Compromise?"

"Compromise."

He shot her a winning smile. "June?"

"Perfect."

They sat and grinned foolishly at each other until the cold got to them again. "Shall we go inside and announce the good news?" he asked.

"In front of everybody?"

"Why not? Once Alice gets a gander at that ring, the whole place is going to know about it, anyway."

She chuckled. "They will be happy about it, won't they?"

"They'll be thrilled. Our engagement will be something else for them to celebrate. And after working with this group, the one thing I know for sure is that they like to party." He stood up and held out his hand. "Shall we?"

Gazing at him with all the love in her heart, Susan rose from the bench and hugged him tightly. A peaceful contentment washed over her. And she knew with a certainty that she'd never be the lonely outsider again. She and Tony belonged together.

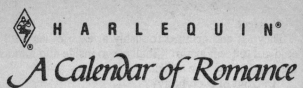

H A R L E Q U I N®

A Calendar of Romance

Be a part of American Romance's year-long celebration of love and the holidays of 1992. Celebrate those special times each month with your favorite authors.

Next month, it's an explosion of springtime flowers and new beginnings in

APRIL

S	M	T	W	T	F	S
			1	2	3	4
5	6	7	8	9	10	11
12	13	14	15	16	17	18
19	20	21	22	23	24	25
27	28	29	30			

#433 A MAN FOR EASTER
by Stella Cameron

Read all the books in *A Calendar of Romance,* coming to you one per month, all year, only in American Romance.

Take 4 bestselling love stories FREE

Plus get a FREE surprise gift!

Following the success of WITH THIS RING,
Harlequin cordially invites you to enjoy the
romance of the wedding season with

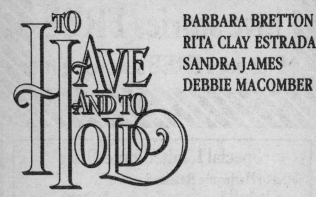

**BARBARA BRETTON
RITA CLAY ESTRADA
SANDRA JAMES
DEBBIE MACOMBER**

A collection of romantic stories that celebrate the joy,
excitement, and mishaps of planning that special day
by these four award-winning Harlequin authors.

**Available in April at your favorite Harlequin
retail outlets.**

THTH